"If you trust ⸻⸻⸻,
"then please ⸻ me up tonight."

He let out a sigh. "Nothing we've said here changes the fact that my mission is the most important thing to me. If you don't wish to be tied to me, we have to find another way that I can be certain you won't escape."

"But this afternoon I didn't leave you when I could have!"

"I know. But what if you change your mind?"

"But if I just sleep next to you, surely you'll be able to tell if I rise."

"I can't sleep next to you again." He sat down on the opposite side of the bed, tilting the mattress dangerously toward him, so close that their knees almost touched. "I kissed you this morning. I won't promise not to try more if you're lying against my side."

He watched the blush heat her skin, and the way her gaze dipped to his mouth. She was remembering the kiss, too.

"Then don't kiss me," she whispered.

He braced his hand beside her knee and leaned closer. "Perhaps I should say the same to you."

Other **AVON ROMANCES**

In Your Arms Again *by Kathryn Smith*
Kissing the Bride *by Sara Bennett*
Masquerading the Marquess *by Anne Mallory*
One Wicked Night *by Sari Robins*
The Return of the Earl *by Edith Layton*
The Sweetest Sin *by Mary Reed McCall*
Taming Tessa *by Brenda Hiatt*

Coming Soon

Cherokee Warriors: The Captive *by Genell Dellin*
Dark Warrior *by Donna Fletcher*

And Don't Miss These
ROMANTIC TREASURES
from Avon Books

His Every Kiss *by Laura Lee Guhrke*
A Scandal to Remember *by Linda Needham*
A Wanted Man *by Susan Kay Law*

ATTENTION: ORGANIZATIONS AND CORPORATIONS
Most Avon Books paperbacks are available at special quantity discounts for bulk purchases for sales promotions, premiums, or fund-raising. For information, please call or write:

Special Markets Department, HarperCollins Publishers, Inc., 10 East 53rd Street, New York, N.Y. 10022–5299.
Telephone: (212) 207–7528. Fax: (212) 207-7222.

GAYLE CALLEN

The Beauty and the Spy

AVON BOOKS
An Imprint of HarperCollinsPublishers

This is a work of fiction. Names, characters, places, and incidents are products of the author's imagination or are used fictitiously and are not to be construed as real. Any resemblance to actual events, locales, organizations, or persons, living or dead, is entirely coincidental.

AVON BOOKS
An Imprint of HarperCollins*Publishers*
10 East 53rd Street
New York, New York 10022-5299

Copyright © 2004 by Gayle Kloecker Callen
ISBN: 0-06-054395-7
www.avonromance.com

All rights reserved. No part of this book may be used or reproduced in any manner whatsoever without written permission, except in the case of brief quotations embodied in critical articles and reviews. For information address Avon Books, an Imprint of HarperCollins Publishers.

First Avon Books paperback printing: October 2004

Avon Trademark Reg. U.S. Pat. Off. and in Other Countries, Marca Registrada, Hecho en U.S.A.
HarperCollins® is a registered trademark of HarperCollins Publishers Inc.

Printed in the U.S.A.

10 9 8 7 6 5 4 3 2 1

If you purchased this book without a cover, you should be aware that this book is stolen property. It was reported as "unsold and destroyed" to the publisher, and neither the author nor the publisher has received any payment for this "stripped book."

To Mark Kloecker,
who's become more than a brother—
a true friend.
It's funny how growing up
makes differences very small,
and the love of family everything.

Chapter 1

A man who looks out of place usually is.

The Secret Journals of a Spymaster

London
August 1844

Charlotte Whittington Sinclair stood at the top of the marble stairs leading down into Lord Arbury's crowded, overheated ballroom. Dressed in her first new ball gown since her year of mourning had finished, she felt as excited and alive as a seventeen-year-old debutante instead of a mature widow of twenty-three years.

Oh, to be out in society again! During the final six months of her marriage, she had been forbidden to associate with her friends and family, practically imprisoned on her husband's remote estate in Cornwall. But now she had shed the sad remnants of her marriage along with her black garments and her wedding ring, and was finally free.

Her mother, Lady Whittington, descended the stairs at her side, forcing Charlotte into the sedate ladylike pace she chafed at. Charlotte noticed that she received the attentive glances of several eligible gentlemen, but thoughts of another marriage were far from her mind. Someday, perhaps, she would do her duty and give her mother grandchildren, but not now. Now was for living, and as a widow of means, she was determined to do so. But she could certainly dance and flirt with those gentlemen.

She had been reborn since becoming a widow, and her excitement had been further heightened when she'd discovered her father's hidden journals just a few days before. She'd always thought her father, Viscount Whittington, was merely an officer in the army of the East India Company. But his journals had introduced her to his world as a spymaster, a secret he'd kept from them all.

Even now, she alone held the knowledge, and guarded it close to her heart where his words enthralled her. Her own life had been stagnant and dull next to her father's, and his journals made her feel a restlessness she'd never imagined before.

At the bottom of the stairs, as friends gathered around them, Lady Whittington gave Charlotte a worried look. Her mother thought Charlotte was fragile yet, a woman who hadn't come to terms with all that had happened to her, but Charlotte felt far from being such a pathetic creature. She accepted the hugs of her longtime friends, and allowed herself to be led away as she fended off their concerned questions. She didn't want to be reminded of the past, so she turned the conversation to the latest gossip.

After a half hour's tales of who was betrothed and who had retired to the country with child, Charlotte moved on to the refreshments for a glass of champagne. She stood alone for a moment, sipping the bubbling liquid and gazing around her at all the familiar faces. She tried to remind herself that this was what she used to live for, the doings of the *ton*, but somehow, it all seemed rather . . . dull.

Dull? she reprimanded herself. After what she'd recently endured, she should be in her glory. But since she'd devoured her father's journals, talk of marriage and offspring seemed rather uninspiring. Her head was still full of dangerous, exciting tales of India and Afghanistan, of barren deserts and bleak mountains. Surely she'd soon settle back into her old ways.

But did she want to? She stood alone in a crowd, full of a knowledge no one else had, ready for the next exciting stage of her life to begin— and what would it be? She tried not to let her expectations overwhelm her.

And then she saw him.

A tall man strode along the edges of the ballroom, his expression set in a pleasant, false smile—nothing new there. But something was wrong. It was his eyes, she decided as he drew nearer; they were very dark, and they constantly swept over the room, as if looking for someone—or avoiding someone.

She tried to stop her imagination, for surely that's all this could be. Her head was full of intrigues that were not to be found in Lord Arbury's ballroom. After all, the man did not quite look like he belonged. He was very broad across the chest, something not normally seen among men of her acquaintance, although he did do justice to his evening clothes. He had black hair, a trifle longer and more unkempt than was fashionable. His face did not have the grace of a nobleman because of its broad bluntness and square jaw, but it was arresting nonetheless.

As he approached her, she found herself holding her breath, some unnameable excitement caught in her chest. Would he speak to her? He came closer and closer, looking bigger and more intimidating than any man she'd ever seen.

Yet his stride did not shorten, and after giving her a single appreciative glance that traveled swiftly from her face to the curves of her breasts, he moved on past.

Charlotte told herself to feel offended that he hadn't even offered a simple "Good evening," that he'd so rudely stared below her face. Yet she turned about and continued to watch him, not caring who noticed her shocking behavior. She moved back into the crowd, slipping between groups of chatting women and bored men. Distantly she heard someone call her name, but she ignored whoever it was to concentrate on the back of the enigmatic stranger. No one called a greeting to him, as if he knew not a soul there. Oh, plenty of ladies noticed his retreat, but turned up their noses at his behavior, as she should be doing.

But she couldn't. She was fascinated and drawn to the mystery of him. Where was he going with such single-minded determination? She stood on her toes and craned her neck; she stooped beneath someone's elbow so she wouldn't lose sight of him. And then he turned, ducked beneath a giant fern, and disappeared down a dark corridor that she knew led to the family's private quarters.

She would lay odds that he wasn't a member of the family.

Even as her feet continued to carry her along, following her mystery man, Charlotte told herself to stop. It was none of her business. One of the servants would intercept him. Yet no one seemed to notice him but her. All around her the orchestra music wafted, people jostled her to get to the refreshments or away from someone's determined mama. It was hot and loud—and the corridor beckoned her. What would Papa do if he were confronted by such a dilemma?

With a furtive glance over her shoulder, she stepped behind the fern and out of the ballroom. After she took a few quick steps into the darkness, the music began to fade, and the stifling heat lessened. Remembering the journals, she pressed herself against the wall and froze, wondering if her mystery man knew she was following him.

But up ahead she could hear retreating footsteps. He was getting away from her.

Keeping as close to the wall and the darker shadows as she could, Charlotte followed him. The corridor twisted and turned and went up to the second floor, but she was able to remain unseen because once, years ago, she had visited a friend here, when another family had owned the mansion.

Since she remembered the layout so well after only one visit, maybe she *did* take after her father a bit, instead of just her mother, as she'd always assumed.

At last, when she peered around a corner, she saw her mystery man disappear into a room and close the door behind him. She crept closer to the door, indecision making her heart race. Holding her breath, she listened, but could hear nothing.

Oh, what did she think she was doing? Perhaps he was a guest here, and this was his room. If he caught her—

If he caught her, she would simply lie and say she was lost.

Having a plan made her feel brave. She would wait a few more minutes and see what happened. But she wouldn't wait down the corridor the way she'd just come—he would likely go back to the ballroom by the same route. She was so proud of herself as she ran silently in her slippers down to the far corner. She ducked around it, then peered out to wait.

When the door suddenly opened, she covered her mouth to hold back a squeak of surprise. She'd almost been discovered, and the thought made her breathing erratic and her body tremble. How did a spy function like this?

And then her mystery man walked back the way he'd come. She caught a glimpse of his face. Now that the fake smile was gone, he looked humorless and cold, with a furrow across his brow that made him look angry.

Charlotte told herself to just keep following him, but the closed door called to her. She stood outside, her hand on the knob, and tried to discourage herself: it was probably a private room for the men to retreat to, just as the ladies had. She might very well surprise another man in a situation humiliating for them both.

But surely such a room would be near the ballroom, not yards' worth of dark corridors away.

Taking a deep breath, she turned the handle and pushed open the door. The room was dark with flickering shadows cast by several wax candles. There was no one inside. She took several hesitant steps in, then closed the door behind her. A large bed with an ornate headboard dominated one wall, decorated with bed curtains tied to four posts. Several candles rested on a bedside table. Two wingback chairs faced the bare hearth, and a desk for correspondence was against the far wall next to a massive wardrobe and a washstand.

Charlotte groaned and covered her face with her hand. She had followed a guest to his bed-chamber.

Yet in the center of the room someone had placed a small table, on which rested a tray bearing two glasses and several crystal decanters. Why in the center of the room? Wouldn't one constantly stumble over it?

As she stood staring at the table, she suddenly heard loud footsteps echo down the corridor, as if her mystery man cared little who heard him coming. And why should he? He was going to his own room!

Mortified, she did the most foolish thing she could—she opened the wardrobe and climbed inside, pulling it almost closed except for a crack. She was surrounded by silks and merinos and brocades, and belatedly realized that these were a woman's garments. They draped over her head and almost interfered with her breathing. Her mystery man must be preparing his lover's room for an illicit liaison—and because of her own stupidity, Charlotte was going to be forced to witness it.

As the bedroom door opened, she called herself every kind of fool. She wished she'd thought to cover her ears, but now if she moved, the rustle of her clothing would give her away. Feeling light-headed, she tried to breathe normally.

"Is the room satisfactory?" said a male voice.

"This is a foolish place to meet," said another man. "The house is full of people."

Her eyes wide, Charlotte stared out through the crack between the wardrobe doors. Thank goodness this wasn't a love affair. The first man who'd spoken had been her mystery man, with a deep, gravelly voice that matched his unusual countenance. The other man was shorter, broader in a stout manner, with a harsh face that looked as if he'd seen much of the streets. Though he was dressed formally, he looked ill at ease.

Her mystery man smiled grimly. "The mansion may be full of people, but they're all clustered in the ballroom, including the servants. *I* had to be at this function. You're the one who insisted on meeting me tonight."

The other man poured himself a drink from the decanter. "You gave me no choice. How did you find out about the woman?"

"Does it matter?" Her mystery man crossed his arms over his chest, looking as comfortable as if he owned everything in sight. "Suffice it to say that I know she betrayed England. She can go on doing it for all I care. I only want to be rewarded for my silence."

Charlotte's disappointment in him felt deep and personal, as if she'd known him her whole life. He was nothing better than a criminal, a traitor himself since he didn't care about England. He knew about a crime being committed, and all he cared about was *bribery money*? She wanted to leap out of the wardrobe and reprimand him, to see that both of these men went to prison.

But such actions would only get her killed, she realized, as a lump of fear settled in her stomach. Oh God, what should she do?

The short man took a long drink, grimaced at the taste, then eyed the other man speculatively. "I could have you killed for this, you know."

"And I could kill you right now," her mystery man countered pleasantly. "But other people know where we are, don't they? Should I disappear, you—and your lady traitor—will have even more men following you."

Charlotte's nose suddenly started to tickle where it was pressed against silk, and her breathing grew quick and panicked. Her life depended on controlling a sneeze!

The short man laughed humorlessly. "You've thought of everything. I'll have to return to my employer and see what she says."

"There might be a problem if she's leaving London. Is she?"

The short man just shrugged.

"Then there's nothing more to say," her mystery man said. "I need my money. I'll pick the time and date of my choosing and leave a message for you at the same inn. When we next meet, you'll have the money with you."

Charlotte's eyes watered; she scrunched up her face, but to no avail. A loud sneeze erupted from her, and she backed as far into the wardrobe as she could, as if the garments could still protect and hide her.

One of the men said, "What the hell—"

She groaned as their quick footsteps approached the wardrobe. The doors were flung wide, and hands reached blindly through the clothing. When an arm brushed her body, she gave a cry of shock. Someone gripped her about the waist and hauled her out into the room. She found herself staring up into the angry face of her mystery man.

She kicked him in the shins and frantically tried to escape. He caught her about the waist, pinning her against his side as she reached her arms toward the door. She opened her mouth to scream, and he covered it with his big hand.

"Ease up, girl," he said harshly into her ear from behind her. "You're not going anywhere, so you can stop struggling."

Panting, she nodded her head and slumped in defeat. Oh why had she read her father's journals? Before, she would never have been so foolish as to follow a stranger. Her eyes stung with tears she tried not to shed, but she was terrified.

The short man glared at her. "I thought you said you'd secured the room."

"I did. Something went wrong."

At her back, her mystery man's deep voice reverberated through her. She hiccupped on a sob.

"She heard too much," the short man continued impassively, his eyes cold. "She has to die."

Chapter 2

There's an art to holding a hostage. Be careful the hostage does not end up holding you.

The Secret Journals of a Spymaster

Nicholas Wright heard the woman's quiet crying, felt her trembling against him and the wetness of her tears on his hand where it covered her mouth. All his training told him that his mission should be his first priority.

But his instincts where women were concerned always led him in another, more vulnerable direction. Was this her room? Had he brought her into danger? Hell, he'd thought he'd been so careful.

He was still in control of this situation; he could be successful at both his mission and protecting the woman. But right now, he had to put

Campbell at ease, before Nick lost his only connection to the traitor Julia Reed.

"It's my fault we've been discovered," Nick said. "I'll take care of her, and believe me, no body will be found."

The woman gave a little squeak and started struggling again. He admired her bravery even as he was forced to squeeze her tighter. Her waist was fragile; her bones felt as delicate as a bird's. He could hurt her if he wasn't careful.

Campbell lifted the woman's chin and stared into her face. "Perhaps I would enjoy it more."

Everything seemed suspended as the woman froze and whimpered softly.

"Go—quickly," Nick said with force. "Someone could be missing her even as you lust over her. At least I belong at the ball. What excuse will you give if they find us?"

Campbell glared at him, then gave a short nod. "I'll look for the message at the inn. You make sure she never talks again."

"Count on it."

Campbell opened the door, looked both ways, and shut it behind him as he left. The woman hung limp in Nick's arms, but at the click of the door, she became wild, flailing her arms and legs, scratching at his hand where it covered her mouth.

"Calm down," he whispered forcefully, his face pressed against her hair. "I'm not going to kill you."

He turned her away from the door toward the bed, and that made her struggle even more. A flowered wreath that had been perched on her dark curls went skittering along the floor.

With sudden comprehension, he tried to gruffly reassure her. "I'm not going to do *that* either. Just be quiet so I can explain—"

She bit down hard on his hand and deliberately collapsed toward the floor. In their struggle he got a handful of one ample breast. After all the work he'd done on this mission, he'd about had it with trying not to hurt her. He picked her up and threw her onto the bed. When she tried to scramble away, he fell on her, forcing her onto her back and pinning her gloved hands over her head with one of his hands and using the other to cover her mouth. His legs and her skirts pinned her lower body. He had an odd, quick thought that she felt very comfortable beneath him.

She stared at him wide-eyed, dark hair sticking out about her face, breathing so hard that her breasts, partially covered and barely contained, shuddered against his chest.

"That's enough," he said in a cold, menacing voice. "You can't escape me, and you'll only be hurt trying. Whether you believe it or not, I don't *want* to hurt you. But I can't risk discovery, either." He rotated his hips until she could feel the pressure of the pistol tucked in his belt against her soft stomach. "Don't force me to use this."

The threat was hollow, and he knew it—but

the woman didn't. She squeezed her eyes closed, and another tear leaked out to slide into her hair. Though her lips moved against his hand, he didn't allow her to speak. The stiffness went out of her body, and she gazed up at him beseechingly with hazel eyes, the flecks of green and gray shimmering with her tears.

"We have to leave," he said in a low, impatient voice, "and it obviously can't be through the ballroom. It will have to be the balcony. Can you be quiet and walk alone, or do I have to gag you?"

Very slowly he removed his hand from her mouth. His weight still held her pinned to the bed, and he imagined she was having difficulty breathing by this point.

Softly she said, "I'll be good. But please, my family has money. Let me go, and I promise they'll reward you handsomely."

"I'm not after money. Now let's go."

"But—"

He slid backward off the bed, pulling her to her feet with the same motion. For a moment their gazes locked, and he saw her fright and desperation. He knew then that he couldn't trust her not to do something stupid. Holding on to her arm, he turned and pulled the coverlet and blanket off the bed.

She gave a ragged cry and tried to tug away.

With his hands on her upper arms, he positioned her beside the bed. He leaned down into her face, and she cringed. "I said I wouldn't hurt you. I don't lie. Now stand still or I'll lose my patience."

He took the sheet and began to rip the fine fabric into strips with only his bare hands in a deliberate show of strength. Taken by surprise when she tried to scramble across the bed in a flurry of skirts and petticoats, he was grudgingly impressed with her bravery—or foolhardiness. Catching her from behind, he pressed her down onto her stomach with one hand, then flipped her skirts up with the other to tie her ankles.

"This is ridiculous, you know," he said casually. "You can't overpower me."

Though her legs trembled, she didn't try to scream. He held her delicate ankles and found himself looking up the length of her legs, past her silk stockings and garters, to her drawers slit to reveal her inner thighs.

In a deliberate attempt to subdue her—and feeling rather disgusted with himself to have to resort to this tactic—he ran his hand down the back of her thigh, letting his fingers brush the bare skin in between. She gave a strangled moan, and he stopped instantly. She had legs to make a man desperate—not that he'd ever get to sample what was between them. He tied her ankles, rolled her over, and secured her wrists in front. After he stuffed a small ball of linen in her mouth, he tied a gag about her head. She glared at him with damp eyes, but no more tears. He blindfolded her.

"This is for your own benefit," he said, as he lifted her into his arms and strode to the balcony. "Remember what will happen to you if Campbell gets ahold of you."

Staring down at her bright blue gown and the smooth expanse of creamy skin and shoulders above her neckline, he realized that she would stand out in the dark alley. He wrapped her in a blanket and carried her outside.

Charlotte could barely breathe, and she struggled to keep her panic from overwhelming her. She'd been bound with ropes once before, and had hoped never to feel such helplessness again. She wanted to cry and sob and start this whole day over. She would stay with her mother and her friends this time, never leave the safety of the ballroom.

If only she hadn't read her father's journals and put such outlandish notions in her head. Yet they were her only guide now. Always her father mentioned keeping calm, no matter how dangerous things seemed. By following his advice, she would be able to think clearly and look for a chance to escape.

Swallowing was dry and difficult, and she had to remind herself that the material in her mouth wouldn't make her choke.

Although her captor wouldn't be able to tell if she did.

Smothered under the blanket, she could hear the muffled sounds of the outside world, the distant rattle of carriages on the city streets, and faint strains of music. Her mystery man carried her easily, powerfully. She flashed back to the scary feeling of his hand on her thigh. He was right—he could do anything he wanted with her. She couldn't believe that included keeping her alive.

Above her, in a soft voice, her captor called, "Are you ready?"

Did he expect her to answer?

"Ready!" came a distant call from below.

Her captor hoisted her aloft, away from his body. For a terrifying moment, she knew she was being dangled off the balcony, felt her body sway and a breeze catch at the blanket.

And then he let her go, and she was plummeting. She shrieked through the gag, but before she could even say her prayers, she was caught in the arms of a man who grunted but didn't even stagger with her weight.

"You're safe," he said softly, in a kinder voice.

She felt her consciousness start to drift away and saw bright pricks of spots in the blackness behind her closed eyes—but she refused to give in to the peace of fainting. She might miss an opportunity to escape.

She paid attention to every detail as she was slung up and deposited on a bench. By the way everything shifted beneath her, she could tell that both men got in opposite her, and someone else drove the carriage away. Hours passed and she as-

sumed she wasn't in London anymore. Where
were they taking her? she thought as her heart
beat wildly in her chest. When they stopped to
change horses, her mystery man made sure she
knew he sat at her side, the threat of his presence
oppressing. If she made a sound, she understood
that he would use force to stop her.

After the second change of horses, some of the
tension waned between her captors.

"So what happened?" asked the second man,
the one who'd caught her.

"I found her eavesdropping from inside a
wardrobe."

Were they going to talk all night and just leave
her like this? She started to struggle, and to her
relief, someone pulled the blanket off her. She
took a deep, cool breath.

"You used a blanket *and* a blindfold?" asked
the second man in an amazed voice.

Her captor didn't answer. He was close now,
just above her, tugging at the knot in her blindfold. The material fell away, and she was left
blinking up at her mystery man, able to see because of the small, rocking lantern hung opposite
the door. All the window shutters were closed.

He rested his hands on either side of her, loom-
ing over her, a weighty presence that frightened
her to death. She tried to glare at him, but she was
certain her teary eyes spoiled the effect.

He grinned, startling her with the sight of
white teeth on swarthy skin. His hair hung di-

sheveled near his cheeks, and if he had an eye patch he'd look like the perfect pirate. Sometime in the last several hours he had changed out of his evening clothes and into a plain brown coat and trousers, striped waistcoat, and shirt. And she'd been sitting right there when he'd done so!

"You're a lively one," he said, then turned her head aside to undo her gag.

When it was gone, Charlotte moistened her mouth and croaked, "You've made a terrible mistake."

The other man leaned forward and peered at her. "I'm thinking the same thing." He had dark auburn hair and a lean, masculine face, which if viewed at a dinner party would probably be attractive.

But she was alone in a carriage with two strangers. She gaped down at her body, where her ball gown was now skewed dangerously low. She couldn't even take a deep breath. Staring from one man to the other, she felt terror welling up inside her again.

"I can see what you're thinking," the second man said soothingly. "Get back in your corner, Nick. You're scaring her like you do all the ladies."

Nick. That was the name of her mystery man. She watched as his dark head bent over her and plucked at the ragged strips holding her wrists together.

Now she knew his name. Another reason for them to kill her.

As her bonds loosened, blood rushed painfully back into her numb fingers, and she wiggled them. She had hoped her long gloves would have offered some protection, but they were too finely made.

"Could you have tied them any tighter?" the second man asked.

"She was struggling," her kidnapper said impassively. He gripped both her hands in his one giant hand and gazed meaningfully at her. "If you want to be comfortable, you will obey me. Do I have your word?"

"What does a man like you care about my word?" she asked with scorn.

"I don't, of course, but you, as a lady of quality, obviously do. Now do I have your word?"

"You have my word that I will not try to escape . . . for now." She tilted her chin and tried to boldly stare him down.

He glanced at his cohort. "Sam, she means to cause us trouble."

Sam, she repeated to herself. Aloud she said, "You told that other man you'd kill me and dispose of my body."

Charlotte was hoping to see where the two men stood with each other, and she was rewarded by watching Sam look startled. But he only crossed his arms over his chest and waited, as if he actually trusted his partner.

Nick shrugged, then opened up a portmanteau

at his feet and rummaged through it. "Campbell threatened to do it himself. It would have been messy."

Sam snorted and shook his head.

"Messy?" she cried. Using her hands, she pushed herself back into a corner. "And it's not messy to kill me here?"

"He's not going to kill you," Sam said gently. "We don't kill people."

"Unless they cause trouble," Nick added, bringing forth several sheets of paper, a capped inkwell, and a pen.

She turned to Sam beseechingly. "Then let me go! I won't tell anyone anything."

"We can't take that risk," Sam said with regret in his voice. He turned to Nick. "But this presents problems. What will we do with her?"

"We have to keep her with us."

Though she tried to control herself, she gasped.

Nick ignored her. "There's no one I trust to keep her safe in London. If she turns up spouting her nonsense, she could get herself—and us—killed."

"She overheard you dealing with Campbell?"

"Everything."

Charlotte tried to sound reasonable. "Surely if you both turn yourselves in, the government will be more lenient with you. I'll testify on your behalf. I'll tell them you tried to be gentle—"

"Stop talking," Nick interrupted coldly. "It's doing you no good. We are not traitors. We are trying to *stop* the traitor."

She gave a little snort, unable to help herself. Sam looked away, obviously hiding his amusement.

Nick watched her impassively. "I don't care whether you believe me or not. If I were lying, wouldn't I have killed you by now? It would make our next few days much easier. We work for the government; that's all you need to know."

"I *don't* believe you," she said bravely.

"You don't have to. All that is required is that you obey unquestioningly. If I have to choose between safeguarding you and finishing my mission, you will not be what I choose."

Trying not to shiver at the coldness in his voice, she thought, *My mission*, and wondered why that sounded familiar. Regardless, he obviously thought himself very important—and he made up lies to reinforce that.

Nick thrust a book at her, then several sheets of paper. "You're going to write a letter. Do you need to remove your gloves?"

She gaped at him, letting everything slide untouched off her lap as the carriage jostled its passengers. "I will not help you in any way."

As Sam patiently retrieved the items from the floor, Nick said, "You will write a letter to your family, saying you've decided to leave London for a few days. Come up with a good reason. Surely you don't want them to worry."

She blinked at him, then folded her arms across her chest. "I will not. I *want* them to send the police looking for me."

He tilted his head and studied her with those dark, black eyes. "We're long gone from London, and heading farther away every hour. No one will find you. Do you *want* your family to be crazed with worry, to spend days—if not weeks—wondering if you're lying dead somewhere?"

Feeling nauseated, Charlotte imagined her mother's reaction to her disappearance. Never a strong woman, Lady Whittington might suffer a drastic decline in health. Could Charlotte live with herself if she were responsible for such a thing?

"But you're going to kill me anyway," she whispered, ashamed of the despair in her voice but unable to stop it. How her mother would suffer because Charlotte foolishly thought herself invincible enough to follow a dangerous stranger.

Nick sighed heavily. "We are not going to kill you. As long as you don't do anything foolish, you will be returned to your family unharmed."

She dashed a tear off her cheek. "Stop lying! I've seen your faces. I know what you're up to. You won't set me free."

Nick leaned toward her, and she shrank back into her corner. "We work for the government," he said, enunciating slowly as if she were a child.

"Campbell, that man you saw me with, is a criminal. He works for a woman who has sold military secrets to a foreign country. We're trying to capture her, so I need to secure Campbell's eventual cooperation. I'll do that by getting him to trust me. I can't tell you any more." He gestured to the paper beside her on the bench. "Now you need to write this letter. What is your name, so we know where to send it?"

Charlotte knew he couldn't be trusted; he was making up stories to confuse her, to win her sympathy. He might think himself good at deception, but he was just another man out to victimize women—Charlotte and the woman he labeled a traitor. After a hellish marriage, Charlotte was through being a victim to men.

But she couldn't make her mother suffer.

Lifting her chin, she gave him a disdainful look. "I am Charlotte Whittington Sinclair. You can deliver the letter to the London home of my mother, Lady Whittington."

Something flickered in Nick's face, and he blinked for several moments, until he finally nodded. "Good girl."

"I am not a girl." But the rebuke was half-hearted, as she was too busy studying the distracted way her captor turned to look out the window, as if forgetting shutters guarded them from the night.

Chapter 3

A spy's mentor is everything to him—and not to
be crossed.

The Secret Journals of a Spymaster

Nick watched the woman—Charlotte Whittington Sinclair—pick up the pen, dip it in
the inkpot Sam held, and begin to write. The
scratch of the pen on paper could barely be heard
above the muted sounds of the moving coach, the
distant rumble of horses' hooves, the rhythmic
creak of wood and leather.

Whittington. It couldn't be.

She paused in her writing and stared into the
distance sadly. She had a delicate, lovely face,
with full lips made for smiling. He wondered
what she would look like happy—how she would
smile for her father, Viscount Whittington. To

her, Whittington was a nobleman, with ties to London society. But to Nick and Sam, he was the colonel, their commander—their spymaster, newly retired.

How the hell had he and the colonel's daughter ended up at the same ball? And how would he explain his behavior, the way he'd tackled her on a bed, how he'd lifted her skirts to bind her, pawed her thighs, and then dropped her off a balcony?

Remembering her legs made him glance at her again. The ball gown's plunging neckline plunged a little more with every hour. For a small woman, she was well endowed. She overflowed the dress, and if she moved suddenly, he might even see—

Shifting uncomfortably, he reminded himself that she had a husband. Sinclair. He remembered the colonel's regret when he couldn't leave India for the wedding. Everyone in foreign service was used to those kinds of disappointments. Luckily for Nick, it had never been a problem.

But if Charlotte had a husband, why did she want the letter sent to her mother? And did she have children to worry about?

Now that he knew who she was, he found himself sliding deeper and deeper into concern for her. She was his hostage, a woman who could hold the fate of his mission in her hands should she escape. But she was also young and frightened, and it was getting harder for him to ignore the sympathy he was starting to feel.

He had to conquer this weakness where women were concerned. Yes, women needed protection—but that didn't mean they weren't also traitors and hostages. He constantly reminded himself that, like men, women should have to live by the consequences of their actions.

The woman in question now threw her completed letter at him, and it fluttered to the floor between them. She drew herself up haughtily, taking a deep breath that did dangerous things to her gown. He kept his eyes on her face, lifting one eyebrow in a show of impassivity he was far from feeling.

Then he betrayed himself by bending over and picking up the letter instead of making her do it herself. Damnation. He ignored her triumphant expression, glanced at the drying letter, and frowned.

"Will she be able to read this?" he asked in an annoyed voice. "It looks scratched by an illiterate. You should have taken off the gloves."

"I assure you, I am not illiterate. But we are in a moving carriage, and it was the best I could do."

He read the contents, noticing with approval that she came up with a valid excuse for a young lady of society. She claimed to have changed her mind about traveling, and decided to catch up with her sister Jane, who was headed north with her betrothed.

"Fine," Nick said briskly. "Sam will see that

it's delivered. He'll also bring you more clothing," he added, glancing with disapproval at the ball gown.

Charlotte blanched as if he'd threatened to kill her mother. "H-he cannot break into my home— either of them! My mother is alone but for the servants. She could be frightened into an early grave!"

Nick felt there was something she was trying to keep hidden. "Are you not concerned with your own home, with your husband's reaction?"

She took a deep breath, hesitated, then said, "Of course I am. But my mother is frail."

"Then you needn't worry. Sam will not be taking foolish chances. He will purchase you a wardrobe that . . . complements our mission."

She opened her mouth to speak, looked between them, then simply frowned and turned away, crossing her arms beneath her breasts. Sam and Nick shared a wide-eyed glance over what she displayed, but she didn't notice.

His curiosity got the best of him, and he asked, "Do you have children, Mrs. Sinclair?"

She hesitated, seeming to struggle with some emotion he couldn't name. Finally she shook her head.

"That's good," he said. "Children might not understand your absence."

"But my mother—and my husband—will?" she asked sarcastically.

"Because you've explained it so well in your letter, of course."

She bit her lip but said nothing.

Soon Nick could tell that Charlotte was fighting a losing battle where exhaustion was concerned. Her eyelids lowered, then fluttered back open several times. Her head dipped forward once or twice, then finally her body gave in, and she sagged into a corner asleep.

After several minutes, Sam softly said, "I think you were a bit harsh with her, Nick."

He knew he had to be, because his first inclination was to protect her, to treat her tenderly. But all he said was, "If she's afraid, she won't cause trouble."

"Did you think that maybe you'll make her more desperate this way?"

"I'll take that chance. What's Will up to?" he asked, changing the subject to their friend Will Chadwick, who'd left the military for a normal life. "Has he spotted you following him yet?"

"Once or twice, but I always escaped before he could discover me."

"He's losing his touch," Nick said with a grin.

Sam shrugged. "Maybe. But I'm not staying very close to him, because we don't care what he's doing—we just need to know where he is if we need him. Will we?"

"Need him? I'm not sure yet. After you deliver the letter—"

"And purchase ladies' garments?" Sam interrupted with a grin.

"Hmm," Nick said in a growling voice. "Yes, after that see what Julia Reed is doing. If she's leaving London, we'll need Will's help keeping track of her."

"He won't want to do it. He made it perfectly clear he was done with this life."

"Maybe, but he's loyal, and I think I could persuade him."

"You, persuasive?" Sam said with a laugh. "I never thought you had to resort to that."

Nick glanced at their sleeping hostage, whose eyelids fluttered with dreams even as she frowned in distress. "I've got a lot of persuading ahead of me."

Before Charlotte finally fell asleep, she heard some of their discussion about another criminal named Will, but none of it seemed as important to her as sleep. She dozed restlessly, and in her dreams, her father was coming to rescue her with his three spies, Mr. North, Mr. South, and Mr. West, code names that had come up often in his journals. They seemed to be very dashing and handsome men, very brave in following their country's duty. What would Papa do in a situation like hers, where brute force was impossible? Try to trick her captors?

She came fully awake when the carriage slowed, disappointed to realize that her reality was still as

daunting and frightening as ever. She made a great
show of quiet acquiescence when Sam brought her
a breakfast tray from the kitchen of an inn before
he left for London. She didn't bother to show them
how difficult it was to remove her gloves, which
were now caked with dried blood at her wrists.
She hoped to lull them both into believing they'd
succeeded in frightening her into submission.

Nick passed a chamber pot inside, saying a bit
too loudly that he hoped her strength returned
soon after her recent illness. Obviously a servant
was waiting nearby. Charlotte desperately
wanted to scream for help, but she worried what
they would do to the servant, regardless of their
protests that they were honorable men.

A few minutes later she overheard them talking
with the coachman, Mr. Cox, a tall, silent man
who kept himself wrapped in dark clothing. How
did he feel about their keeping a hostage? She
would try to determine if he was someone she
could appeal to for help.

She ate to keep up her strength, munching
gratefully on biscuits and cheese. After the horses
were changed, Nick alone climbed back inside,
and the carriage pulled away again. She noticed
that their speed had greatly diminished, as if they
didn't want to stay too far ahead of Sam.

The kidnapping reprobate sat opposite her, his
long legs spread wide, as if he'd previously been
restrained having to sit beside his partner. She
knew he was trying to intimidate her, and she

had to admit he was succeeding. She fought the instinct to draw her legs up beneath her and cower away.

She wished he would sleep, because all he did was watch her. And his gaze did not always remain on her face. The upper slopes of her breasts felt hot with embarrassment at being the recipient of so much male attention. Never had a man been so forward as to leer at her. She felt bare, stripped raw by his attention.

She finally pulled the blanket up to her shoulders, and he gave her a brief smile that did not reach his eyes. They were as cold and black as the remote depths of hell must be, where all heat and flame had long since fled. He could hardly convince her that he was a government agent when he looked at her so thoroughly, so dispassionately. And he had fondled her legs!

Charlotte fervently hoped that her letter would convey the clue it was intended to give. She didn't want to alarm her mother, but she hoped her deliberately poor penmanship would alert Lady Whittington that something was wrong. She just wanted her mother to think she was distressed and sad about her widowhood. Surely Lady Whittington would send a letter to her husband, telling him to take special care of Charlotte's feelings once Charlotte arrived in Yorkshire. And when she didn't arrive, her father would realize that something ominous had occurred, and would know what to do.

She knew it was a remote possibility that such things would all come to pass, but she had to take a chance—like the chance she took pretending that her husband was still alive. Surely her captors would treat her more cautiously if they thought that her husband would be demanding justice if they abused her.

She waited until the carriage stopped again to take another, even riskier chance. The blackguard stepped outside, and she saw a wince cross his face, as if he'd grown stiff. Stiff! Her ankles had been tied for almost a day now. He didn't know the meaning of stiff!

When the door closed, she awkwardly pressed herself against it to listen. She heard him speak to Mr. Cox, who then climbed into the coachman's box. Perfect. She lay back on the floor, bound legs raised toward the door. When Nick opened it, looking down to place his foot on the step, she kicked hard, aiming for his face. But his height deceived her, and she landed a blow to his chest that sent him staggering backward.

His hard, angry face was enough incentive to move quickly. She tried to jump from the carriage, yelling for help, but in her brief glimpse of the outside world, she saw only the rear of a stable and a deserted yard. Then he hauled her back inside and the carriage sped off, leaving them in a tangled heap on the floor.

"That was foolish," he ground out, pushing her down, then rising on his knees to loom over her. "I told you things would go better for you if you behaved."

Using her hands, she pulled herself up to a sitting position against the far wall, trying to stay away from him. That was difficult when his legs straddled hers, and she felt weak and helpless. "Wouldn't *you* try to escape if someone held you against your will? How can you expect me to do otherwise?"

He eyed her as if considering her words, then shook his head tiredly. "These are dangerous times, Charlotte."

"Mrs. Sinclair," she said, lifting her chin in defiance.

One corner of his mouth curled up in a smile. "But your name is lovely, Charlotte. It would be a shame not to use it."

She frowned at him with incomprehension. Was he teasing her? Pointing her finger, she started to lecture him. "Don't think you can—"

He suddenly grasped her wrists and pulled her up, her body dangerously near his. The wide skirts of her ball gown offered only meager protection against the weight and heat of him.

"And now you'll have to pay the price for your disobedience," he said in a low, rumbling voice.

She froze, waiting for terror to surge through her, immobilize her—but it didn't, and she felt relieved. She allowed him to manhandle her back onto the bench. She offered a token struggle when he tied up her wrists again, but she knew she could not fight the strength of his long fingers. She would look for other ways to manipulate him.

Several hours passed, and when the carriage slowed, Nick pulled the gag back out of his pocket. Charlotte watched him quietly, knowing this meant that they were finally going to leave this moving prison. When the carriage stopped, she felt it swaying as Mr. Cox climbed out of the coachman's box, but he didn't knock on the door.

"I'll keep quiet," she said, even as Nick loomed over her.

He snorted his disbelief. "Open your mouth."

She hesitated but finally obeyed him. He stuffed cloth into her mouth and tied the gag about her head. He stayed at her side, his face above hers, his black eyes so near she could see a faint circle of gray about the pupil, a hint of something soft inside that she couldn't believe about this ruthless man.

"I wish that you would accept the truth," he murmured.

She remained still as he tucked her stray hair back behind her ears. His finger slid along the shell of her ear, and then he touched her chin. Something inside her trembled, though she wasn't afraid.

"We are not the ones you should fear," he continued.

She put as much scorn into her eyes as she could.

He suddenly chuckled. "You're very bold, Mrs. Sinclair. Or perhaps it's *Lady* Sinclair. Such nobility would suit you."

They remained still, staring at each other, until he shook his head and backed away.

"I can't force you to accept the truth," he said brusquely. "Now be a good girl and keep quiet if you'd like to spend the night in a real bed."

Then he pulled her toward the door and stepped down. After throwing the blanket over her, he tossed her over his shoulder. She grunted with the impact against her stomach, trying to kick him, but he held her legs still. He started to whistle, then he had the gall to pat her backside.

When he began to walk, she gasped as he lurched to one side, then the other. His whistle took on a decidedly drunken warbling. What was he doing?

A door banged open in front of them, and she could tell he started ascending stairs. With another drunken sway, her feet hit one wall.

"Sorry, lass," he said rather loudly in a slurred Scottish accent.

When they reached a corridor, his drunken sway got even worse. Her head brushed against a wall.

"Can I help you?" called a timid voice.

For just a moment Charlotte felt every muscle in Nick's body tighten, including his hand on her backside. Then he laughed as she gave a muffled shriek and tried to kick.

"It's the wife, sir," Nick said, trying to sound conspiratorial even with a booming voice. "Got angry at me, she did. Stormed out wearin' only her nightclothes."

The other man said nothing. Nothing!

She tried to kick for all she was worth to dislodge the blanket, but with that reprobate's hand tightening on her backside, all she got for her efforts was a deeper cut where the linen ties bit into her ankles.

"A good day to you, sir," he called as he continued walking.

She heard a door open, then slam behind them. When he tossed her onto a bed, Charlotte sat up quickly, shook the blanket off her face to glare at him, then used her bound hands to pick at her gag.

He returned her glare even as he pushed her hands away and caught her face in his hands. "I am doing important work, and you almost destroyed it. If you can't promise me you'll stay quiet, I'm leaving that gag on permanently."

She looked into those dark, cold eyes, and though she didn't think he'd kill her, she did think he'd follow through on this new threat. She glared her ire at him.

"Do you promise to be quiet?" he demanded again. "Don't think I can't convince people you have a pleasurable reason for screaming."

She knew she blushed, and though she tried to hold his gaze, she couldn't. Did women of his ac-

quaintance . . . scream their pleasure? She couldn't
imagine feeling anything more than duty—or unease.

He was waiting. Finally she looked up and
nodded with resignation.

He gave her a look filled with more weariness
than triumph, then tugged loose her gag. She spat
out the linen wad, then lifted her bound hands to
him. He shook his head.

Her tongue felt thick and dry, and she sounded
hoarse as she said, "I'm locked in this room with
you. Where can I go? Please untie me."

Standing above her, his hands on his hips, he
said, "You've repeatedly promised not to escape,
then you break your word and try to."

"I never broke my word! But look at my wrists
and—" To her shame, she tugged at her skirts
and exposed her ankles, but couldn't quite say
such intimate words to a man.

To her surprise, he frowned and knelt in front
of her to inspect her wrists. Instead of treating
her brusquely, his touch was gentle as he turned
her wrists over to inspect both sides. She watched
his dark head, bent so near to her, and felt a
strange reaction she couldn't identify. She wanted
to push him away—yet she remained still, allowing his nearness. When he looked up at her, she
held her breath.

"Very well," he said. "I'll untie you briefly. But
there's only one door, Charlotte, and I will be between you and it."

Chapter 4

A true spy never really leaves the service of the Crown; the bonds of patriotism and duty are ingrained.

The Secret Journals of a Spymaster

Charlotte bit her lip and said nothing, watching as he very gently untied her wrists. With the strips gone, raw welts were revealed, and one or two places oozed blood. He untied her ankles next, and she gave a sigh of relief. But there were raw spots on her ankles, too.

"You shouldn't have struggled," he said shortly.

"I'll keep struggling. The government needs to know what you're doing—"

He looked up at her wearily. "I've told you, they already know."

"And they're trying to capture you."

"They're *backing* me." He sighed. "Just wait here. We need to clean your wounds."

We? she thought in disbelief. To her surprise, he poured water into a basin and brought several towels to the bed. With soap and water he washed her wrists with a gentleness that amazed her. When he reached for her foot—and she was tempted to allow him to continue—she knew she had to stop this trance she was in. She took the cloth away from him, brought her feet up onto the bed, and turned her back to him. Her skirt and petticoats puffed up around her, and she pushed them down.

"I can finish this myself," she said quickly.

"But I already touched your ankles," he said with dry amusement in his voice.

"Only to bind them cruelly."

She could hear his hesitation. "It's necessary, Charlotte."

She ignored him then, wincing when her cloth touched a particularly sore spot on her ankle. He was going to tie her up again, further aggravating her injuries, and there was nothing she could do about it, except plan another escape. She took her time washing her skin and looked about the room for help. There was a small table and chairs, and a standing screen for privacy in the corner. She'd thought there were windows in the far wall, but then she realized they were doors. There must be a balcony or gallery outside. Did he even realize it yet?

Nick stared at Charlotte, who huddled on the bed with her back to him, bright blue silk rising high on petticoats all around her. With all that material gathered up around her, it was practically impossible for her to reach her ankles, but she was doing her best.

She would do anything rather than let him touch her.

This was good, he told himself. Just looking at what he'd done to mar her smooth skin made him feel uneasy and guilty. If only she were a man, the wounds wouldn't bother him a bit.

But if she were a man, he wouldn't have the pleasure of looking at her.

She was merely a hostage, he reminded himself as he turned away and began to pace in front of the bare hearth. She was a hostage with a husband who would be missing her.

Yet he couldn't help but admire her stubborn insistence in trying to escape. When he'd opened the carriage door and she'd kicked him in the chest, he'd almost laughed and applauded her bravery. She stubbornly continued to defy him, no matter how overwhelming her task seemed.

He was watching the way her bare shoulders seemed to gleam in the near darkness, when a soft knock sounded at the door.

Charlotte lifted her head and met his gaze wide-eyed.

He frowned at her and called, "Aye?" in his Scottish brogue.

"It's me," Sam said.

Nick unlocked the door and Sam slipped inside, carrying an overstuffed portmanteau. Sam had changed clothing and was now wearing the coat and top hat of the country gentry.

"How was the trip to London?" Nick asked.

Sam dipped his head to Charlotte as he set the portmanteau beside her on the bed. "Good afternoon, Mrs. Sinclair."

"Sam," Nick said impatiently, as his partner seemed lost in the loveliness of her smile. He hoped she didn't think she could pit them against each other with feminine wiles. That had been tried many times before, and it had always failed.

Sam only grinned, as if he knew what Nick was thinking. "That horse moves like the wind. It was a quick journey."

"And Julia?"

His face sobered. "She's left London, heading north."

Finally the culmination of a year's worth of work was at hand. If only they didn't have to worry about Charlotte. "And you have no way of knowing if Julia is on to us?"

"None. She could be racing us to Leeds—or heading for Kelthorpe's house party."

"Then we'll need Will's help. I'll go to him tonight."

"Who's Will?" Charlotte asked as she knelt on

the bed and opened the portmanteau. She pulled out a plain brown dress and frowned at it.

"No one you need to know," Nick said abruptly.

That delicate chin lifted higher into the air. "I need you both to leave so that I may change."

"We're not leaving you alone." Nick pointed into a shadowy corner of the room. "There's a changing screen right there. You may use that."

"But—"

"Or you can change in front of us."

She blushed in a very lovely way, he thought, almost wishing she'd accept his challenge. But then he'd have to kick Sam out of the room. All so he could drool over a married woman. He sighed heavily.

"Does that mean I cannot bathe?" she asked.

"Not any time soon."

Frowning, she lay three dresses side by side and then chose one, along with several feminine items she tried to keep hidden from them. Sam had even brought her one of those useless little bags women liked to carry.

"If you need help unfastening your dress, just call," Nick said.

She hesitated. "Can I not have the services of a maid?"

"You cannot."

Glaring at him, she said, "You are a wicked man."

"Only a practical one. Now, do you need help?"

He thought her eyes glistened with tears, and he felt guilty. But he couldn't change anything. He started to walk toward her.

She looked past Nick and appealed to Sam. "There are just a few fastenings at the top that I cannot reach."

While she turned her back and Sam walked forward, Nick fisted his hands and tried to tell himself it was better this way. He was too drawn to her, his hostage, a married woman. Let her show her disdain—it would help him remember the situation between them.

When Sam was finished, Charlotte walked regally to the screen, displaying a long line of skin. When she disappeared behind it, Sam eyed Nick as if he were enjoying himself.

"Be wary of her," Nick said in a low voice. "She's still trying to escape."

"Can you blame her? But I'm off to follow Julia. I assume while you're gone that Cox will be handling our lovely hostage."

Nick nodded.

"That ought to be interesting." Sam shook his head and grinned. "When I left Will he was headed for Huntingdon. I'm sure that's where they'll spend the night. There are only three inns; you should be able to find them easily."

"Them?"

"He has a woman with him."

"Ah, to have time for such things," Nick mused.

"She appears very wellborn. He met with her frequently in London, but I kept my distance. I didn't think it important to know who she was, as long as I could find Will when I needed to. And now they're looking at estates as if to purchase one."

"Maybe Will really is settling down. I'd better go before we lose him. Stay here a minute, Sam. I'll explain everything to Cox and send him up to take over for you."

But before Nick could escape the room, their hostage made her appearance. She was wearing a gown of plain dark green, which buttoned up the front. It covered every part of her but her neck and head, yet across the bodice it stretched rather . . . tightly, outlining her assets.

Sam winced. "I did my best estimating her size."

Charlotte frowned and looked down at herself. "It is not too uncomfortable, although I wasn't able to wear a—" She broke off, her face flushing red.

"A corset?" Nick finished for her. He had noticed immediately that her shape was womanly instead of confined.

Her mouth snapped shut, and she glared her contempt at him.

Once again he'd embarrassed and angered her. But he preferred her this way, rather than frightened of him.

"Sam and I have to go," he told her as he rummaged through his portmanteau for a long, shabby cloak.

She looked wary, as if she didn't understand where the conversation was going.

"My coachman, Cox, will be with you. He's not a man who takes his duties lightly, so I would not cross him. I'll return as soon as I can."

"But—" She broke off, the worry in her voice evident. Then she collected herself, gave a cool nod, and turned away.

After an hour's ride on a fast horse through mists and occasional rain, Nick reached Huntingdon. He looked for the most disreputable lodging first, over a tavern, and took a room there so that he had a private place to meet with Will. Then he went back out into the streets, walking slowly as he limped and leaned on his cane. Twice women came out of the shadows to offer themselves. He kept walking, knowing Will wouldn't bring a lady near such a place.

The next inn he came to was made of uneven stone, built near an ancient bridge that spanned the Ouse River with many arches. The innkeeper knew Will by Nick's description. Nick went inside the public dining room, eased himself onto a wooden settle before the hearth, and propped his leg up.

The room was crowded with travelers and local people, and it didn't take long for him to spot Will Chadwick and his companion taking a seat at the table. Will was much better dressed than the last time Nick had seen him, though there was more gray in his brown hair. In Afghanistan he, Sam, and Will had all sported beards and turbans, and had wrapped themselves in sheepskin cloaks to fight the bitter winter winds of the Hindu Kush mountains. They'd passed as natives and kept watch for the East India Company on the Russian plans for the country. The three of them had relied on one another and had been as close as brothers. But then Will's cover had been blown, and he'd been ambushed by Afghani tribesmen and almost killed. He had had to leave the country and work in India.

And now Will was in England, ready to begin a new civilian life. Nick promised himself he would use Will as little as he needed to.

To Nick's surprise, Will's companion began talking to other people in the room, and eventually walked over to smile at him. She was an attractive woman, with black hair and the most direct green eyes.

"Good evening, sir," she said in a cultured voice. "I've been looking for some local people who might be able to tell me where some unusual historic sights are. Might you be able to help me?"

Nick glanced behind her at Will, and saw the moment that recognition dawned in his eyes. Will frowned at him.

Nick turned a smile on his lady. "Sorry, miss, I'm but a stranger here like you."

Though she would have politely continued their conversation, he rubbed his leg a few times and looked pained, until she said she didn't want to disturb him. She and Will left eventually, but Nick knew Will would be back.

It took him only an hour, and this time he came alone. He ignored Nick and sat at the bar for several beers while he talked to the innkeeper. Occasionally, Will let his arm drop, and his hand made the gesture they'd long used for "meet outside in the back." After Will left, Nick waited a few minutes, then went out the back door, following an alley toward the stables. In the gloom a man passed him going toward the inn, and Nick was certain it was Will's servant Barlow, but neither of them acknowledged the other.

Will stood near a carriage parked beside the stables, and Nick limped toward him. There was no one else in sight.

"Is the wound real?" Will asked.

"No," he said. "Nice to see you, too."

Though Will shrugged idly, his gaze was direct and challenging. "I'm not sure I'll be able to say the same. The disguise doesn't reassure me."

"It shouldn't. There's trouble. I never would have bothered you otherwise. But let's not talk here. I have a room above a tavern nearby. Follow me."

Chapter 5

A spy keeps tight hold on all information until
he needs to use it.

The Secret Journals of a Spymaster

Nick led Will back through the decaying alley that paralleled the Ouse River, then held
up a hand when he reached his lodgings. "This is
the place. I'll go in first. Take the steps in the
back, right corner. I'm the first door on the right
at the top."

He went in ahead of Will, limping through the
smoky, loud taproom to the far staircase. His
room was in one corner, where the ceiling slanted
over the bed and he had to duck if he wanted to
pace. After tossing his cloak and cane on the bed,
he threw another piece of peat on the iron grate
in the fireplace, and it belched out smoke.

When Will gave a soft knock, Nick let him in. They sized each other up for a moment, and he saw the suspicion Will didn't bother to hide.

Nick looked at Will's fine garments. "I should have given you the cloak. You stand out around here."

"They thought I was drunk, so I fit in well enough. Now what do you want?"

"Sit down," Nick said, nodding toward a wooden chair. He had never had to figure out a way to talk to Will before. They'd always known each other's thoughts, yet this well-dressed Will, this fine gentleman who'd recently become a baron, was almost a stranger.

After explaining to Will where Sam was, Nick was able to get to the most important question. "So who's the woman? She looks of quality, yet she's traveling with you."

"*I* am of quality now, old man, thanks to our good queen. But her name will tell you who she is—Jane Whittington."

This new information sent Nick's thoughts ricocheting in another direction, but he had to be sure. "As in Colonel Whittington?"

"She's his daughter. I'm bringing her north to see him."

How had they *both* gotten tangled up with the colonel's daughters? There was no such thing as a coincidence. "And she doesn't mind traveling alone with you?"

"We're engaged."

Nick pretended casualness with a whistle. "Well, look at you—a nobleman, a dandy, and soon a married man. Hard to believe."

"Miracles happen."

But even Will's assurance seemed forced.

"Now why did you feel the need to find me?" Will continued.

"Do you remember General Reed?" Nick asked. "He had a sister named Julia."

"I remember. He was with the Bengal army."

"Yes. Do you remember how his sister came with all the other army families into Kabul? She was always foolishly brave, even more so than her brother, I think."

Nick tried not to let his bitterness show, but Will was too clever for that.

"You knew her?" Will asked, tilting his head to study him.

"Intimately. We both agreed it was only for a short while because I wasn't going to be in Kabul long. Sam had introduced us. He grew up in the same parish as the Reeds."

"So what does this have to do with me?"

For a moment, Nick stared into the fire. Was it still so difficult for him to believe that Julia had committed treason without him even knowing? "She was sending British troop information to the Russians."

Will stiffened. "How can you accuse a woman of treason, let alone be certain she actually did it?"

Nick hadn't anticipated how difficult it would

be to talk about something so personal—and embarrassing—even to Will. "The Reeds didn't have much money. They were from an old family whose investments had long ago gone bad. I knew then that she wanted more than someone like me, a mere cousin to nobility, could give her. She took matters into her own hands."

"All right, you've given me motive," Will said as he stood up to pace, "but not any proof. I assume you know for certain this happened?"

"Originally, the word 'treason' was whispered by one of my Afghani informants. I knew he was playing both the Russians and us, but he could be useful. I think he was shocked when he realized that a British woman was involved. She sent the information in a coded letter, and he saw her deliver it."

"And you know it was Julia?"

"He described her perfectly—how many women can there be in Kabul with hair so blond as to be almost white? One who would roam the bazaars dressed as a boy?" Nick had been drawn to her independence, to the wild, unfettered way she lived her life, so different from the other European women he knew.

"Maybe she spurned his advances," Will said thoughtfully, "and he's decided to punish her."

Nick shook his head. "She left a necklace I had given her with a certain Russian officer. I saw it myself." He didn't want to see the pity in Will's eyes. Will must have suspected that Nick sympathized with women. Had Will realized Nick's weakness as an intelligence agent?

"Nick, you might be only one of many she bedded," Will said cautiously. "How do you know she wasn't simply involved with this Russian?"

Nick refused to allow his emotions to get the better of him, and he hardened his tone. "Because I traced her accomplice back to England. He's here now, ready to testify against her. He gave me one of the letters, and he has the matching code letter. They look innocent—except for little blobs of ink, certain letters filled in, as if someone just randomly scribbled on them. She would send two letters, by two different routes, and you could not read the code until both letters were side by side. The accomplice will give me the matching code letter when I reach Leeds and get him to safety. He's afraid she's going to have him killed for what he knows."

Will leaned back into his chair, his expression wary. "But why now? This all happened over a year ago."

"It's taken me a long time to track this man down. But the main impetus is that my lovely Julia has made a good match for herself. She's supposed to marry the Duke of Kelthorpe."

When Will gave a low whistle, Nick scowled and said, "I can't let a traitor to England marry into one of the highest families in the land—hell, the groom is a distant cousin to the queen!"

His outburst sounded loud even to his own

ears, and the silence that followed was awkward. He was making this assignment too personal, and he had to get past that. He understood Will's reluctance to return to a life he'd left behind, but Nick explained that he needed Will to get himself invited to a house party that the duke was holding. If Julia hoped to marry the man, she could hardly afford to miss the event. Will only had to watch her, and inform Nick about her movements.

But Nick was surprised by what worried Will the most: Jane's welfare. Had he fallen in love so quickly? He hardly remembered Will ever making time for women, in all the years he'd known him. Nick was unmoved by this new side of his friend. England's safety had been weakened, and he would be damned if he didn't stop it from happening again. Will's eventual agreement made them both relax, and Nick told him about the location of Langley Manor.

Nick had one last thing to reveal, and he knew this would be the hardest. "I have Jane's sister with me."

"*Charlotte?*"

That got a good reaction, from Will's stunned expression.

"I didn't mean to bring Charlotte with me—frankly, she won't tell me why she was at Lord Arbury's party—"

"You were there?" Will said, looking guilty.

"It's my fault *she* was there. I didn't want her traveling with Jane and me, so I had Arbury send her an invitation. Of course she couldn't refuse."

"You had to send her to *Arbury's*?" Lord Arbury was a man well known to the Political Department. He'd done them favors, and had favors done for him in return. He'd spent much of his youth in India, and now used his experience in the hallowed halls of Parliament. Arbury had rather enjoyed the idea of Nick holding a clandestine meeting during his ball.

"Who else did I know so highly placed?" Will continued. "Hell, Queen Victoria was going to be there. Charlotte was beside herself with anticipation for her first ball since coming out of mourning."

Everything Nick thought he knew about Charlotte disappeared in an instant. "Mourning? For who?"

"Her husband. Didn't you know?"

"She's not exactly speaking to me." His mind raced with the implications, with how this news helped ease some of his problems.

"Why not?"

He wished he didn't have to tell Will quite everything.

"Because I've gagged her."

Will's mouth fell open. "Why the hell would you need to gag a gently bred woman—the colonel's daughter?"

"Because she thinks I'm a traitor," he replied, unable to stop his laughter—and his relief.

Charlotte's husband had died over a year ago.

Nick explained the kidnapping to Will, then insisted he could not tell Jane any of this. His friend reluctantly agreed.

When Will stood up to leave, Nick followed him, saying, "Maybe I'll just hand Charlotte over to you. After all, her sister would be anxious to comfort her." Even as he said it, he knew he could never go through with it.

"I think not," Will said. "When Charlotte finally understands the importance of your mission, send her back to London. I'm sure she won't want to miss the end of the Season."

But she didn't seem like a woman who cared about such things. She was more alive, more vibrant than those boring ladies of the *ton*. If he'd kidnapped one of them, he'd have a hysterical woman on his hands, instead of the challenging, wily Charlotte.

Charlotte laughed at the joke Mr. Cox had just finished telling, more relaxed and at ease than she'd felt in two long days. But then she heard the sound of Nick's footfalls before he even opened the door. How she knew, she wasn't certain, but a prickle of awareness raised the hair on her neck. She stared blankly at the cards in her hand, where just a moment before she had sworn she would beat Mr. Cox this round.

After being unlocked, the door swung open, and Mr. Cox, his face redder than before, raised his shaggy head to glance over his shoulder.

Nick leaned inside. "Sorry to interrupt your private party. Cox, can I speak to you for a moment?"

Mr. Cox rose to his feet, drawing on his long black overcoat and swathing his skinny neck in a black scarf though it was a hot August evening.

"But our game was not finished," she said, hearing a hint of desperation in her own voice. He would probably send Mr. Cox away, leaving her alone with her kidnapper again.

Mr. Cox nodded formally to her. "Mrs. Sinclair, ye surely had me beat that game."

"You're only humoring me. Do give me one more chance."

"I got to see to the horses and carriage, ma'am. A good evenin' to ye."

With a nod to Nick, Mr. Cox disappeared into the hall. The door closed behind both men with a finality that was suddenly nerve-wracking.

But she was alone for the first time in more than a day. Here was her chance to escape. She jumped to her feet and raced to the other door. She opened it and stepped lightly onto the balcony in the cool night air.

Not a sound rose from the inn yard below. It was so late that even the laughter of drunken men in the taproom had died away. Off in the distance she could see lanterns hung in the darkness and

hear the sound of neighing horses. That must be
the stable. She could steal a horse.

Luckily lanterns were hung in several places
along the inn itself, as well as in the yard down
below. It didn't seem too far to drop.

She climbed over the balustrade and faced inward, holding on tightly. The breeze picked up
and lifted her skirt and petticoats, and she
swayed with terror. But she couldn't back down
now. She had to get away.

Crouching, she slowly went down on her
knees, holding the balustrade hard against her
stomach. The ground faded into murky blackness. Why didn't it seem any closer? If she lowered herself and hung from her hands, surely she
could drop down lightly.

Why hadn't she followed Jane's example as a
child and escaped the house once in a while? Jane
knew which tree grew close enough to the manor,
which stair creaked on the servants' staircase. It
would have prepared Charlotte for this.

She leaned away from the balustrade and lowered one leg.

From below her, a voice said, "You are so pre-
dictable, my fair Juliet."

It was *him*. And he didn't sound amused.

Squeezing her eyes shut, she clutched the
balustrade. "You are no Romeo!"

"It's a long drop down. Do you want to risk it?"

Very carefully, she drew her leg back up beneath her, then rose to her feet. One hand slipped, and she swayed backward for a moment.

"Stand still!" he said in a soft, angry voice.

He was directly beneath her now, and she muttered every curse she knew under her breath. She put one leg over the balustrade, turned, and brought the other over, which left her standing on the balcony, looking down at his furious face.

He suddenly leaped and caught the beam that braced the balcony. She gasped and fell back, even as his hand gripped the floor. He was coming after her!

She turned and grabbed for the door, which rattled in her hand and wouldn't open right away. She finally flung it wide, stepped inside, and tried to slam it on him. He stopped it with his boot and then began to force it open. Although she braced all her weight against it, she slowly slid backward.

When it was obvious she'd lost, she let go and tried to run around the bed, but he vaulted it easily and put his back to the door before she could get there. He crossed his arms over his chest and glared at her.

Even in plain country garments, he looked very powerful, very masculine, very dangerous. His jaw was stubbled and shadowed. How could eyes so black seem to blaze out at her, reminding her that she was alone with him, that she'd angered him?

This man was her kidnapper, a criminal, she insisted to herself. But it was so difficult to think of him that way. Had she really interrupted a mission of British agents? How could she tell? She forced herself to remember every line she'd read in her father's journals, but nothing came to mind. She knew no secret code words that would ferret out the truth. She could only judge him as a man.

And he was not wanting in that area.

A dark cloak swirled about his shoulders as he began to walk toward her. He removed the cloak and tossed it over a chair, then his frock coat followed. She kept retreating backward across the room. His faded white shirt stretched taut across his shoulders, and a pair of suspenders flattened it to his chest. His threadbare pants clung to his thighs and hips. She was no virgin who didn't know what a man's naked form looked like. After her experiences with her husband, she thought she'd never want to see that sight again.

But instead her mind betrayed her, and a kidnapper's body had secrets she suddenly wanted to see revealed.

Charlotte controlled a groan of mortification. She was alone with him. His gaze dipped to the bodice of her too-tight dress. Her late husband had never shown an interest in her form unless in the privacy of a bedroom. But Nick couldn't seem to stop. Sometimes she wanted to cover her chest with her arms, but other times—like now—

she wanted to straighten her spine, take a deep breath, and let him look his fill, show him what he would never have, prove that she wasn't afraid of him.

Raising her chin defiantly, she said, "So what are you going to do?"

He kept advancing until her back hit the wall and she had nowhere else to go. And still he kept coming, until his chest pressed into hers, and every inch of him seemed to touch her. She could feel his arousal, and she should have felt threatened. She was trembling, and she told herself it was out of fear, but to her shame, she knew it wasn't so.

He leaned down into her face, his breath hot against her skin. "Don't do that again," he said menacingly. He stayed there, their lips almost close enough to kiss. She gasped as she breathed, and that only made her breasts ever more sensitive to the pressure of his chest. When his gaze dropped to her mouth, she stopped breathing altogether.

He suddenly stepped back, and she almost sagged to the floor.

He glanced at the second door. "And I'll make sure to tell Sam no more balconies."

He wiped a hand through his hair and sprawled into a wingback chair before the cold hearth. "You know I can't let you go. Not until this is over, anyway."

She put a hand on the other chair to steady herself. "And did this evening bring you closer to the end?" she asked, remembering his meeting with someone named Will.

"We'll see." He stared about the room, lit only with tallow candles on the table where she and Mr. Cox had played, as if he were looking for something. "I thought you'd be abed by now."

Clasping her hands loosely before her, she made a show of pretending to be calm. "I am not in the habit of sleeping in front of strangers." Were they going to act as if he hadn't pressed himself against her?

"So cards were in order?" he asked lightly.

"Mr. Cox suggested it. It kept my mind off . . . things."

His expression sobered. "Did you have supper?"

"The innkeeper sent up what you'd ordered. Heaven forbid Mr. Cox lock me in so he could go find us food."

"After what just happened, I wouldn't put it past you to pick the lock."

"My accomplishments do not extend so far, but I am sincerely grateful for your praise." She smiled at him sweetly, falsely.

His answering grin shouldn't have warmed her, but it did.

"You have a wicked, bold tongue on you, *Mrs. Sinclair*, and I discovered a few other bold things about you tonight."

A chill went through her, but she remained

standing before him, trying not to notice how near to his spread legs she was. With but a step or two, she would be between his knees. A discordant thought that made her breath catch and her resolve harden.

"And what did you discover? That I am but an ordinary woman? That I have nothing to hide compared to a criminal like you?"

His head dropped back against the chair as he watched her. "I discovered you've been lying to me. Your husband is dead."

It was as if he'd ripped away a layer of clothing to expose her, leaving her more vulnerable to him. She'd lost that card to play.

"Nothing to say?" he continued. "No protests, no explanations?"

"I owe you neither. It should be obvious to you why I let you believe what you wanted."

"You thought you could use the fiction of a husband to make me treat you better, as if knowing someone could seek revenge on your behalf should affect my behavior."

Again she said nothing.

"Charlotte, I would not care if you were an eighty-year-old grandmother. I would still treat a hostage with the same resolve and force—and with fairness."

"And you would look at her bosom as much as you look at mine?" Oh God, where had *that* come from? What new, brazen woman was she becoming, to dare him so?

Nick's smile was slow and seductive. "Every man looks at your bosom, Charlotte. I wager you don't normally mention it to them. But now that you've brought up the subject—"

"It does not bear discussion," she quickly interrupted, feeling hot and mortified and no longer so clever.

Because now he rose out of the chair and to his full height, which made the ceiling seem low. She made herself remain still, instead of scurrying to put a piece of furniture between them. Her face flamed as he deliberately studied her breasts, walking back and forth as if to judge them from all angles. Hadn't he just felt them against his chest, for heaven's sake?

When she could take his perusal no more, she surrendered and crossed her arms over her breasts.

"Now you see," he began softly, "I do enjoy looking at your chest. I try not to, because I'm sure you think I'll attack you in your sleep—which I would not, by the way."

"And I'm supposed to take the word of a criminal, especially a man who would intimidate me with his much larger body?"

His expression momentarily darkened, then cleared. "I am not a criminal. But I am only a man. I would not attempt to seduce you. On the other hand, should you offer—"

"I beg your pardon!" she cried.

"No begging necessary, of course," he said,

stepping closer, looking into her eyes with a dark amusement she tried not to find fascinating. "As I said, you might invite me, since it has been over a year since you've been with a man, and a woman has certain needs . . ."

"As if I would ever need such a thing!" She was trembling with anger now. She couldn't help remembering how her husband had used that same phrase, "certain needs," but applied it only to men. She couldn't imagine a woman needing to be treated the way her husband had treated her.

But Nick's knowing smile and the languorous way it made her feel called into question everything she'd ever known about relations between men and women. She had women friends who were blissfully happy with their husbands—and she had never understood why.

Nick hadn't admired a woman this much in a long time. Charlotte Whittington Sinclair had a smart answer for every barb he sent her way. And although she was flustered by the direction their conversation was taking, she was not backing down.

Hell, he wanted her. He admitted it to himself, knowing he could let nothing come of it. She was exciting and unusual, and not afraid of him. He had pressed her into the wall and still she'd not shown fear, only surprise. He'd wanted to rub his thigh between hers and rub other parts as well. But she didn't understand her power over him, and he wanted to keep it that way, much as he longed to explore her insistence that she didn't miss sex.

But he'd been down this path before. His deference to women left him vulnerable to their manipulations, especially in bed. Julia Reed had done that to him—made him so besotted with her that he hadn't seen beyond the façade she presented, hadn't bothered to ask what she did when she was roaming Kabul dressed as a boy.

But he put Julia from his mind and concentrated on his lovely hostage, whose fair skin still blushed from the paths their conversation was taking. She didn't turn away from him. He allowed himself the forbidden, and gently stroked his finger along her soft cheek. For the space of a second he could feel her trembling, feel the softness of her rapid breathing, see her dazed expression.

Then finally she pulled back, and he knew he'd succeeded in driving her away. She broke his gaze, looked at the bed, realized where she was looking, and whirled toward the balcony door. Would she be so foolish as to try that again?

Clearing her throat she asked, "So who told you this secret about me? This Will person I don't know?"

"You don't need to hear the details." He sat down on the edge of the bed to remove his boots. "But I know more than one secret."

Chapter 6

Be careful what you reveal—it can bind you.

The Secret Journals of a Spymaster

When his boots were off, Nick leaned back, bracing his weight with his arms. The mattress felt soft, and his body betrayed him by showing him how much he wanted this woman he couldn't have. He sat up quickly. Charlotte was no innocent virgin not to know an aroused man when she saw one.

"I have no other secrets," she said with conviction. "I wouldn't even have had the one about my husband, if you hadn't assumed he was alive."

"Your full name is Charlotte *Whittington* Sinclair."

He was satisfied to watch her lovely brows

compress in a frown. Clearly she had no idea why her father's identity should matter to him.

"I told you my maiden name," she said in a puzzled tone of voice.

"And your father is Colonel Whittington."

She gave him a superior grin. "Then you now know he's in the military. When he finds out what you've done—"

"He'll find out rather soon. I eventually tell him everything."

Her face reflected her thoughts like a disturbed pond, each ripple outward revealing another emotion: confusion, doubt, then dawning understanding and suspicion.

"You know my father?" she asked softly.

"He's been my commanding officer for many years."

"Everyone knows he was in the military."

"But does everyone know he was a spymaster?"

Her eyes went wide, and her lips parted soundlessly.

"Did you even know?" he gently asked.

"Only recently."

She practically whispered the words. Then once again, she drew her strength about her like an overcoat and straightened her back. He swallowed hard over what that did to her magnificent breasts.

"But there are many ways you could have discovered that secret," Charlotte said scornfully. "This proves nothing."

"It proves I'm telling the truth. I could go into plenty of detail about the work I did for your father, but I'm sure he didn't share such dangerous things with you. I can tell you one thing, though—watching you wrap Cox around your finger certainly told me you take after your father."

He watched the blush bloom in her cheeks and spread down her delicate neck until she turned away from him. She almost seemed . . . pleased.

Her shoulders drooped as she said, "There's no way you can prove any of this to me. You could have been in the army and deserted."

"I could have," he agreed pleasantly, then began to unbutton his shirt.

Charlotte didn't know where to turn, what to think. Nick claimed to work for her father! Her mind was scattered, unfocused, and she tried hard to think of the journals, but could remember not a single line. Besides, her father never mentioned people's actual names, just code names. She had to think calmly, logically, find some way to trip Nick up using the journals, but she was exhausted. She looked at the bed longingly, not even remembering how one felt.

She turned back toward Nick. "I'm tired, and I'm ready for b—"

He opened the few buttons on his shirt and pulled it off over his head. He was naked from the waist up, every inch of him as sculpted as the museum statues her sister had dragged her to see. She hadn't thought a real man could look that way, but she was wrong. He'd looked broad and powerful in clothing, but she hadn't imagined his true impressiveness. And in several places, there were tiny white nicks, and even one long scar, marks of a life no society gentleman led. It should be disturbing—but it wasn't. It made her think of the dangers he'd escaped, and the skill it must have taken to survive.

He watched her calmly, arrogantly, as if he knew how he affected her. She couldn't allow such a thing, of course.

"Where will you be sleeping?" she asked pointedly.

He smiled and silently turned down the blankets on the bed, his answer obvious. Deep inside her, something dangerous stirred to life.

"Since you forced me to sleep bound in a carriage," she said coolly, "I deserve the bed tonight. You may sleep in that chair. Light the coals in the grate. You'll be comfortable."

"But then how would I keep an eye on my lovely prisoner?"

"You could pull the chair in front of the door. Surely there are only a few hours left before dawn, and you'll be up doing whatever secret things you have to do."

"There *are* some secret things I'd like to show you."

He looked down her body in that way that worried her, because it made her feel all shaky and hot inside. Where was his menace now? Why couldn't he make her frightened of him again?

"But now is not the time," he continued. "Let's get you out of that uncomfortable dress."

With a squeak of surprise, she rushed to put the bed between them. "Mr.—Nick—!" How could she speak to him when she didn't know his last name? "Do not insult me so!"

"I'm not insulting you," he said, striding with animal grace to stand opposite the bed. "I just know Sam misjudged your size. You couldn't possibly sleep in that dress."

"I will manage, thank you!"

"As you wish. If you need a moment's privacy, step behind the screen."

"Aren't you going to leave?" she asked faintly.

He only arched a brow at her stupidity. He continued to study her, and she must have succeeded in looking sick and desperate, because he suddenly sighed.

"All right, but I'll be right outside the door. I assume you now realize you can't escape me. Cox is with the carriage nearby, and trust me, he doesn't sleep well when we're traveling. If you try to escape off the balcony again, he'll hear you. If you shout for help, we'll only have to tell people that my poor, crazy wife is bound for Bedlam. Don't make me embarrass you like that."

Charlotte remained silent, watching wide-eyed

as he pulled his shirt back on. He didn't bother buttoning it, and his skin gleamed in the opening.

"You have two minutes," he warned, then stepped into the hall and closed the door.

Tiptoeing frantically, she found his portmanteau, then dropped to her knees and dug inside. Nothing but clothing—and a book on politics. A book! That was a waste of a minute.

Next she ran to the balcony door and opened it. She leaned out and saw the carriage nearby, just as Nick had said.

Down below, a man leaned against a hitching post and looked up at her, the whites of his teeth gleaming.

Nick.

She slammed that door shut and raced for the other one. Flinging it open, she only ran four steps down the hall before she ran squarely into Nick's broad chest. Desperate, no longer thinking, she opened her mouth to scream, and he covered it with his hand. Dragging her back inside, he flung her onto the bed, where she bounced once and rolled off the far side onto her feet.

She faced him across the bed, her chest heaving with each breath, feeling that she wanted to slap him.

Nick lifted his portmanteau onto the bed. He glanced down at the contents. "Looking for this?" he asked, pulling the pistol from his trouser pocket.

She gasped.

He rolled his eyes and set the gun inside the portmanteau. "I hope you at least refolded my clothes."

He reached in again and this time removed real rope, not just strips of torn sheets. How had she missed that?

"I warned you," he said when he saw her backing up. "Now get into bed."

"But I still have to use . . ." Her voice died away.

"Then use the damn chamber pot!"

He was almost shouting by the end, and she scurried behind the screen.

Several minutes later, when she'd delayed all she could, she stepped out from behind the screen and saw that Nick was once again wearing only trousers. He blew out most of the candles until they seemed wrapped in shadows. But she could see the rope in his hand.

"I wasn't planning on tying you up, but you've left me no choice. Come here."

"I promise I won't—"

"Charlotte!" He said her name calmly, firmly. "We both know you'll lie to get what you want. I admire that. Now come here."

After she did as he requested, he wrapped a handkerchief around her right wrist, then knotted the rope over that. With a sigh she held up her left.

He ignored her, let out a yard's length of rope, then tied the end to his own left wrist. He didn't use a handkerchief to protect his skin, as he'd done to hers. Surely such consideration only aided his purpose. If her wounds festered, he'd need to seek treatment.

After pulling tight on the ropes one last time, Nick said, "Now get into bed on the left side."

She hesitated, staring at the turned-down blankets, remembering when she'd last gotten into bed with a man, and what had happened.

"Charlotte."

After saying her name, he didn't wait for her compliance, but climbed into bed and slid to the far side. The rope between them went taut, and she was pulled, stumbling, to the edge. She put a knee up, then gingerly lay back, so close to the edge that her shoulder hung off. The weight of him sank in the old mattress, making her panic that she would slide against him in her sleep.

Not that she was in any danger of sleeping when her heart raced so and her mind fluttered with images of Nick's naked chest and his dark eyes, eyes that she'd caught unguarded once. They'd betrayed a hunger she'd never seen before, which even now made her shiver.

She lay frozen, listening to the sounds of her captor relaxing into sleep. First she heard his breathing deepen and slow, then she felt the brush of his elbow against hers, sending her nerves into a panicked skitter.

She pulled her arm across her chest, but he didn't move again. How could he have fallen asleep so quickly? Surely he was trying to deceive her.

But minutes passed, and only one soft snore escaped him.

Nick had turned her into a liar.

With a sigh she watched the shadows dance through the curtains and flash mingled patterns on the ceiling. She'd always prided herself on her honor. No matter how coldly her husband had treated her, no matter what degrading things he'd forced her to do in the dark of the night, she'd had her honor. Sometimes she'd even fooled herself into thinking Aubrey Sinclair had admired her for it.

But when forced into desperate circumstances, the first thing she'd done was lie so that she could escape. And what had it gotten her? The admiration of a criminal—and the certainty that he'd continue to watch over her closely.

What was she becoming? she wondered, even as tears stung her eyes. She called herself desperate, yet Nick had touched her cheek and ignited a firestorm of yearning in her that she still didn't understand. She knew nothing about him—yet he'd treated her gently, showed more restraint than her own husband had. Nick was amusing and exciting and—

Was she starting to believe him? Just because he'd said he knew her father? Or was she misinterpreting everything out of some sad need to change her life?

She'd succeeded in doing that, all right. She'd been kidnapped, tied up, threatened, and now forced to sleep bound to a man who confused her—scared her—drew her.

Slowly she turned to look at Nick. His head was turned toward her in sleep. He wore no frown, no look of intense concentration, just relaxed peacefulness. He looked . . . different, younger, so very handsome.

With rising dismay she realized she was succumbing to his charm. She had no proof of his allegiance except what she'd witnessed with her own eyes. She had to make her escape before she lost herself altogether. She'd find her father, and he would help her sort out the truth. She spent several fruitless minutes picking at the knot of rope at her wrist, then gave it up as hopeless.

But how else to escape? Nick was stronger than she was, and he had two other men to help him watch over her. He'd warned her again tonight to behave. And if she did, would that help her situation? Could she remain calm, outwardly docile, and lull them into forgetting that she was still a threat?

She rolled onto her side, trying to make herself comfortable in the tight dress, slid her hand beneath her cheek, and stared at Nick until she finally fell asleep.

Chapter 7

Every relationship formed is a vulnerability for a political agent, one which can come back to haunt you.

The Secret Journals of a Spymaster

Nick was the first thing Charlotte saw when she awoke. He was much closer this time, also turned on his side, staring at her. When he looked at her mouth, all her plans from the previous evening flew out of her head. She felt the warmth of his breath, the intensity of his regard as he seemed to study each part of her face. She couldn't move, frozen in place by a feeling so very foreign to her—so very exciting.

She told herself she was lying there to placate him, but that was a lie.

She told herself she would understand him better if she waited to see what he would do. That was a lie, too.

When he leaned toward her, it was all she could do not to let these powerful feelings overwhelm her. Instead she watched this confident, arrogant man hesitate, then gently brush her lips with his.

His touch was rain-shower soft, moist, so very different than anything she'd ever experienced. Each small kiss was a separate exploration of her lips, from the corners to the full bottom. She breathed in the scent of him, her eyes half closed as she immersed herself in the wondrous sensations.

She thought she heard him faintly groan as he nibbled at her bottom lip, drawing it gently into his mouth to exert a soft sucking pressure. Something shuddered to life deep inside her, awakening her to a rising passion she'd never experienced before.

She gasped and they came apart, both breathing heavily, both staring at each other in surprise. Then his eyes narrowed, and he cursed and rolled to sit on the edge of the bed. The rope that bound them together gave a gentle tug on her wrist, and she remembered that he'd had to bind her to keep her in bed with him.

Once her husband had tied her up for his pleasure, and the humiliation had made her cry and beg to be freed. So why did she now feel something fleeting, something unnameable for Nick?

Was she doomed to keep repeating the mistakes of her past? She didn't even know his full name!

Biting her lip to hold back a sob, Charlotte rolled away from him, only to have her right arm caught behind her by the rope.

"Wait, I'll release you," he said coldly.

She didn't turn back, but a moment later her arm was free. She drew it back to hug herself, shivering. To her surprise he pulled the blanket up over her.

"Go back to sleep," he said. "It's early."

She didn't think she'd be able to, as her thoughts roared with confusion in her head. Surely her plan to placate him didn't include accepting his advances.

She must have eventually dozed, because when next she was aware of her surroundings, she could hear low voices in conversation.

"Julia is still heading north," Sam said. "But she's moving at such a leisurely pace, making no attempt at secrecy, that I can't believe she knows we're on to her."

"I wonder if Campbell said anything about my blackmail attempt?" Nick asked. "You'd think she'd be in more of a hurry then." He sounded impatient and frustrated, a man who wanted to be moving, but couldn't.

"Regardless, I think she's definitely putting in an appearance at Kelthorpe's house party."

"Good," Nick answered. "That's where I've

sent Will. He's heading to Yorkshire anyway, with the girl he's engaged to."

"So he agreed to return to the service?"

"No . . . but he agreed to help us just this once. He's out of the army, ready for a new life. I can't take that away from him, not after all he's been through."

Charlotte wondered if they knew she was listening, if this was all an act for her benefit. But why? Wouldn't real criminals just dispose of her, rather than try to make her think they were on England's side?

"What did he have to say about Julia?" Sam asked, and Charlotte could hear reluctance in his quiet voice.

"He was surprised at her duplicity. Frankly, I told him I wish I would have killed her."

She stiffened as the cold loathing in Nick's voice unnerved her. Whenever her feelings softened toward him, she should remember this moment.

"No, Nick, you can't do this to yourself," Sam said sadly. "We couldn't have known what she was capable of. I've known her since childhood, and I suspected nothing."

"You were with her brother more than her. Whereas I was in her bed."

The bitterness in Nick's voice confused her. He'd had a relationship with this woman he claimed was now a traitor? If he really was a spy for England, that must make him feel . . . even more betrayed.

But he was holding Charlotte prisoner. If he wanted Julia dead, couldn't he easily kill Charlotte, too?

Yet both men sounded so—convincing.

In a low, furious voice, Nick said, "Do you know what it's like to have a woman under your control, to think there was . . . something between you, when all the while she's trying to betray you and everything you stand for? If I would have killed her, then maybe the army wouldn't have been slaughtered."

Charlotte hadn't heard this part of his story, and she couldn't imagine the kind of person who could be responsible for so many deaths, let alone a woman.

"You did what you could then, just like you're doing now. We'll capture her. And with Will on the inside, we can't fail."

Nick lowered his voice, and a touch of amusement crept in. "It didn't go well when I told him who I had hostage."

Though she wanted to hold her breath with anticipation, she forced herself to breathe deeply, normally. She opened her eyes the barest slits, so she could see the two men sitting in chairs before the hearth, leaning close together.

"Why?" Sam asked. "Surely he understood the necessity."

Something was wrong. Sam looked different, but she didn't want to stare just yet.

"When you were following him," Nick continued, "didn't you ever wonder who he was engaged to?"

Suddenly he turned to look at her, followed by Sam, who was wearing some sort of wig. Sam looked confused until his face cleared with understanding—and worry. Charlotte found herself staring back at them, not caring if they knew she was awake. Why did they look at her as they discussed some girl Will was—

Will? Heading for Yorkshire? Were they referring to . . . William Chadwick, her sister's future husband?

"Now Charlotte—" Nick began.

Thinking only of protecting her sister, she bolted out of bed and ran for the door. Nick caught her easily, holding her tight to his body. Facing him, she squirmed and pushed at his chest, feeling the hard pressure of his hips, but more concerned about her sister than the threat to herself.

"You're talking about William Chadwick!" She hit him hard enough in the stomach that she heard his breath catch.

"Yes, we are. Now stop struggling, or I'll have to tie you up again."

He gave her a last tight squeeze, which, through her thin, old dress, allowed her to feel the hard, muscular length of his body. She gasped and went still. Before he pushed her away, she felt his erection against her stomach. Though she experienced a momentary anxiety, she forced it from her mind. Her sister's very happiness was at stake!

She put her hands on her hips and glared up at Nick. "You must let me go! I have to warn my sister."

"Warn her about what?" he asked, leaning back against the door and crossing his arms over his chest. He glanced at Sam, who raised his palms as if to say he was staying out of it.

Charlotte was briefly distracted. Was Sam wearing . . . cosmetics? But she forced herself to turn away and glare at Nick. "That Lord Chadwick is one of you!"

"Will left the military. He's starting a whole new life with your sister. That's why he—"

Nick stopped himself, but not in time. He could see Charlotte's worry turn to suspicion, and he heaved a sigh.

"That's why he what?" she demanded, advancing on him.

She was so tiny; what was she going to do—shove him aside? "He wanted to be alone with Jane, so he made sure you were absent. He procured an invitation he didn't think you could resist. He didn't know about the meeting I'd planned with Campbell."

Her mouth opened and closed, but she didn't seem to be able to find the words.

"He wanted to be alone so he could—compromise Jane?" she gasped out.

She looked as if she was ready to take on the

world to defend her family. Hell, this wasn't good. More and more he admired her, more and more he had to force away thoughts of getting her into bed. The excuses were varied in his head—she wasn't a virgin, she hadn't gotten pregnant while married. But the biggest obstacle of all was that he knew himself too well: he would grow to care for her, and he had vowed he wouldn't let that happen again until he was done working for the government. He wasn't leaving the army yet, no matter how his family thought they could trap him.

Yet like a fool, he'd kissed Charlotte. He'd tormented himself with a taste of her sweet lips. It had been a long time since he'd slept with a woman, because he was not a man to take what was offered and leave.

He couldn't leave Charlotte, and for a moment she'd been very willing to have him stay in bed with her.

But now she was looking so affronted that he raised both hands to placate her. "Will just wanted the chance to get to know Jane. You do remember how that felt when you were engaged to your husband?"

A strange look he couldn't read came over her face. He suspected it didn't involve happy memories. Was her marriage not as idyllic as he thought?

Through gritted teeth she said, "And so he disposed of me by putting me in your way?"

"He didn't know I would be at Arbury's. He didn't even know I was back in the country. I've already told you, he's out of the military, done with spying."

"Even if I believe any of this, now thanks to you he'll be putting my sister in danger."

That's what Will had worried about, and though it made Nick uneasy, they had no choice. "There's nothing dangerous in a duke's house party. Julia might be marrying Kelthorpe—she wouldn't risk exposing herself."

"This woman you're chasing is going to marry a duke?"

"Yes. Now don't you see why it's so important that we have the evidence to stop her? The Duke of Kelthorpe is related to Queen Victoria. Can you imagine the scandal should Julia marry into that family?"

She looked frozen with indecision, until she finally covered her face and turned away. "I can't listen to you! I don't know what to believe! All I know is that you're holding me against my will— and now I discover you've embroiled my sister in all this danger—and she doesn't even know it! She never read my father's journals, she won't understand—"

When she broke off, looking horrified, he read her face as easily as any newspaper.

"He kept journals? He let you read them?" Nick was stunned that the colonel would ever do something so foolish.

"Oh don't worry," she said bitterly, "they prove nothing. He doesn't even use real names. It's Mr. West this, and Mr. South that."

He tensed as she recited Will's and Sam's code names, then exchanged a look with Sam.

"I found them hidden—he certainly didn't allow me to read them. But I kept them to myself," she said, lowering her voice and slumping down to sit on the bed. "I should have showed them to Jane. They might have better prepared her to figure out what Lord Chadwick is up to."

"And did they prepare you?" Nick asked.

She wore a sad smile, and to his surprise a single tear slid down her cheek. "If I hadn't read them I never would have followed you out of the ballroom."

When he'd been walking through the ballroom, intent on his meeting, he had still noticed her. Her face and figure had penetrated his determination, almost distracting him.

"My foolish head was filled with intrigues," she said sadly. "It was so good to have something else to think about after—after everything that had happened."

She must mean her husband's death. Had she loved him that much?

"So when I saw you looking so suspicious—" she said.

"I didn't look suspicious."

Nick heard Sam abruptly laugh, then choke it off when Nick glared at him.

Though she looked as if she were thinking of other things, Charlotte slowly shook her head. "No one at a ball moves with as much purpose as you did. And then when you went into that private corridor—what was I supposed to think?"

"That I belonged there?" he answered dryly.

"I just knew you didn't. I thought—I thought maybe I had some of Papa in me after all."

"You definitely have some of him in you," Nick said shortly.

Sam cleared his throat. "I've got to get back to Julia."

Nick had the absurd wish to make Sam stay. Did he now think he needed protection from a single small woman? But all Nick did was nod.

"I'll return when I have news."

"We'll start heading north. We'll keep to the prearranged roads. And do me a favor—when Will's coachman Barlow has time on his hands at Langley Manor, have him deliver this note to London for Campbell. Everything's spelled out inside."

Charlotte glanced briefly at Sam, and then she stared as if she hadn't really looked at him before. Nick hadn't had the chance to explain Sam's penchant for disguises. As Sam stood up out of the shadows and took the note, his cloak flowed out over a skirt. Sam knew he was being stared at, so with a fluidity surprising in a man, he sank into a curtsy before Charlotte.

As a slow smile spread across her face, she said, "Take off the cloak."

Wearing a grin, Sam dramatically whirled the cloak from his shoulders. Though he was not a very broad, muscular man, it seemed ridiculous to see him in a woman's red dress, buttoned clear up to his neck, and fully flounced with petticoats that spread his skirts wide.

Charlotte said to Sam, "Surely you realize you fool no one with that *disguise*."

Sam cocked his head, and the curls in his wig danced. "And you've never seen a very tall woman before?"

"Of course I have! But the rest of you is not—"

She broke off as Sam began his transformation, and Nick watched her astonishment grow. Sam was legendary in his ability to hide himself within the physicality of a character. His every movement now became graceful, his walk womanly as he retrieved his cloak, and even the breadth of him seemed to shrink.

Sam wrapped the cloak about himself and spoke in a soft, throaty voice. "I shall see you both in just scant hours. Do play nicely with each other." He glided from the room.

Nick watched Charlotte gaze blankly at the door, then turn an astonished look on him.

"What did you expect?" he asked. "We're good at what we do."

She just shook her head and turned away.

They were quiet for a long time, and he couldn't think of a thing to say. It was still morning, and he had no duties until Sam returned with news about whether Julia was heading for Kelthorpe's house party.

And he was alone with a beautiful woman next to a big bed.

Chapter 8

Intimacy encourages all sorts of revelations, including the ones you don't plan on revealing.

The Secret Journals of a Spymaster

Nick went to the window as if he were looking for something important, instead of merely keeping busy. But he noticed when Charlotte raised her head and stared at him.

"I heard you say you had . . . relations with this woman, this Julia."

Well *that* wasn't a normal conversation for a society lady. He studied her, pretending an impassivity he didn't feel. "Yes."

"Why do you men do that, sleep with women so readily?"

He could only blink at her for a moment. "You want to have this conversation with *me*?"

"Why not?" she said with exasperation. "I've already slept tied up in the same bed with you."

And I've already kissed you.

"Lying side by side, fully clothed, is hardly the same thing as *relations*," he said, emphasizing her word.

"But for women it is something treated with the reverence of only a wedding night and begetting children."

"Men usually hope those two things aren't involved," he said dryly, "unless one needs an heir, of course."

But she only glared at him. "That's what my husband wanted—children. And I didn't give them to him."

There was a pain in her words that called to him, but he refused to acknowledge it. He'd let down too many people in his own life—and his own father had let him down.

She sighed. "My husband used to tell me about the women he'd consorted with before we were married."

Nick didn't know what she wanted from him, but it seemed to require conversation. "And did he continue to consort?"

"I don't think so. He seemed faithful . . . to a degree."

"To a degree?" he echoed.

She waved her hand and didn't look at him. "Never mind. I should never have brought up such a subject—not with my kidnapper."

"A very unwilling kidnapper."

"Of course you *could* let me go."

He was glad to see some of her spirit return. He found himself fascinated by her, drawn to her and these hints of a past that did not always seem so wonderful.

"I think we're done with this conversation, Charlotte."

There was a brisk knock on the door, and he couldn't help feeling relieved. Cox walked in, carrying a large tray for breakfast.

There were plates of eggs and bacon and toast, and the three of them ate in uncomfortable silence.

Charlotte's restless mind could settle on no single thought. She thought about innocent Jane, who didn't know the truth about her future husband. Jane was innocent because Charlotte had selfishly kept their father's journals to herself. She'd also foolishly told Nick about their existence. All he had to do was have them stolen, and he would have access to all her father's work.

But she didn't believe Nick needed those journals to craft a believable story. Was he telling the truth? He and Sam had been speaking when they thought she was asleep. Could they really have faked their whole conversation to lull her into a falsehood? Why would they have bothered?

All right, they might want her cooperation to make things easier on themselves, but if they were truly traitors, killing her would accomplish the same purpose. And no one would ever know. But she was already cooperating, although for her own reasons. She had to get away, before her mother thought something horrible had happened to her, before Charlotte told every dreadful marital secret she had to this stranger—before she succumbed to more of his kisses.

Charlotte behaved herself as she left the inn on Nick's arm. He didn't tie her up, though his look was threatening as they got under way. He tossed a newspaper on her seat, stretched out his long legs and fell promptly asleep, as if the past night hadn't rested him. Could it have been as difficult for him to sleep in the same bed as it was for her?

She stared at him with dismay, then peeked past the shutters out the glass window. The rural countryside of Huntingdonshire rolled by at an alarming rate. What was she going to do—jump? And risk breaking her leg?

She decided to behave as she thought her father would, biding her time and waiting for a better opportunity.

It came only hours later, when the carriage suddenly thumped. The newspaper slid to the floor, and Charlotte braced herself on the bench.

Nick frowned and leaned toward the window. "I wonder if we hit—"

A shudder wracked the frame, and with a great groaning of strained wood, the carriage suddenly lurched sideways, and she tumbled to the floor.

She watched in shock as Nick's head slammed into the window frame, and then he fell heavily on top of her. For several minutes she flailed beneath his weight, then the carriage shuddered to a halt, tilted at an angle.

She finally succeeded in sliding out from beneath Nick. She didn't know what to do first, as he was so ominously still. There was another tug on the vehicle, and she remembered stories of frightened horses continuing to run, pulling a carriage to pieces. Moving carefully, she ducked her head out the open window. Mr. Cox had both hands raised before the two pairs of horses, who were whinnying and tossing their heads. Each jerk of the harness sent another shudder through the carriage.

"Ye're good beasts now," Mr. Cox said soothingly.

Very slowly he reached down and unhooked the horses' harness from the carriage. Charlotte breathed a sigh of relief, but the cessation of tension seemed to intensify the horses' fear. The paired leaders pawed high in the air as Mr. Cox dove to the side. All four took off at a gallop down the tree-lined road, and the coachman followed at a surprisingly swift run. Charlotte sagged back onto the edge of the bench.

But Nick hadn't moved. He lay in a crumpled heap on the floor at her feet. Her heart renewed its pounding as she slid her hand down his neck to feel the strong beat of his pulse. Breathing a shaky sigh, she gently lifted his head. A lump swelled just above his left temple, and a trickle of blood oozed from the small cut in the center. He was unconscious, but he would probably be just fine.

And she was alone on a road surrounded on both sides by a wooded forest. If she hid long enough in the trees, someone was bound to drive by eventually and help her. She would be free to appease her mother, to warn her sister.

Her throat tightened with helpless tears, and a battle began in her mind. Nick looked as peaceful as he had that morning, when she'd awakened in bed beside him. This was the man who'd gently bathed her cuts, who'd kissed her as if she were made of precious glass that might break if he exerted force—who'd promised to protect her from the villain who wanted her dead.

And what if Mr. Cox had gone to the next village for help? How long would Nick be alone, helpless, if she left him?

She closed her eyes and gave in. She couldn't leave him like this. He needed her help. After pulling a handkerchief from her reticule, she climbed down from the carriage and listened for the sound of running water. It took her several searches of both sides of the road to find a tiny stream that gurgled over a few rocks before disappearing underground again. She wet the handkerchief and walked back to the carriage.

Nick loomed in the doorway unsteadily. He

blinked several times, then shook his head as if to clear it. Wearing a frown, he asked, "You didn't run away?"

She put her hands on her hips. "Maybe you're not the only one whose head is damaged."

He blinked again. "You're hurt?"

She shook her head as her attempt at humor went right by him. "I went to dampen a handkerchief. You have blood on your face."

He lifted his hand to his head and winced.

"Nick, why don't you take my hand and I'll help you dow—"

He tried to step down on his own and ended up staggering. He would have pitched forward onto his face if she hadn't steadied him. Swaying, he propped his arms on her shoulders and stared down at her.

"Sorry," he murmured.

She didn't think he was. "Sit down here in the shade and let me wipe your face."

He complied, resting his back against a carriage wheel, then remained silent as she knelt beside him and began to dab at his wound.

"Does it hurt?" she asked quietly.

"Not the cut, but my head feels like it's going to explode."

She pressed the cool handkerchief to his temple, and this time he caught her hand and held it.

Searching her face, he asked, "Why didn't you leave? It was the perfect opportunity."

She shrugged and avoided his gaze, pretending intense interest in his injury. "I'd probably get eaten by wild animals."

"In Huntingdonshire?"

"Or killed by that man you were talking to in London, the one who wants me dead. Trust me, it was a purely selfish decision on my part."

He didn't answer at first. Several minutes passed before he pushed her hand away. "I'll be fine. Where's Cox?"

"He went running after the horses, back the way we'd come."

"There's probably a wheelwright in a village nearby," Nick said, nodding. "Cox will be back soon."

But several hours passed while she was forced to hover over a drowsy Nick. The coachman returned, riding in a wagon that carried a new wheel behind it, and four harnessed carriage horses attached at the rear. The driver was a blacksmith—the village was too small for a true wheelwright—but the man had brought along his strapping son to help.

Regardless of Charlotte's protests, Nick helped lift the carriage so the new wheel could be put in place. He was sweating, and his face looked pale. When he finally stumbled back from the carriage, she slid beneath his arm and steadied him.

Looking down at her, he gave her shoulder a squeeze. "Be a dear, love, and break out the ale I keep beneath the bench. This is hard work for a hot autumn day."

She nodded, knowing he was playing her husband again. "Are you sure we shouldn't have the blacksmith find you a doctor, dearest? Your bruise is turning an ugly color."

He grinned. "I've had worse. But your concern is touching."

He gave her a quick, hard kiss that made her feel as unsteady as he was.

Between gritted teeth and a forced smile, she said, "Anything to help." But she couldn't remain angry when she could feel the tremor in his muscles as he held himself upright. The blow to the head had done more harm than he wanted to admit.

When they'd all drank their ale, and the blacksmith was paid for his efforts and on his way home, Mr. Cox went forward to check on the horses one last time. Charlotte felt Nick's arm around her shoulders again. As she put her arm about his chest, he began to sag against her, dropping to his knees and bringing her with him.

"Nick! Let me get Mr.—"

"No, don't worry him," he said heavily. "I'm fine."

"But I'm all that's holding you up," she insisted.

"Then let's get into the carriage, and you won't even have to do that."

With a lot of pulling on her part, she managed to get him to his feet. After they'd taken a couple of shaky steps toward the open carriage door, Mr. Cox suddenly called out in a loud, worried voice.

"Nick!"

Nick detached himself from her so suddenly that she staggered. She watched in shock as he sprinted past the horses, the picture of his usual athletic grace. Mr. Cox stepped out of the horses' shadow and shook his head mournfully.

"As I thought," the coachman said as Nick skidded to a halt, "ye're not quite as sick as ye pretend."

Charlotte gaped at the two of them, and then Nick turned to face her.

"Now Charlotte—"

She threw up her hands with a groan, then turned and strode away from him, back down the road from where they came.

"Where are you going?" he asked in a laughing voice.

She could hear him advancing behind her. Glaring at him over her shoulder, she said, "I should have just left you!"

"But you didn't."

He was trying his best to look serious, but to her disgust he wasn't succeeding.

"Were you even unconscious?" she demanded, turning to face him so quickly that she was able to push him backward.

He leaned his chest against her hand. "Truly, I

was *quite* unconscious. Senseless. Unaware. I might have *died* without you."

Against her palm his heart pounded with surety, with safety, with confidence. When she didn't answer, he bent and lifted her up, his arms behind her shoulders and her knees, and walked back toward the carriage.

She pushed at his chest. "Put me down!"

"I can't take that risk. I might collapse again. Who would nurse me back to health?"

Their room at the next inn that night was considerably smaller than the last, although thankfully it still had a screen for Charlotte to retreat behind when she needed privacy. The bed dominated the room, and she tried not to look at it. Would they sleep there again? Would he attempt to do more than kiss her? That afternoon, when he'd swept her off her feet, she'd found herself imagining him kissing her deeply, as if he really needed her.

And would she still be able to resist? What was it about him that called to her? He had taken her prisoner, but he'd tried to be gentle. He was a man on a mission, and she was beginning to think he was on the correct side of the law. Good heavens, she'd given up a chance to escape for that. She'd seen evidence of his desire for her, but besides one kiss, he'd not acted on it, or tried to force her into anything, when he so clearly had all the power. Was it this restraint that she thought exciting? Or the gentle playfulness she'd occasionally glimpsed?

Mr. Cox brought up a dinner tray, and once again they ate together. Mr. Cox was not a talkative man, and Nick seemed to have something on his mind. Charlotte let them have their silence as she worried about the coming night.

When the coachman had finally departed with orders to send up a bath for Nick, she sat down on the edge of the bed, deciding the best way to ask for the favor of her own bath. She hoped he wouldn't require something in return.

There was a quiet knock on the door. Nick walked over to her and put a hand on her shoulder, and she found herself tensing.

"That will be the bath. I suggest you sit here as docilely as any wife until the servants are gone."

"And what will you do if I don't—kill the maid?" The day's frustration made her speak more sharply than she had intended.

"Don't become a threat, Charlotte."

They stared at each other as another knock sounded.

Finally she lowered her gaze, knowing this was not the way to placate him. "Very well."

As two kitchen boys carried in a copper tub and placed it before the hearth, Charlotte listened in surprise to the new character Nick had adopted. No longer was he a Scotsman, but a very proper British gentleman, with the subservient air of a banker's clerk, and an undercurrent of a man who thought he was entitled to more. She watched him in amazement. The arrogant, powerful Nick was gone.

Who was he?

The servants made several trips, bringing steaming buckets of water. They lit the coals in the grate to warm the room, and even left two buckets of cooler water behind. After Nick tipped them handsomely and they left, she stared at the tub.

"I don't know how you're going to do this," she finally said. "Of course I could go sit in the dining room."

He folded his arms across his chest. "The bath is for you."

Stunned, she couldn't look at him, so she let herself stare longingly at the bath. Steam rose from the water, and there were thick towels and scented soap set on the nearby chair.

He had ordered this for her?

She felt confused and uncertain over his motives.

"Why did you do this?" she asked, raising her gaze to meet his. This didn't make sense from the man who had kidnapped her, who'd tied her up in bed, who'd pretended illness to see how she'd react. Did he want something more from her? Or was this another hint of the gentle man who'd washed her wounds?

For a fleeting moment, he looked as confused

as she felt. Then he gruffly said, "The odors in here might become rather ripe."

He was lying. Was he embarrassed that he'd shown a softness he didn't want her to see? Or was his final goal seduction?

"And will you wait somewhere else?" she asked.

"No."

She wasn't surprised. Even her behavior today seemed to have given him no reason to think he could trust her. She allowed herself a sigh as she stared longingly at the tub.

"I'll move the screen for you," he said.

She couldn't help but smile at him. She swiftly gathered up a change of clothing—maybe the next dress would fit better—and when he was finished she ducked behind the screen without meeting his gaze.

"Promise you won't come over here," she called.

She thought she heard him snort before he said, "I give you my word."

Since she was trying to lull him with sweetness, she resisted the urge to remind him that he had admitted he admired her lies. He too would lie when he thought it necessary. But she didn't think he'd lie about this. And the fact that she believed this about Nick was something she didn't want to examine.

So although she was uneasy with his nearness,

she undressed swiftly, and with a sigh of pleasure sank into the tub.

Nick found himself pacing. Charlotte's blissful sighs put him on edge, for he kept imagining more erotic ways he could make her sigh like that. They were separated by a thin screen—and she was naked.

He should have had Cox send him up a brandy.

What had Nick been thinking? He was pampering her with a bath, as if he was going to enjoy her scented flesh. What happened to his own insistence that he would treat her as he would a male hostage?

Listening to the splashing of water, he paced even faster. When she began to softly hum he wanted to groan his frustration. He'd been trapped with her all day, watching the graceful way she'd held the newspaper, the strain of her bodice to control her breasts, the way she'd refused to sleep, although her lovely eyes had sagged with weariness.

After the carriage accident she could have escaped, yet she'd stayed to tend him. He'd woken up, his vision bleary, and thought for certain she'd run. But she'd been fetching water for his wounds like a concerned wife. What the hell was he supposed to make of that?

And now he was alone with her again, in an even smaller room with what seemed like an enormous bed. He *couldn't* spend another night lying at her side. He would have to think up another plan.

He glanced at the screen again, then stopped cold. She had taken the only lamp back there with her, and as light flickered against the far wall, he could see the faintest shadow of her through the screen. He should quickly light some candles. But he didn't move.

She was only a blurry shape, almost indistinguishable, but he found himself staring like the celibate he'd lately been. As she rose out of the tub, he could see her silhouette, the roundness of her breasts, the fall of her hair, the surprisingly full curve of her ass.

Cursing under his breath, he turned away.

When she finally folded back the screen, a waft of sweet-smelling woman greeted him. Her hair fell in damp, tangled waves down her back, and she'd donned another gown. He couldn't decide whether he was grateful Sam had forgotten a nightdress.

With her eyes cast down she murmured, "Might I borrow your brush?"

He gave it to her without comment, then sat down to watch the next torture as she bent before the hot coals, spread out her hair, and repeatedly combed through it.

When she was done and turned to stare at him hesitantly, he couldn't take it anymore.

"Is the water cold?" he asked brusquely.

"Yes."

"Good."

Charlotte watched with rising shock as Nick pulled off his coat and then his shirt.

"What are you doing?" she asked breathlessly, trying not to stare at his bare chest.

"Using the tub."

"But I just—"

"I'm too lazy to wait. Did you use all the towels?" he asked over his shoulder as he set the screen back up.

She cleared her throat, hoping her voice sounded normal. "No. But I hung my wet . . . underthings back there."

He disappeared behind, and she swallowed as she saw his trousers tossed to hang over the screen. As he sat in the dirty water, surely he must be shuddering with the cold.

And looking at her drawers and petticoats.

Suddenly the whole screen fell forward, landing partially on the bed. Her mouth sagged open as she watched Nick lean his head back in the tub. His bare wet knees were plainly visible.

"Couldn't let you think of escaping from me, now could I?" he said.

And then he started washing himself. She was frozen with shock—and something that made her feel overheated and vulnerable. He grinned at her as his soapy hands slid slowly down his chest and disappeared from sight. With a gasp Charlotte turned her back. She could hear his laughter and much splashing, but she certainly didn't have to watch. It was a shame she couldn't turn off her mind, though, because she couldn't forget his wicked smile, and how . . . pleasantly it transformed his face.

And sad to say—she hadn't even thought about escaping while he was bathing.

"I can't believe this," she muttered to herself, sitting down on the bed and clutching a pillow.

"What?" he called.

She could hear his amusement. She found herself wanting to put him in his place, to saunter over there and prove that his nudity did not bother her. She'd been a married woman, after all.

But she'd never been at a man's bath before, even her husband's. She couldn't do it. "I only said how incongruous it is that we're bathing in the same room—in the same *tub*—and I don't even know your name."

"I'm not lying about my name."

"Your full name."

There was a pause, and she almost looked over her shoulder to see what he was doing. Almost.

"It's Nicholas Wright. With a W."

"Wright?" she echoed. "I'm sure you think it's perfect for you."

He chuckled. Had she heard him laugh before? For the first time he sounded truly relaxed.

"Have you heard of my family?" he asked.

"Should I have?"

"I don't know. They've never been much for London."

"And were *you* much for London?"

"My father wouldn't allow it."

Even that thought-provoking statement couldn't distract her from the ludicrousness of their situation. She groaned. "I can't believe we're having this conversation while you're . . . bathing."

"Frankly, I'm relaxing. You can look at me if you want. I promise I won't stand up without warning you."

"I don't think—"

She realized he was assuming she wouldn't look! Before she could think through the consequences, she swiveled on the bed until she faced him, crossed her arms over her chest, and lifted her chin.

His wet hair was slicked back from his face, and his muscular arms glistened where they rested along the edge of the tub. His bent knees pointed to the ceiling. She was decidedly daring and brazen, altogether unlike herself. It felt very much like freedom.

He was grinning widely at her. "You're very brave."

Ignoring his words, she said, "If your father didn't allow you to go to London when you were young, I hope your estate was at least pleasant. Where is your family from?"

He leaned his head back and eyed her from beneath lowered lids. "A village in Kent called Folkestone. It's near the cliffs overlooking the English Channel."

"Isn't there an earl by that name?"

His smile faded a bit. "There is."

"And you don't like him?" she said, tilting her head as she studied him.

"I didn't say that."

"You don't seem to want to say much."

"Not my favorite subject. Let's move on."

Knowing she had to take this opportunity to discover things about him while she could, Charlotte fluffed two pillows against the headboard and leaned back.

"Do you have brothers or sisters?" she asked.

"My mother died when I was fourteen. After my father married again, they had another son and two daughters." His expression grew thoughtful. "I've never met my youngest sister, and the others were very young when I left the country."

"How old are they now?"

He looked up at the ceiling for a moment. "My brother would be sixteen now, and my youngest sister twelve."

"Such a shame that you're not a part of their lives."

"I've sent them gifts and the occasional letter. They've never written back."

She felt a catch of sadness, knowing that she'd

been lucky to have Jane at her side, even if they did not always agree. "I'm sorry."

"I know it's not their fault. I ignored my father's wishes when I joined John Company, and he never forgave me."

"John Company?"

"The East India Company. I'm part of the Political Department, although I used to be an officer in the cavalry."

Though she wanted to question him about his military career, she could not imagine not being close to her father. "Did it . . . disturb you greatly to go against your father?"

He smiled. "No. He controlled me by the purse strings, even after my stepmother convinced him to let me attend Oxford."

"Well . . . that was decent of her."

"She wanted all my father's attention on her own children," he said dryly. "But that suited my purposes."

"It sounds like your family life was not ideal," she said in a soft voice, realizing how lucky she was, even though her marriage had turned out badly. At least she had a family that loved her.

Nick shook his head. "I don't want your pity. My father was a cold man and my family emulated him, so I found my relationships elsewhere."

" 'Was'?"

"He died several months ago." His voice lacked all emotion.

"Were you even in the country then?"

"No. Word reached me as I made my way through Paris on my way to England."

"It must have been terribly difficult on your stepmother, not to have you to lean upon."

"I wouldn't know. I haven't been home yet."

She gaped at him. "But surely when you came across the channel—you said your home was on the coast, did you not?"

"I couldn't abandon my duty, Charlotte. You better than anyone know how important it is to me. My father's death was months ago. A few more weeks' delay will not harm matters."

They stared at each other quietly, while she tried to imagine how different their lives were. And then came the realization that he might not be telling her the truth.

Yet . . . she believed him. And deep inside her she wanted to believe it all. He didn't seem like a criminal.

Or was it that she didn't want him to be?

Chapter 9

Guard evidence of a crime with your life. It's all
that stands between you and ignominy.

The Secret Journals of a Spymaster

Nick watched Charlotte's expression cloud
over with pensiveness instead of the interest
she'd just shown in him. He hadn't thought he'd
ever want to talk about his family, but she only
had to ask, and he'd told her private things.

Well, not everything.

But he didn't want to stop talking, even though
the water was cold. If he told her he had to get
out, it would break this tenuous thread of com-
munication that was strung between them. She
was a woman; she wanted to hear about family
relationships. It was a good way to keep her calm
and interested—and not a threat to his mission.

Maybe she would finally believe the truth. And what harm could there be in her learning a few carefully selected facts about his family?

"Over the years," he began, "I've heard a thing or two about you."

Those changeable, hazel eyes focused on him again, and he relaxed.

"Surely there has not been much gossip about me," she said. "We lived a very quiet life."

"I haven't been in England for thirteen years, so any gossip wouldn't reach me."

"Thirteen years!" she breathed. "How did you bear it?"

"I enjoyed almost every minute of it—unless I was fighting for my life, of course, and then I was too busy to enjoy things."

"Nicholas!"

Her scolding voice warmed him, and he tamped down that part of him.

"Your father spoke of you and your sister often."

"He did?"

"He was very proud of both of you." Deliberately he added, "He regretted that he could not be here for your wedding." He wanted to hear more about her marriage.

She glanced toward the dark window, as if she were looking far off. "I missed him terribly. I have often wondered if things would have turned out differently."

"What do you mean?"

"Maybe he would have seen that Aubrey Sinclair was not the husband for me." She bit her lip and looked down at her clenched hands. "I shouldn't be saying these things to you."

He sat up straighter, controlling a shiver induced by the cold water. "No, go ahead and say it. Maybe you've needed to."

She tilted her head and smiled. "But you don't need to hear it. Suffice it to say, my mother was overjoyed when Aubrey showed his intentions, and I went along with it without questioning how well we might suit."

"It sounds as if your mother didn't expect you to find a husband—which is ridiculous, with your beauty and your father's title."

She blushed and looked down, smoothing out her skirt. "I think she just allowed herself to be caught up with the excitement of my first serious suitor. 'He was a gentleman of exemplary character and fortune,' as she liked to say."

"How did he die?" he asked carefully.

Her gaze dropped to the bed, and she smoothed the coverlet. "His horse threw him into a river. He drowned."

"So sudden. That must have been difficult."

"I guess it was better than if he'd suffered."

He wanted to draw more from her, but then an uncontrollable shudder raced through him.

Charlotte stiffened. "My goodness! I've been prattling on and you must be freezing. Should I put the screen up?" she asked doubtfully.

"And risk coming near a naked man? No. Just turn your back. I trust you."

After she turned to face the wall, he quickly dried off and pulled on a clean pair of trousers. When he walked around to the side of the bed, she looked up at him. He noticed how quickly her gaze skimmed over his bare chest.

"If you trust me," she said quietly, "then please don't tie me up tonight."

He let out a sigh. "Nothing we've said here changes the fact that my mission is the most important thing to me. If you don't wish to be tied to me, we have to find another way that I can be certain you won't escape."

"But this afternoon I didn't leave you when I could have!"

"I know. But what if you change your mind?"

"But if I just sleep next to you, surely you'll be able to tell if I arise."

"I can't sleep next to you again." He sat down on the opposite side of the bed, tilting the mattress dangerously toward him, so close that their knees almost touched. "I kissed you this morning. I won't promise not to try more if you're lying against my side."

He watched the blush heat her skin, and the way her gaze dipped to his mouth. She was remembering the kiss, too.

"Then don't kiss me," she whispered.

He braced his hand beside her knee and leaned closer. "Perhaps I should say the same to you."

Her gaze flew to his face, her lovely lips parted, but she didn't say anything. How could she? She hadn't immediately pushed him away when he'd kissed her. Deep down, he wondered if he could seduce away her inhibitions, show her that there was more to life than what she'd experienced in an unhappy marriage.

"I won't kiss you," she said, but her voice spoiled her resolve by quivering.

Smiling, he said, "I'm glad I'm safe from your unsavory intentions."

She frowned. "Don't tease me. My situation with you is precarious, through no fault of my own."

"I know."

Taking a deep breath, she asked, "So where will you sleep?"

"I'll put a chair near the door."

"But you refused to do that last night."

He reached toward her and tucked a long curl behind her ear. "Last night I didn't know the bed would be worse."

This was dangerous. Charlotte was a woman who could test his resolve as perhaps no other ever had. He could read every emotion on her face, and he wondered how she would look if he was inside her.

He pulled back and stood up. He had to re-erect a small barrier between them.

"I want you to remove your clothes. You'll be less likely to try to escape in the night—and if you do, I'll be more likely to hear you."

He waited for her outrage, but the expression on her face remained almost calm. She rose slowly to her feet, the bed between them. He looked about, wondering what was nearby that she might throw at him. Or did she mean to go behind the screen?

But then her fingers went to the buttons at her throat, and she started opening them.

What the hell?

Nick's uneasiness intensified. There was something wrong. Her face looked almost blank, resigned, as if she weren't really aware of what she was doing, where she was. Her dress parted farther and farther over her bodice, as the tight material finally sagged with relief. He could see her chemise now, but it was cut low over her chest, as if it had been the one she'd worn under her ball gown.

She had to pull hard to tug each sleeve down, and he wondered if she'd have marks on her skin from how tight everything was. And she'd never complained a bit.

But she wasn't saying anything now. The dress fell to the floor in a pile, and she began untying the petticoats at her waist.

She was undressing for him, but it was far from provocative.

He couldn't look at her blank expression anymore. He came around the bed and took her hands when she would have reached for the neckline of her chemise.

"No, Charlotte, you can stop now."

The emptiness in her face began to fade away as she looked up at him. "Nick?" she whispered, sounding so confused.

Something in his chest began to ache as he looked into her frightened eyes. "That's enough, Charlotte. I didn't mean—I only meant your outer clothes. Sleep in your chemise."

She took a sudden, deep breath and stepped away from him. "That wasn't very nice," she said, projecting sternness over the quiver in her voice.

He began to relax as color blossomed in her pale cheeks. "You're right, it wasn't. I should have explained myself better. Now get into bed and go to sleep. We should hear from Sam tomorrow, and it might be a busy day."

As he watched her slide beneath the light sheets, he thought about her behavior. She'd begun to remove her clothes at just a suggestion, as if she'd done this before and it hadn't ended pleasantly.

What kind of man had she married? Or had something else happened to her that he didn't know about? Hell, he didn't know much about her at all, and he shouldn't be so curious to find out.

Yet he didn't want her dwelling on the hurt she'd suffered in life. A depressed hostage was far worse than an angry one. But how to distract her?

After turning down the lamp and dragging a chair near the door, he sat down and leaned his head back, thankful at least for the high back and the armrests. But he knew sleep wouldn't come easily, for in the shadowy darkness he could still see his hostage.

It took a long time before Charlotte finally felt some of her tension dissolve away.

What had happened to her?

Was mention of her husband's name enough to resurrect the ghost of her old response to him?

And that's what her behavior had been, a response she'd long been used to having when given an order to remove her clothes.

Would she have just kept going if Nick hadn't stopped her? What else would she have done in that trancelike state?

She covered her face with a pillow out of embarrassment. She would not let herself respond to a man's command like that again. Her old life was finished, and she had embarked on a new one, where she stood up to kidnappers and fought back as best she could.

Now if only she could stop these feelings of attraction that made it hard to think when she was around him. With frustration she tossed the pillow onto the end of the bed.

"Can't sleep?" said Nick's deep voice out of the darkness.

She drew in her breath on a gasp. "You startled me."

"Sorry. Sleep is eluding us both, I gather."

He hesitated, and she found herself listening for his voice in the silence.

"So would you like to talk?" he asked.

She closed her eyes against the darkness and wished she could will herself to sleep. "About what?"

"Well, you started an interesting subject this morning about having—what was your word?" He chuckled. "Ah, yes, *relations*."

She felt her face flush. "I did not talk about us having relations!"

"I didn't say *us*, now did I? You've revealed how your mind works."

Mortified, she rolled onto her side, away from him. "Go to sleep."

"Now, now, don't get all upset with me. So, very well, you talked about men having relations, and how to a woman such a thing is treated with—reverence? Was that your word?"

She groaned and pulled the pillow over her head again.

"Perhaps now that you're a widow," he continued, "you should remind yourself that sex—how crude of me to refer to it correctly—is also a union of pleasure."

If he wanted her curiosity, she would give it to him. "And do you not worry that you might accidentally get the woman . . . with child?"

"There are ways to safeguard against that."

She was shocked. "There are?"

"Aren't you the innocent."

She looked up into the darkness, where she could see nothing, including Nick. She felt bold, even reckless—and consequently didn't trust herself. "I don't wish to hear such things."

She heard his soft laughter. "Don't you want to play the merry widow?"

"No!"

"Of course you wouldn't," he said, soothing and teasing her at the same time. "Sex is for begetting children. And that's the only reason to be married, correct?"

"No, I—" She broke off, confused by the turn in the conversation. "I never said that."

"But you said you didn't give your husband an heir, and that's all he wanted."

She frowned. "Maybe."

"But is that all you wanted in a marriage? Children?"

"I guess not."

"But it was all your husband wanted," he said softly.

There was a long, awkward silence while she tried to understand why this made her so sad, that her husband had only wanted children from her, and not any other relationship. Most couples lived separate lives, with little in common. Had she expected—hoped—to be different?

"Good night," she said firmly.

Charlotte climbed out of the depths of sleep and rolled over. The room was bathed in sunlight, and the smell of ham and eggs made her stomach gurgle. She stretched away her stiffness, arching her back and sighing. She glanced at the window, only to see Nick watching her with an inscrutable expression.

What must she look like? Her hair was a mass of curls and snarls, and as she looked down herself, she saw that her chemise revealed a shocking amount of her breasts. In fact an inch more to her stretch, and all her assets would have been revealed. She quickly pulled the sheet up to her chin. His lips twisted in a smile before he turned back to the window. He was looking at several sheets of paper in his hand.

She wrestled with her neckline until it was as respectable as possible, then she climbed out of bed. Breakfast was laid out on the little table, and although it was obvious he had eaten some of his, he now seemed very preoccupied. She pretended her chemise was a nightgown—as if that was any better!—and after throwing a blanket around her shoulders, tiptoed toward the window, craning her neck to see what he was reading.

"It's a letter," he said over his shoulder.

She stumbled to a halt. "Oh. I will admit I was curious. Was this just delivered? I guess I was sleeping deeply."

"You were. Cox brought us breakfast, and you never knew. But no, I've had this for quite some time. Julia Reed's former accomplice, Edwin Hume, the one who is willing to testify against her, sent this to me. It's the way Julia gave secrets to our enemies."

She peered over his arm. In the sunlight the paper was so bright, she couldn't make out the exact words. "Her penmanship is rather poor."

"Like yours?"

"I was in a moving carriage," she reminded him, hoping he believed her.

"Then unlike you," he said, with a touch of sarcasm, "Julia wrote the letter this way quite deliberately. Can you see a pattern?"

"A pattern?" To her surprise he handed her the letter, and she lifted it nearer to read. It was addressed to someone named Helen, and seemed a simple account of what Julia had been doing at a market fair in Kabul. "Where is this strangely named village?"

"In Afghanistan. Julia's brother, General Reed, was the head of a division of the army of the East India Company. Their parents are dead, and she'd been traveling with him for several years. There were quite a number of families in our encampment on the plains below the city."

Charlotte studied the letter closely, seeing that Julia had even turned the paper and written up the sides of the margin. She hadn't noticed originally, but now she saw that Julia's penmanship wasn't poor. But there were plenty of stains and blots of ink, as if she were in too much of a hurry. She'd even randomly filled in the loops, perhaps scribbling while she collected her thoughts.

"There are drops of ink everywhere," she said. "If Julia wasn't flinging her pen about, then I don't know how she did this."

"Exactly," Nick said with satisfaction. "Although it looks random, it isn't. Every mark on the letter is part of a code. This was how she told our enemies about the strength of our forces."

She squinted at the paper. "I must confess, I see nothing."

"I wouldn't have either, if not for Edwin Hume. He knew I was trailing Julia and him. He sent me word that he fears she means to kill him. He included this letter, and promised me the second letter, to use as proof against Julia. He demands our protection in exchange for this."

"But how is the second letter proof?"

"Julia sent two letters, by two different routes." He held the letter between them, and they both bent over it, their heads close together. "You notice that if the letters are intercepted, there is nothing suspicious to condemn her. But once the two letters are side by side, you use the second letter to figure out the code. That will be part of our treason case against her."

"Part?"

"We have other evidence."

When Nick didn't elaborate, she asked, "To whom did she betray England?"

"The Russians. Afghanistan is a buffer between Russia and British India. Much of my mission was keeping track of what Russian agents were doing, and how the various monarchies of countries were receiving them."

"And these hostile countries—they just let you sneak about?"

"Of course not." He grinned down at her, and she saw his gaze drop to her chest, where the blanket had sagged a bit. "I'm very good at . . . blending in."

His statement was very innocent, but somehow she had thought he was going to say something else. Her blood had heated before the words could even come out of his mouth. What did she want him to be very good at?

"And my father coordinated all this?" she asked, bringing up a topic she knew would refocus them both.

He straightened. "Especially for three of us."

Three of them, she thought, remembering the men most often mentioned in her father's journals. Everything Nick was saying corresponded to what she had read. How could she know what the truth was? Goodness, he could have merely been in the army, and still know enough to fool her.

"Why don't we eat?" he said.

She watched him put the letter away in a flat leather pouch that he slid inside his portmanteau. Then he sat down in a chair and turned to watch her approach with a bit more attention than she felt necessary.

"I'll dress first," she said, disappearing behind the screen with her own bag.

When she was covered well in the drab brown dress, she returned to the table and sat down opposite Nick.

He glanced at her. "Are you terribly uncomfortable in the garments Sam brought you? I regret he didn't choose the size well."

"It is manageable. They seem to stretch a bit as I wear them."

"Understandable," he said dryly, and again she watched his gaze roam her figure.

She cleared her throat and cut her first bite of ham. "So tell me about the countries you've worked in. The only long journey I've taken was to Scotland."

He told her about the Afghani mountains which towered so high they made Cumberland look like lowlands. He talked about fierce winters and hot summers, where one couldn't escape the elements. But her favorite part was listening to him talk about how the people lived.

It was all so foreign to anything she'd ever heard before. How could he be making it all up?

He was leaning toward her, smiling with intense interest in his subject, seeming so relaxed and civilized. His demeanor had changed much in just the last day. She should probably be suspicious.

"You know," she said, when the conversation lulled, "I have noticed something about you."

"What?"

"You try very hard to portray this inflexible, hard man that no one should cross." She leaned even closer, feeling bold, daring. "But I think it's not true."

He frowned.

"It's almost like another part you play in this spy game."

There was a sudden knock on the door. Both of them straightened, but from his expression, she knew Nick wasn't done with her.

Chapter 10

Coercion involves more than the threat of force.

The Secret Journals of a Spymaster

Nick raised his voice as he emulated an army clerk who used to irritate the hell out of him. "Who is it?"

Sam answered, and Nick let him inside. With her eyes demurely downcast, Charlotte took a sip of her tea, but when she glanced at him, Nick frowned at her, masking his unease at her ability to see through his performance.

Sam glanced suspiciously between them. "I was right. Julia's heading for Kelthorpe's. She should be there by this afternoon."

"Regardless of our threat to her, she couldn't avoid the house party of the man she's trying to marry," Nick said, nodding.

"We aren't certain that she even knows we have Edwin Hume ready to talk. She might think she's safe."

Charlotte set down her teacup. "But that man you were meeting when you kidnapped me—Nick, didn't he say he would tell Julia about your bribery attempt?"

Nick reluctantly smiled. "Yes, he did. He has to have caught up with her by now and told her about me. So are you saying you finally believe us?"

"I don't know," she said primly. "I have a few other questions."

Nick turned back to Sam. "Will is already in place at Kelthorpe's, isn't he?"

Sam nodded. "He secured an invitation as effortlessly as always."

"My sister hates house parties," Charlotte said. "Your friend won't have an easy time with her. Especially since she's anxious to see Papa."

"I don't know about that," Sam said with a shrug. "There seems to be the beginnings of an intimacy between Will and Jane. The colonel might have been right to pair them up."

She folded her arms over her chest indignantly, and Nick kept his gaze on her face.

"But it was still wrong of Papa to force Jane so," she said firmly. "Every couple needs a chance to see if they suit."

"And they're getting that chance," Nick pointed out, enjoying provoking her.

"Then let me go to her. She needs to know the truth about her situation."

"I won't interfere with Will's personal life."

"It's my sister's life as well!" she said heatedly.

He held up a hand. "We can argue later. Sam, even though Will is at Langley Manor, he won't be able to keep Julia in sight twenty-four hours a day. We need to watch the roads leading to the estate."

"There are two of them," Sam said, glancing pointedly at Charlotte.

Nick followed his gaze to find her watching him with interest. She obviously understood his limited choices.

"You and Cox won't be able to do this without sleep," Nick said. "We'll take turns."

"What about me?" she asked.

He arched an eyebrow. "You and I will discuss that later. Sam, if Julia is only just arriving there, surely she'll be occupied simpering to Kelthorpe for the rest of today. You and Cox get some sleep now, then begin your watch at midnight. I'll take turns relieving you both tomorrow."

Charlotte again said, "But what about—" then stopped when he gave her a black look.

"Go talk to Cox," Nick said to Sam. "Leave our *guest* to me."

After Sam left, Charlotte found herself locked in a staring contest of sorts with Nick Wright. She wasn't afraid of him.

"If you escape," he said, "Campbell will try to kill you—and maybe go after your family."

She felt the blood drain from her face at his bluntness. "And if I remain with you, I'm a hostage, with no say in my life."

He rolled his eyes. "It doesn't have to be this way. I've told you everything about our mission. I've never confided so much to an outsider in my life."

"You just need me to be pliant."

"I call it cooperative. After everything I've told you, why can't you trust me?"

She wanted to trust him. Was there some part of her still afraid that if she gave herself over to another man's care, she'd finally lose herself for good?

In a low voice, she said, "If you were in my situation, at your captor's mercy, you wouldn't find it so easy to trust."

His dark eyes were mesmerizing, flaring with heat. He paused, and then seemed to make up his mind about something. "Then I'm at your mercy, if that's what it takes. The rope is still in my bag. Tie me up."

Her breath caught in a gasp of shock at the thought of doing to Nick what he'd done to her—what her husband had done to her. A flood of power made her face flush with heat and excitement, but the good girl inside her said, "Tie you up? What would that prove?"

"You could ask me questions about my mission from things you've read in your father's journal.

If you don't like the answers, you can leave me here, and I won't be able to stop you."

"Sam and Mr. Cox would still be in my way."

"They're sleeping for the rest of the day." He leaned forward, hands pressed to the table, and challenged her with his grin. "What are you afraid of? I'm the one with the most to lose. You could tell someone about everything that's happened and endanger the mission."

"I wouldn't do that."

"If you left, you'd be in danger from Campbell, and what do you imagine your father will think of me then?"

She got to her feet, angry that he'd use her father as his argument. "Where are the ropes?"

He slid his chair back from the table, his smile full of triumph. "In my portmanteau."

He looked so darn comfortable sprawled in that hard wooden chair, so sure of himself.

When she felt the ropes in her hand, something terrifying moved through her. She knew what it was like to be tied up and helpless. Did Nick?

When she saw his smug expression, she hardened the uneasiness in her heart. Maybe he needed to know what it felt like to be humbled.

"Put your hands behind you," she said coldly.

He slid those long, well-muscled arms behind him, and she walked around the chair. Forcing her fingers not to tremble, she crossed his wrists, then began to wrap the rope around them, even using the lattice of the chair back.

"Good thinking," he said.

Moving in front of him, she used two more pieces of rope to tie each of his ankles to the chair leg. Then she stepped back. His chest looked wide and expansive with his arms pulled back. His shirt was drawn taut across his muscles, his trousers snug across his thighs and pulled tight between his legs, outlining the part of him that made them so different from each other. Again she felt that flare of heat deep in the pit of her stomach. His head was tilted as he watched her, and she noticed a sheen of perspiration on his forehead, and an answering warmth in his gaze.

He was enjoying himself, and that thought hardened her resolve. She closed the curtains against the sunlight of midday, leaving the room in dusky shadows. For only a moment she thought of escaping, but it flashed and was gone from her mind.

How could she believe in Nick once and for all? She took a deep breath and forced herself to relax, recalling the journal. She'd had only a couple days to read it, but surely she could use it to her advantage.

She moved to stand directly in front of him, almost—but not quite—between his knees. "In what city did my father first land in India?"

He dropped his head back and laughed.

"You're not playing fair. He reached the country long before I did."

She smirked at him.

"But I know the answer. It was Bombay."

With a tilt of her head and a smile, she acknowledged his correct answer.

His smile faded as he watched her. Then very deliberately his gaze dropped down her body, lingering on a rounded area he had already professed a fascination for.

"So what's my prize?" he asked in a deeper voice more husky than normal.

"Prize?" Her voice broke, and she inwardly cursed herself.

"I had the right answer, didn't I?"

"Surely you don't think I'm going to untie you after just one answer?"

"No. But you can come closer. I'll take that as my first reward."

First reward? She suppressed a shiver. But something was uncoiling inside her, like a serpent in the Garden of Eden. There was a guilty pleasure in knowing that Nick was at her mercy, that he could not move. Boldly she stepped between his legs until the chair itself stopped her, until her full skirts pressed against his legs. She thought he drew a deep breath, but she could not be sure, for his expression never wavered from amusement.

"Next question?" he prompted.

It was hard to think so close to him, especially

when he no longer even made a pretense of keeping his gaze on her face. Her breasts burned beneath his regard, and she felt constricted in the too-tight dress, as if she couldn't take a deep enough breath.

"What did my father call you?"

"That's an easy one. Mr. North."

She sucked in her breath. "I already told you about Mr. South and Mr. West. You could have—"

"Made it up? Will is Mr. West and Sam is Mr. South."

"You heard me say that!"

"And your father is Mr. East, because even before the sun rises—"

"He's awake," she interrupted, repeating the end of the quote her father, Ernest Whittington, had often used when he wanted his daughters to remember that he knew everything they were doing—or not doing, as far as Charlotte's studies were concerned.

Damn. She almost cursed aloud. She put her fists on her hips and narrowed her eyes at him.

"I'm right again," he said, and this time, to her surprise, he betrayed himself by wetting his lips. "So what's my next reward?"

Her hand flattened below her neck, and his gaze followed. What could she use against him? She smiled and undid the top button at her throat. He gaped at her. This was easy. It would take ten buttons before her dress even reached the provocative neckline of any ball gown, and she certainly didn't intend to let things get that far. But he seemed to take such pleasure in teasing her that she actually looked forward to giving it in return.

Yet her heart raced as the wanton inside her took control. "Ingenious," he said.

Did his voice sound different? "Thank you."

"But would you mind asking questions about the other spies or me? Talking about your father feels—indecent. I'm thinking thoughts about his daughter he wouldn't approve of. Now ask me another question."

She should stop now. She knew the truth about Nick—he was no criminal. Who else would know these things but an associate of her father's? But she found herself whispering, "What mission did you and your fellow spies almost ruin?"

His grin was wicked. "A mission to the fort in Jalalabad. And do you know *why* it was almost ruined?"

She swallowed and shook her head.

"Because my disguise as an Afghani tribesman was so good, I was picked out to marry a local girl."

She held her breath.

"She didn't exactly want marriage."

"What did she want?"

"To be pleasured."

His husky voice hummed through her.

Softly he asked, "What would give you pleasure, Charlotte?"

She opened her mouth, but nothing came out. She didn't know.

"I need my reward," he prompted in a hoarse whisper that dared her, excited her.

She popped open another button, wondering if she was revealing the frantic pulse in the hollow of her throat. But why should *she* be the only one unbuttoning? After all, he was at *her* mercy.

Before she could think things through, she removed his cravat and opened several buttons on his shirt, even as his mouth fell open in surprise. Her thumb brushed against his skin, and he hissed in a breath and looked up at her. Their faces were close, their breaths mingled. Daringly she placed her open palm flat against his skin below his neck. She could feel the heat of him, the frantic pace of his heart.

But he couldn't touch her. She was the one in control.

Lifting her hand, she let her fingers lightly caress him, feeling the coarseness of chest hair. "What happened to Mr. South in the Turkestan desert?"

He watched her hand move, then with a groan he looked back up at her face with an intensity that was riveting. "He was captured and sold as a slave."

"Who rescued him?"

"I did—but that's two questions, so I'll need a large reward."

The sound of his desperation ignited a surge of something deep in her blood—desire. This was what it felt like to desire a man, to want his touch, to want his kiss. Brazenly she opened five more buttons, then glanced down at herself, seeing a path of skin and a just a bit of white lace from her chemise.

Suddenly he strained forward in the chair, but she didn't let herself recoil from him.

"Untie me," he whispered. "I want to span my hands around your waist, feel the curves of your—"

"No. You're not in charge anymore."

He tilted his head back and grinned up at her. "You like this feeling of power?"

"Maybe. Now which spy was presented to the Shah of Persia?"

"Will. He was acting as an emissary from the British government."

He'd answered everything correctly—what more could she ask? And what reward could she give?

She put her hands on his face and kissed him.

Chapter 11

A bond of dependence can form between captor and hostage and surprisingly, it goes both ways.

The Secret Journals of a Spymaster

Charlotte kissed Nick softly at first, wanting to experience the gentleness she'd only known from him. She explored his lips a kiss at a time, each moment parting her lips more and more. With the tip of her tongue she tasted him, and then his mouth opened on a groan. Their tongues met and played, hers hesitant at first, but soon she was as caught up as he was in the frenzy of new exploration.

She leaned against his chest, then slid her knee onto his thigh to brace herself.

"Straddle me, Charlotte," he whispered against her mouth.

She stared into his eyes and let herself drown in the emotion she saw there. Never before had a man shown this kind of desperation to possess her.

Before her sense got the best of her, she gripped his shoulders, then eased her knees across his thighs, her skirt bunching up between them, her muscles shivering as she held herself up. She felt as if she were climbing a solid rock mountain.

"Closer," he whispered, then leaned forward and pressed kisses to her neck. He nuzzled against her, and she felt his hair brushing her ear, felt the moist warmth of his mouth.

She dropped her head back, and with a moan let herself fully settle on top of him. His hips were nestled between her thighs, and the hard ridge of his erection pressed up against her.

She kissed him again, letting herself be taken away by sensations she'd never known before. After a deep thrust of his tongue, he suddenly rolled his hips, arching against her in a shocking way that made her nerves scream inside her.

She cried out against his mouth as she clutched his head to her. He rocked against her hard, over and over, until she felt an exciting, building tension that required all her concentration.

He broke from their kiss, and his mouth found the sensitive skin beneath her ear. "Unbutton my trousers," he said hoarsely.

It was then she realized where this was going. She had him tied to a chair, and she was riding him.

"You were married, you know what to do," he said urgently. "You know what we both want."

She knew what *he* wanted: a merry widow. She couldn't see herself as that woman.

Lifting her head, she slid her fingers from his hair. "What I want and what I should have are two different things."

Nick had known when he started this game how it would end. He just hadn't thought she would let it get so far. He rested his forehead against her shoulder and tried to calm his ragged breathing, inhaling the warm, intoxicating scent of her. When had he last allowed a woman to become paramount to his every thought? It had been many years, and even now he did not often look back on his youth.

But now there was Charlotte, experienced yet innocent, captivating, maddening, and mysterious. It took every bit of his strength not to thrust against her one last time. He was losing himself in her, and he couldn't seem to stop—didn't want to stop. Surely he could control his work, his mission, and keep it separate from her. He was only feeling this way because he was closeted with her almost constantly.

But he had promised not to seduce her, so he let her climb off his lap, watching her blush as she pushed her skirts to the ground. He went on letting her think she'd tied the ropes tight enough to contain him.

But she didn't turn away. She met his gaze, and

although her face turned even more fiery, she raised her chin and dared him to challenge her.

He grinned. "Would you mind untying me now?"

She put her hands on her hips and grinned back. "You said I could leave."

"Only if you don't believe me. But surely you can have no more reservations."

"That's true. But what mostly keeps me here with you is knowing that Mr. Campbell might go after my family if he thinks I'm alive."

"Good thinking."

She went around behind him and tugged on the ropes with her fingers. She leaned over his shoulder to look at him, and he found himself again feeling overwhelmed by her nearness.

"These weren't tied very well, were they?" she asked, wearing a sheepish expression. "You could have escaped any time."

He lowered his voice. "But I didn't want to."

She met his gaze only briefly, then his hands were free and she stepped away. He untied his ankles, then stood up and stretched his arms high over his head.

They were too aware of each other now. For several minutes the silence between them stretched taut with the memories of what they'd done—what they still wanted to do.

"So what was that about?" he asked.

She turned her back. "I don't wish to discuss it."

"You might prefer to forget about it, but I don't. I asked for a reward, but I admit I'm stunned by the one I received."

She seemed to sag a bit. "I assure you, I don't usually go around kissing men."

Taking pity on her, he softened his voice. "I didn't think you did. I assumed it was my natural charm that simply made you lose your head."

"It wasn't your natural charm," she said dryly, glancing at him over her shoulder. "It was—" Then she stopped, frowning.

"My handsome looks?"

"Appearance is not everything."

"Then it was my sparkling conversation."

He could see her fighting a smile.

"Since you try not to tell me anything substantial," she said, "it was hardly that."

"Then why did you kiss me?"

"Because I wanted to," she breathed. "I don't know what's wrong with me. I'm doing all sorts of things—stupid things, like following you from a ballroom. I've never been like this—reckless, unthinking."

"You've never been a widow before."

"And you know so much about it?" she asked sharply. "Are you trying to tell me that you understand my motivations better than I do?"

"I wouldn't presume such a thing. But I know what it feels like to be uncertain of one's place in life, to wonder what decisions one should make."

Her lips thinned. "So while other widows attend society functions for camaraderie and the chance to marry again, I foolishly choose to kiss a stranger?"

"I'm not exactly a stranger."

"Oh, my mistake. You're my kidnapper. You've worked for my father—in a dangerous, unstable profession, I might add."

"But you trust me," he said simply.

"I believe your story," she countered. "There's a difference."

"So can I hope that you'll kiss me again?"

"No."

He gave a dramatic sigh. "Then if we cannot kiss, here is a book and newspaper. Which do you want?"

When the day's shadows lengthened, and the last of the sun hid behind low clouds, Nick looked up as Charlotte set the book down with a thump.

"Nick, can we go down to supper this evening? Surely I've proven myself. I could have tried to escape, but I believe you now. And I'm feeling rather . . . trapped."

He stood up. "Let's go."

When she would have hurried past him in her eagerness, he took her upper arm to stop her. The spark between them caught fire again, and he was suddenly breathless.

"Just remember who I am," he said, fighting

the effect of her nearness. "I'm Mr. Black, a London clerk in the employ of a duke. You're my wife. We're going north to visit relatives. We haven't been away from London in many years, so you can be excited."

She smiled. "I'll remember."

He pulled her closer. "Be careful, Charlotte. This isn't a game. Over a year's worth of work has gone into these final days."

Her expression grew serious. "I understand."

The public dining room of the inn was faded and drab, with only hints of the former glory it had enjoyed before the railroads had taken customers away. But the dozen or so locals and travelers made the most of the hot food and good company. As Nick guided Charlotte to a table, he was reluctantly impressed by the change in her manner, the sedate, pleasant expression on her face, the unhurried way she moved. She did not look like a woman imprisoned for the last several days.

A serving maid took their order, and there was something so subtly different about Charlotte that it took him a moment to place it.

And then he realized she'd changed her accent, coarsening it just enough for the middle class.

He stared at her. When she took notice, she lowered her head modestly, and while spreading a napkin across her lap, murmured, "My maid speaks just like this. How did it sound?"

"Excellent. Your father would be impressed."

She blushed with pleasure.

During the meal he allowed his gaze to linger with heartfelt earnestness upon her, as he would a wife. It wasn't difficult to do, for she was so easy to watch. She had a timeless, classical beauty that made him ache to possess her. She was curved in all the right places, so delicate and feminine. Yet she had a spine of steel, going toe-to-toe with him when not many men would.

When she was finished with dinner, she looked at him hopefully and asked, "From our window I glimpsed a walled garden. Might we go walking?"

How could he deny her? Soon they were strolling down gravel pathways as dusk became full dark, listening to the quiet voices of the servants as they lit torches to illuminate the garden. The rich scent of roses wafted through the air, and Nick, with Charlotte on his arm, glimpsed a contentment he'd never felt before. What would it be like to really be Mr. Black, with a wife like her waiting at home for him?

But he was Nick Wright, with a duty to his government that had kept him out of his home country for many years. He loved his exciting life. How could he ever think a quiet home with one woman would be enough?

Wasn't it his weakness for women he'd been trying so hard to get rid of?

And his family would make sure he never had a quiet, simple life.

Charlotte felt the warmth of Nick's body as she slid her hand deeper into the crook of his arm. She let her mind float with the contentment of a good meal, with freedom, with fresh air—and Nick.

She tried not to think about him, to just enjoy the beauty of the well-tended garden and the night air. But he was there at her side, and hard to keep from her thoughts—especially when she still felt tender between her thighs, still tingled with a frustrated need she'd never felt before.

She wanted him.

It was as if, now that she knew he was an honorable man, she'd given herself permission to think about being with him.

She shivered at the thought, and when Nick said, "Cold?" she shook her head and leaned closer against his arm.

He could be a considerate man.

She withheld a giggle at the thought that a man who'd kidnapped her could ever be called considerate.

But he was. He saw to her bath, he cleansed her wounds, he thought of her pleasure as well as his.

Oh, he was a rough sort of man, too, but there was a line of chivalry that he didn't cross. He could easily have tried to seduce her with their first kiss, but he hadn't.

And today it had been such fun to tease him, to taunt him—and to know she was safe. She could explore the feelings that burned hot between them.

But would she dare? Could she live with herself after a night of passion, only to be left alone when he went on with his life?

Yet her time with him might be the only tender moments she ever shared with a man.

He looked around the garden constantly, his gaze sweeping from side to side. He was always alert, always ready for danger. She should be flattered that he protected her.

But she was uneasy, wondering if he ever really left a mission behind.

"So," he said quietly. "This morning when we were talking about Jane and Will, you said couples should get to know one another before they get married."

She groaned. "We both know you don't subscribe to the institution, so why are you mentioning it?"

"We're portraying it as we speak, so I feel I should know how my character would think."

She only rolled her eyes.

"Since I don't have much experience, how am I supposed to act as a husband?"

"You've done just fine tonight," she said grudgingly.

"But not this afternoon?"

In her memory flashed the image of herself writhing on top of him. She couldn't control a blush. "I wouldn't know."

"But you've been married."

"There are private things between a husband and wife that should never be discussed with another."

"But a husband can be playful," he continued, tugging a little on her arm.

"I would imagine." But she didn't know.

"I tried to look into your eyes with adoration during dinner. Did I do it correctly?"

Reluctantly she met his gaze. "You made me feel special, and I guess that's very important. You don't often see a husband show affection for his wife in public."

She waited for him to ask why she never felt special before, but he didn't. He only studied her face, making her feel foolish as much as grateful.

She took a deep breath and tried to hurry the conversation on. "Did I look suitably besotted when I stared into your eyes?"

"Besotted?" he echoed, frowning thoughtfully. "Come to think of it, you did. I must admit, I don't often remember seeing open affection with many married couples."

"And it's sad." Her whisper sounded so forlorn that she forced herself to smile brightly up at him. "So if we seem too happy together, will we look like lovers instead of a married couple?"

"I don't know."

"We'll just have to take that risk, because I like seeing you suffer."

"I'm not suffering. And a husband wouldn't

suffer either, because I imagine he and his wife don't spend much time together. She would live mostly in the country, wouldn't she, while he does business in town?"

"But what if she loves London society?" she countered. "Would you force her to stay in the country?"

"I'm supposed to say . . . of course not!"

She smiled and tried to read his face through the flickering shadows. "Which means you really think it's a husband's decision."

"No, I do not. What kind of adoring husband would I be if I did not involve my wife in every marital decision?"

"Now I *know* you've never been married."

"Surely a compromise is in order—time in the country, time in town."

"The diplomat's solution. If only it were that easy."

They finally went upstairs to their shadowy, overheated room. Nick threw open the window, then lit a lamp. Together they stared at the bed. She looked away and realized that the only chairs were straight-backed wooden ones. Hardly comfortable for a sleeping man.

She cleared her throat and didn't look at Nick as she said, "You know I won't try to escape. Perhaps we should get a second room . . ."

He shook his head. "We're married, remember? This husband and wife don't spend their nights apart."

"Oh." She straightened her spine and forced herself to meet his gaze. "Well you can't sleep in one of those chairs."

His eyes began to smolder in that way that made her want to swoon. In a deep, soft voice, he said, "You could invite me to sleep with you."

She knew what he meant. And suddenly her thoughts of an affair seemed wild and too daring, full of hazards she had not yet foreseen. She couldn't make such a decision. She shook her head, not trusting her voice.

He nodded with resignation. "I've slept on far rockier surfaces than this floor. Just give me a blanket for bedding."

"Take them both, please. It's far too warm."

"But promise me you'll cover yourself with something," he said, in a voice gone hoarse.

She nodded swiftly. "The sheet." Then she ducked behind the screen before her scarlet face could further embarrass her. She disrobed to her chemise and let her hair down, only to tie it in a simple braid, hardly an alluring coiffure.

When she hesitantly emerged, Nick had already made a pallet for himself between the bed and the wall. There was hardly enough room for the width of his shoulders, but she said nothing.

He glanced at her, then looked away with a

curse. "I'm going to go talk to Sam and Cox. I won't be gone long."

She bit her lip, uncertain if she should apologize, or wear all her clothes to bed. How could either of them forget what had happened between them?

"You'll be all right?" he asked, striding to the door.

"As in, will I escape?"

"I know you won't. But this is a dangerous situation. Do you mind being alone? It might start happening frequently."

"I'll be fine."

He nodded, and his gaze openly slid down her one last time before he left. She crawled into the bed and pulled the sheet up to her chin. She really was alone for the first time in days. She should feel relieved.

But as the minutes sped by, she grew more and more worried by her mental state. She missed Nick. What kind of foolishness was she allowing herself to feel?

Knowing she couldn't sleep, she got out of bed and dug the book out of his portmanteau. She sat down before the cold hearth grate and tried to read.

She wasn't sure how much time passed before she heard the creak of footsteps in the hall. The flood of warm relief she felt should have worried her, but she couldn't help it. The doorknob rattled, but didn't open. Had Nick forgotten his key?

Setting her book aside, she went to the door and almost opened it, then stopped. He hadn't called her name. Was it even Nick?

She leaned near the door and spoke in a raised voice. "My dear Mr. Black, have you forgotten your key again?"

The door suddenly burst open, slamming into the side of her face and flinging her back onto the bed. As her head pounded, her vision went out of focus. She heard the sound of the door shutting. When she could see again, a strange man dressed in black stood over her, grinning.

She came up on her elbows and tried to keep her voice from quivering. "You must have the wrong room, sir. Me husband and I—"

He clapped a hand over her mouth, and leaned hard against her chest. She tasted horse mixed with tobacco. The intruder wore a tattered hat pulled low over his dark eyes, and a couple of days' growth of black and gray whiskers.

"I've got the right room," he said, grinning. "Campbell tol' me what the bloke looked like, just in case, and sure enough, 'twas him havin' dinner without a care in the world. But who could *you* be? Perhaps a bed toy instead of the corpse ye're supposed to be?"

Oh God, he knew. Campbell thought her dead. If this man were permitted to tell Campbell the truth—

She shook her head and tried to push his hand away, but he leaned on her harder and she couldn't breathe. Tears of terror stung her eyes as she gasped and frantically flailed her legs. Her knee connected with something solid, and a giant whoosh escaped the intruder's mouth as he fell beside her on the bed.

Air rushed back into her lungs as Charlotte surged to her feet. She felt a catch at her chemise, and she sobbed as her hand fumbled for the door. She was dragged backward.

But the door suddenly opened and there was Nick. "I thought I heard—"

She cried out, and his face went deadly with comprehension. Instinctively she dropped to her knees, and he vaulted over her, slamming into the intruder. She looked over her shoulder as they both tumbled off the far side of the bed. She staggered out into the hallway for help, angry that she'd never asked which room Sam and Mr. Cox were in.

But the door across the hall opened and the two men emerged. She pointed into her room, and all three of them pushed inside.

Nick was on his knees, gasping, with the intruder standing behind tightening a garrote about his neck. Nick had one hand inside the wire. The intruder looked up at the commotion, and Nick dropped forward, flipping the man over his shoulders onto the floor. Mr. Cox and Sam turned him onto his stomach and began to tie his hands with his own belt.

Praying that no one in the inn thought much of

the commotion, Charlotte quietly shut the door and went to Nick. When she touched him, he put up a hand, and she let him stand by his own effort. There was a nasty red line marring much of his throat, and she imagined the same across his hand.

"Are you all right?" she asked.

He cleared his throat, and his voice came out husky. "I should never have left you alone."

She tried to smile. "I knew you'd never trust me."

He chuckled and wiped the back of his forearm across his perspiring brow. "So what did he say to you?"

She sobered and looked toward the intruder, who was being forced into a chair. Blushing, she tried to forget what had happened on that chair earlier. "He said he recognized you from the description Campbell had given him. He wondered if I was supposed to be a corpse."

Nick swore and turned to look at the man, who glared back at them, his shoulders held by Sam and Mr. Cox.

"Where's Campbell now?" Nick demanded.

The intruder tongued a cut at the corner of his mouth and said nothing.

Sam yanked hard on the man's hair, pulling his head back, and spoke in a deadly voice Charlotte could never have imagined him using. "Speak when you're spoken to."

"I don't know where he is," the intruder finally said with desperation. "He was supposed to find me."

There was a sudden knock at the door, and as everyone turned to look, the intruder broke free, took two running steps, and dove out the open window.

At Nick's side, Charlotte leaned out the window and saw the intruder's body lying in an unnatural heap only one story below. Bile rose in her throat as she thought of the lengths he'd gone to to protect his secrets.

"It's a good thing I never tried to escape that way," she whispered.

Nick said nothing, only waited for Sam and Mr. Cox to seat themselves at the table as the knocking continued. She gaped as they brought out cards and started to play. Nick motioned her toward the screen and she hid herself, sliding down to sit against the wall.

She heard the conversation at the door rather distantly, as she fought to keep from trembling, relief and fright still coursing through her.

"Can I help you?" Nick asked, in that polite, deferential voice he used for the clerk disguise.

"Good evenin' sir. Me wife was cleanin' tankards below and thought she heard a noise."

"She has good ears, then sir. Yes, my companions and I were playing cards, and Mr. Sherman here doesn't take losing well. He kicked over a chair in his anger. Do forgive us for bothering you at this time of night."

The man was soon appeased, and when the door shut, she knew she could stop hiding. But she hugged herself and couldn't seem to stand.

"Charlotte?"

Nick folded the screen back and stood above her. The concern in his voice was her undoing, and she angrily wiped away her tears.

"Are you all right?"

She nodded and took his hands, allowing him to help her stand. He put an arm around her waist and she let him, swaying into the warmth of his body. Even as her trembling eased, he pulled her into the safety of his embrace.

Sam and Mr. Cox abruptly left, and she realized they were going to deal with the body. She closed her eyes, shuddering, and pressed her face into Nick's chest.

"He deserved to die, Charlotte."

His voice rumbled through her, became a part of her.

She wasn't sure she was supposed to be comforted by that, so she only sighed. "I know. He would have told Campbell where we are, would have told him that—" Words deserted her.

"That you were alive?"

Clutching him tightly about the waist, she only nodded.

"But we didn't let him. You're all right. And I won't leave you alone again."

"Held hostage once more," she murmured.

She heard him chuckle. "But in a trusting sort of way. Now why don't you get some sleep."

He tucked her into bed, and she tried not to notice how carefully he pulled the blankets up around her shoulders, how gently he brushed the hair back from her forehead. He tilted her face toward the lamp and frowned at her.

"Did he strike you?" he asked.

She shook her head. "I was standing near the door when he flung it open, and my face bore the brunt of it."

"You'll have a nasty bruise in the morning."

"I'll swear to people that my husband doesn't beat me. Only sheer clumsiness on my part."

He smiled, even as his fingers traced down her cheek before he released her. "My thanks for protecting my reputation."

"Then you must come up with a reason for that line on your throat, so people don't think I tried to strangle you."

He was sitting on the bed staring at her as their smiles slowly died. She could lose herself in the vivid depths of his eyes.

He finally looked away and stood up. "Time for bed."

He went behind the screen. Before he came out, she told herself to roll over and go to sleep. But then he emerged, half naked, and she inhaled swiftly and stared. She would never get used to the thrilling sight of him, to the way he made her ache inside. For one crazy moment she wanted to change her mind and throw back the sheets for him.

But she was a coward. Instead she watched him stretch out beside her on the floor. He never met her gaze again, just faced the wall to sleep.

Before dawn Charlotte awoke to the sounds of Nick moving about the room. She was almost relieved to be awake, because she'd had horrible dreams about Campbell trying to kill her. She pushed herself to a sitting position, then swept wisps of hair from her eyes.

"Nick?"

By the light of a low lamp, he turned to face her, fully dressed. He had a small, empty satchel in his hands.

"Charlotte, I was just going to wake you."

"You're going to relieve one of the men?"

"Yes."

"And I'm to stay here alone."

"No." He hesitated, and she could almost see his mind working. "My first thought was to leave you with whoever I relieve. But he won't get his sleep if he has to worry about you. So you're coming with me."

She flung back the sheet and stood up, suddenly eager for the day. She would be helping to protect her sister, who even now might be dining with Julia Reed. And she could keep her mind occupied instead of reliving her attacker throwing himself out the window.

"Wear the darkest gown you have and the largest bonnet you own," he said sternly. "Obey me instantly, in everything, because it could mean our lives."

Chapter 12

When keeping watch on a suspect, drowsiness is not all you should guard against. Any distraction, however welcome, can result in failure.

The Secret Journals of a Spymaster

As the sun rose behind her, Charlotte sat astride a horse for the first time in her life, her arms clinging tightly about Nick's waist, her cheek pressed against his warm back. It was all she could do to occasionally tuck her skirts back under her calves and ignore her shocking ankle exposure.

The morning gallop was wildly exciting, with the wind catching at her hair, tugging a few strands free. She could feel the movement of Nick's back muscles against her chest, and it was oddly stirring. The day held the promise of important work, the opportunity to look out for her sister, the chance for her to help her father, though he wouldn't know it.

And a chance for her to be with Nick, something that was important, though she warned herself not to think that way.

She spoke over his shoulder. "Where are we going?"

He turned his head toward her so that she could catch his words. "Sam told me that there's an old barn near the property border of Langley Manor. We'll be able to see the road from there."

They left the town of Stamford behind and passed several miles of farmland sectioned off with hedgerows. When the trees began to thicken, they moved off the road and followed a path through the woods. She was the first to spot the weathered old barn, and as she pointed excitedly, almost slipped off the horse. He caught her thigh and steadied her until she wrapped her arms around him once again.

"Shh," he murmured, his hand still on her thigh.

She obediently bit her lip and leaned into him, as if making herself inconspicuous. But her eyes looked at his hand, felt its hot imprint.

They circled the barn, and she noticed its dilapidated condition. It was made of ancient stone, a relic of another era, and seemed to be in the early stages of crumbling in on itself. But its walls still held, though its thatched roof was full of holes.

As they came upon the wide door, she heard a strange sound from the dark interior, like an animal, but not one she'd ever heard before.

Then Nick brought his hands up to his mouth and returned the sound with uncanny precision. He shot her a grin, and said simply, "Camel."

When a tired-looking Mr. Cox emerged from the barn and she realized it was a special call between the spies, she almost laughed at her stupidity. Hadn't she read about this very thing in her father's journals?

When Mr. Cox stopped short on seeing them, Nick only said, "It's all right. Charlotte believes us now. She won't get in the way. Can you help her down?"

She leaned toward the waiting coachmen, panicked as she started to slide, but he caught her neatly about the waist and set her down.

"Thank you, Mr. Cox."

"Ye're welcome, ma'am."

She took a deep breath, rubbing the spot at her waist where the too-tight dress aggravated her. Her legs felt a little wobbly, and she wondered if she would be sore the next day.

While the two men spoke in low tones, they tightened the saddle on Mr. Cox's horse and loosened the girth of Nick's. Charlotte wandered the interior of the barn. The morning light angled in through bare windows, and dust rose through the beams as she walked. Besides the door, a window faced the road. There were scattered bales of straw in broken-down horse stalls.

And somewhere nearby was the mansion itself, where her sister Jane was. Charlotte stepped close to the door, wondering at the distance between them. Was Jane happy? But that really didn't matter, because if she *was* happy, it was because of a lie. Jane's only thoughts were probably about visiting Papa, while all around her prowled men intent on foiling treachery and a traitor trying to escape punishment. Unless Lord Chadwick had truly captured Jane's interest . . . but that seemed so unlikely when Charlotte thought about his foppish behavior.

Mr. Cox departed, and she watched Nick take a seat on a bale of straw beside the window, his face in the shadows. He squinted as he watched the road, and subtle lines fanned out from the corner of his eyes. For many silent minutes she studied him. How many hours would he remain like that—watchful, alert, just waiting?

She asked, "How will you know who you're looking for?"

His head turned quickly toward her, as if he'd forgotten she was there. As usual, his gaze didn't remain on her face for long. She stood still, letting him look, playing this dangerous game between them, and wondering if he would soon tire of it.

She couldn't imagine tiring of this feeling of lightning that crackled between them, making her aware of everything he did.

He looked back out the window. "I know what Julia looks like," he said dryly.

She rolled her eyes, then pushed another bale beside him and perched on the prickly edge. She wouldn't be able to see much out the window—but she could watch *him*.

"I'm sure you know much more than what her face looks like," she answered tartly.

He grinned. "True. But I'm also looking for Campbell, or another of her henchmen."

"Besides Campbell, have you seen any of these other men before?"

"No, but Hume, our traitor-turned-witness, described one man to me in a letter, and it wasn't our visitor last night. Hume was dead-on where Campbell was concerned, so I trust him."

"In a letter?"

Charlotte wrapped her arms about one bent leg and rested her chin on her knee. Her petticoats were a flounce about her ankle. Only Nick's pointed glance made her realize the picture she presented, but she chose to remain in the comfortable position.

"If I'd spoken to Hume in person, he'd be in custody already."

"Oh, of course." She winced with contriteness.

He turned back to watching the road, and within a half hour they finally heard the rumble of what might be a carriage. He put his arm across her chest, pressing her against the wall, while every line of him stiffened with readiness. But when the sound of wheels crunching on road crested and began to fade and he relaxed, she allowed herself a glimpse. It was only an open-ended wagon, driven by an ancient farmhand.

Though Nick resumed his watch of the road, his arm still pinned her to the wall, the long muscles pressed into her breasts.

She stirred, and his arm fell away.

"Sorry," he said without looking at her.

"Quite all right. A woman doesn't mind feeling protected."

"Then you've been fooling me."

"Pardon?" she said in puzzlement.

"All I've ever tried to do was protect you, even at the beginning. You fought me at every turn."

She primly raised her nose in the air. "Being bound and gagged did not feel like protection."

"I only bound and gagged you because you kept trying to escape. You would have put yourself right in Campbell's path."

"How was I to know—"

"Never mind. I'm sorry I brought it up."

She let the silence stretch on for part of the morning. The sun rose higher, bees buzzed in and out of the window, and once or twice she caught herself dozing. But Nick never ceased his narrow-eyed search of the road.

Soon she heard the approach of an open carriage full of wellborn laughing ladies. When they'd passed she leaned back against the wall and opened several buttons at her throat. How practical of Sam to think only of dresses that buttoned up the front.

She caught Nick watching her with an expression not unlike the one he'd had when she sat astride him the day before. He shifted a bit on his bale of straw, then looked back outside.

She blushed furiously, for she hadn't meant to remind him of their passion. She needed to distract them both. "So what does Julia look like?"

He shot her a puzzled look.

"If I'm to look for her, I should know what she looks like," she added.

He smiled. "She's very tall, a robust, healthy woman, but not plump. Rather small in the chest area."

Charlotte gasped and felt her face flame. "I cannot believe you said such a personal thing to me. As if it matters."

"I'll explain why soon enough. She has this shock of blond hair that is almost white. You'll know her when you see her."

"And is that what drew you to her when you first met her?" she bravely asked.

"Hardly. She was dressed as a boy, prowling a Kabul bazaar, where no woman should ever be. Now do you see why I mentioned her chest?"

Ignoring his crudity, she gasped, "A boy? Whatever for?"

He turned sideways, his head leaning back against the rough stone, where he could easily see the road, but also glance at her.

"Just for the freedom of it. Surely you long for a little freedom now and again, Charlotte."

He reached out and touched her hand, where it was clasped in the other around her bent leg. It was as if something inside her had waited breathlessly for this moment, as if somehow she knew he would touch her and she would allow it. How could she not? Wasn't every dance they did with each other leading to this?

She licked her dry lips, knowing he watched the movement of her tongue. "Was she trying to be free like an Afghan woman?"

"They're not free, Charlotte. Women live a very different life in Muslim countries."

She slowly straightened her leg, letting her foot drop to the ground. His fingers remained covering hers, tracing the bones of her hand, just a bare inch above her thigh. The need for him to touch her there was like a madness; she couldn't stop watching his hands, feeling as if he wove a spell of desire about her. The gentleness of his touch was something she'd longed for for so many years. He'd moved up to her wrist now, teasing the skin beneath her sleeve with gentle, tantalizing strokes.

"Woman are kept away from the sight of men," he continued, "veiled when they're not in their own houses."

He moved his hand as he spoke, letting his thumb run along her lower ribs, just above her waist. She caught her breath.

He looked into her eyes, and she found herself breathing shallowly, waiting. Did he want her to make the first advance?

"This dress is too tight," he murmured. "It surely must chafe you."

She could only shrug.

"Show me where."

She couldn't look away from the dark blaze that was his eyes. Her unsteady fingers moved to the buttons on her bodice, and as she undid them, she could swear his gaze blazed brighter with each one. She hesitated at her waist, feeling on the precipice of a new part of her life, where impulse and danger ruled.

As if in a trance, she reached for the ties at the neckline of her chemise and tugged, loosening the fabric. He wasn't touching her now, but his heavy gaze was enough to urge her onward. She stretched the gathered neckline and began to pull downward, feeling the rasp of fine linen across the sensitive peaks of her breasts. But they only truly tightened and ached when they were revealed to the warm summer air.

He made a hoarse, choked sound, but only said, "Show me where the dress chafed, Char."

As the chemise sagged lower, she arched her back so that he could see the faint raw marks across her waist.

Murmuring his shortened version of her name contritely, he bent over her and pressed a gentle kiss to the nearest scrape on her abdomen. Her flesh tightened and tingled, her breasts ached at the brush of his hair. Then he turned and looked up into her face, her breasts between them.

She took a deep breath, feeling light-headed, silently begging him to touch her. But he did more than that. Slowly, reverently, he leaned upward and closed his mouth over her nipple.

Her groan of pleasure was too loud in the silence, but he did not berate her. Instead he suckled her, teased her, let his tongue dart out and lick her. Every sensation shot downward through her body, until between her thighs she throbbed with a desperate feeling of tension she'd never felt before.

Nick had spent the ride to the barn tormented by the feel of her breasts bouncing and rubbing into his back. Now to see them bared before him was like a welcome feast after a long day's labor.

Her skin was soft and delicate, and he worshipped her tight little nipple with each stroke of his tongue. He moved to the other breast, tasting, exploring. When he sucked hard, she shuddered against him, and her moan was as intoxicating as a caress. His fingers teased one breast, his mouth the other, until her trembling told him she was ready.

He was consumed with the promise of what

lay beneath her skirts. He knelt down in front of her, letting his hands skim up the outside of her calves beneath her petticoats. He looked up the length of her, past her spreading skirts, to the roundness of her bare breasts—

And then he saw her face.

The Charlotte he knew was suddenly—gone. Two days ago, when he'd told her to remove her clothes, she'd donned this same, blank expression, as if her personality, the woman she was, had retreated behind a wall. Now she reached for his coat like a blind woman, as if she meant to undress him.

And his passion for her dimmed and banked in concern.

"Charlotte?" he said, taking both her hands in his. "Tell me what you're seeing."

She froze, and for a moment he thought she would speak. Then she shook her head and blinked several times until she finally saw him. Her face whitened, and with a gasp she grabbed at her garments.

He caught her hands again. "Char, don't. Whatever you're seeing in your mind, don't make it a part of what we shared." He replaced her chemise and tied it at her neckline.

The color returned to her face as she straightened. "I don't know what to say," she murmured.

"Just tell me what happened to you."

But they both heard an approaching carriage.

Nick's concern for her became swamped with the realization of his purpose, his mission. Somewhere in his mind, as he'd begun to seduce Charlotte, he'd told himself he would remain alert to sounds outside the barn.

Instead he had been drowning in the tastes and smells that were uniquely hers.

But his hearing was once again finely tuned, and the carriage had pulled to a stop outside the barn. He turned to Charlotte, who was still trying to button up her dress. "We have company."

She went still and gaped at him. To his surprise she grabbed him by the lapels and pulled him down on top of her in the straw. She kissed him passionately, even as her hands fumbled between them to finish buttoning her dress. Never one to resist a good idea, Nick joined in wholeheartedly. When her tongue teased its way into his mouth, he almost forgot everything else.

But then a throat was cleared, and someone giggled.

They both rolled to a sitting position, straw caught in their clothing and in their hair. Two young women and a man stood in the barn door. The man looked amused, while the women giggled and spoke to each other behind their hands. From their elegant clothing, it was obvious they were guests at Langley Manor. Were there more arriving? Could Julia Reed be one of them? She would recognize him immediately. Before he could even begin to create an explanation, Charlotte was blushing and smiling and patting her hair.

"My goodness, John," she said to Nick in a scolding voice, "I thought ye told me this barn was abandoned."

He chose his character by the tone of her voice. He wrung his hands together, ducking his head. "M-mistress, I t-told what I kn-knew. B-Billy said—"

"I'm not interested in what Billy said," she interrupted, speaking between gritted teeth. She stood up and made a hurried little curtsy to their guests.

Nick got to his feet behind her, keeping his shoulders hunched. He was so impressed by her behavior that he could have almost forgotten this was Charlotte Whittington Sinclair. Her curtsy was brusque, her voice had an unpolished edge, as if she were the daughter of minor gentry, one who thought herself deserving of more.

He placed himself behind her and kept his gaze lowered respectfully, guiltily.

"We didn't mean to intrude," said one of the women, who was small and plump, and so pale that her blush made her face very red.

The man stepped forward and boldly looked Charlotte up and down. He had the swagger of a man who relished his position in life. "We're not intruders but invited guests. Do you have the Duke of Kelthorpe's permission to be here?"

Charlotte smiled like a woman used to being

admired, and Nick could have sworn she subtly
thrust her breasts forward. Maybe this was carrying the character a bit too far, he thought darkly.

Charlotte gave a flirtatious gasp. "This is the
duke's estate?"

"M-mistress," Nick began, "your f-father
wouldn't like—"

"Hush, John," she said, waving him back with
her hand. "Milord," she addressed the man, "this
is an old barn in the woods. If the duke doesn't
want it . . . *used* by the villagers, he should tear it
down." She swished her skirts and swayed
provocatively. "But he leaves it be, doesn't he?
Perhaps he's young at heart."

The women put their heads together and giggled. Charlotte and the young lord watched each
other as if they wished everyone else would leave.

"You have a nasty bruise on your face," said
the gentleman. "Did he give you that?"

Nick held his breath.

"My goodness, no," she said with a trilling
laugh.

"Her p-pa done it," Nick muttered, scraping
one boot in the straw. "She s-sasses him too
m-much."

"John!" she cried. "These people needn't
know my private business."

He tugged on her sleeve, bowing nervously.
"But m-mistress—"

Then out of the corner of his eye he saw
through the window someone riding by on horse-

back. He could just see the back of a man, top hat pulled low over his ears and a bulky coat hiding his broad torso. The man was heading away from the mansion, skirting through the trees, the horse's bridle jingling softly.

Charlotte turned and gave him an angry frown. "John, you had better—"

"M-mistress, we 'ave to g-go! I t-told yer father we'd b-be right back, b-but we're not. I think he j-just rode by!"

After a moment's hesitation, her eyes went wide with comprehension. She gave a dramatic sigh and turned back to the onlookers, while Nick deliberately stumbled on his way to ready the horse.

"I'm sure John is just seeing things, milord," she said, "but when he gets upset, he's miserable for days. We'll have to be on our way." She watched the gentleman in particular, putting regret in her voice.

Nick mounted the horse, then reached down for her. "M-mistress!"

Charlotte made another curtsy look like a sexual prelude before catching Nick's hand. He pulled her up behind him, heard her call, "Farewell!" before he followed Campbell's path.

Chapter 13

Secrets, if not guarded carefully, can be used against you.

The Secret Journals of a Spymaster

As they rode the galloping horse, Nick felt Charlotte lean into his back.

"Was it Campbell?" she said into his ear.

He could feel her trembling, and well remembered the aftereffects of escaping danger. She must also be thinking that Campbell had threatened to kill her slowly.

"Yes. But he's leaving the estate, and we never saw him arrive. I need to discover where he's going next."

His stomach tightened with a spasm of anger. But now was not the time to castigate himself for the day's failures.

They followed Campbell for several miles, keeping far enough behind so as not to be seen in the open countryside. He thought fleetingly of Charlotte's brilliant "disguise," and knew he would have had a harder time explaining his presence in the barn without her.

In the narrow, cobbled streets of Stamford, they were forced to slow down. Campbell continued to ride recklessly. Charlotte gasped in Nick's ear when Campbell forced an old woman selling flowers to stumble and fall to keep from being run over by his horse.

Nick thought he was being more careful, until Campbell turned a corner far ahead of them. He picked up speed, took the corner, and there in his path was a little boy, who flung his arms over his head and screamed. Nick pulled back on the reins, the horse pawed wildly in the air, and Charlotte fell off with a cry. The horse bolted through the alley, and it took several minutes to calm him. All the while Nick felt sick with fear for Charlotte, and wondered if he could learn to pray again.

When he was able to return to her, she was on her knees with her arms around the little boy, who was crying for his mother. Nick controlled the trembling that seemed to want to engulf him and quickly dismounted.

He put his hand on her shoulder and she looked up. "Charlotte, are you both well?"

She nodded and smiled at him, shushing the little boy against her shoulder. When the boy calmed down, he was able to lead them to his home just down the alley, where his mother seemed rather shocked that they were worried about him.

Afterward Nick and Charlotte spent a half hour combing through the streets of Stamford, but never caught sight of Campbell again. Finally Nick guided the horse in the direction of the barn to finish his shift.

During the ride his thoughts of guilt roared back to prominence.

He'd seen Campbell leaving, but not arriving.

Had he been so wrapped up in his obsession with Charlotte and his own pleasures that he had ignored his duty? He'd thought he was being watchful. But had he honestly believed that with his face between her breasts he could listen for traffic on the road? How could he have heard anything above the blood pounding in his ears?

So Campbell had been on the estate. Had he been meeting with Julia? If Nick had seen him entering, he could have followed and known for certain. He reminded himself that he could not have interrupted them—Julia wasn't to know she was being followed.

Campbell could have entered by the other road, and surely Sam would have seen him and followed. And since Sam hadn't appeared, Nick knew with certainty that Sam hadn't seen Campbell's arrival.

Now at least he knew Campbell was in the vicinity. Had Campbell told Julia about the meeting with Nick and the blackmail attempt? Did this mean he would not receive the note Nick had sent to London in time to make the meeting? Hell, the meeting was supposed to be in two days' time.

Charlotte held on tightly to Nick and tried to find a comfortable position for her sore backside. The cobblestones hadn't made for a soft landing. But at least their horse hadn't run over the little boy. She was still shaky and thanking God for that small miracle.

But her circling thoughts eventually came back to her surrender to Nick. It had been so easy, so very natural to offer herself, to let him touch her. Though she'd often had to disrobe in front of her husband, this hadn't seemed the same in any way. Nick's eyes had been aglow with admiration and longing. When he had chosen to give her pleasure, it had been a revelation to her.

Then why, when she was with Nick, had her mind sunk back into those dark nights of her marriage? Was she forever doomed to be haunted by the ghost of her husband?

When they reached the barn Nick guided the horse in a slow circle about the building, but their earlier guests had departed. After they dismounted, Charlotte sat on the straw bale near the window to keep watch while he loosened the horse's saddle girth and rubbed the animal down with a cloth from his saddlebag.

She gave up his seat when he approached, then sat beside him. "Are we going to keep watching, in case Campbell comes back?"

He nodded silently, his face grim. She understood his mood. He had let himself get too close to her while he was working, and Campbell had eluded them. Nick would not make that mistake again.

She braved one more question. "How long does our shift here last?"

"It's a twelve-hour shift, so roughly six more hours."

"Oh."

"Sleep when you need to, Charlotte," he said gruffly. "This isn't your problem."

"But along with your friend, it's my sister in that house with Julia Reed."

He dipped his head in acknowledgment and looked out the window.

When Sam relieved them early that evening, they went back to the inn. They had a meal and a bath sent up to the room, and when they began eating, Charlotte remained quiet, wondering at Nick's mood.

But after taking a bite of his roast duck he sat back in his chair and smiled at her. "That was quite a performance you put on for our guests today."

She felt her face heat with a blush. "I—I surprised myself."

"Now you're picking up my stutter?"

She laughed. "The stutter was inspired. You were quite the subservient country boy."

"I think I made it clear I'd obey any order you gave." He deepened his voice and wiggled his eyebrows at her.

She let her eyes flash at him flirtatiously. "I rather enjoyed being in control."

"So I noticed," he said dryly. "And so did your admirer."

"Don't call him that." Even now she shuddered. "I was afraid for our lives every time he spoke to me!"

"You certainly didn't show it. I had the distinct feeling—and believe me, so did he—that you would have gladly pulled him down in the straw, too."

She shrugged and felt bold and wicked. "If I had to. Why—were you jealous?"

Her smile died as she realized what she'd said, how she was behaving. Did she *want* Nick to seduce her?

But his grin remained. "I'm not sure John the serving boy is capable of jealousy."

"Of course he is," she said, relaxing. "He's innocent, not stupid."

"And his mistress doesn't mean to keep him innocent for long."

"Nick!" Waving a hand to dismiss his teasing, she shoved back her chair. "And with that, I think I'll retire for my bath."

* * *

Nick only had a few hours to sleep before his next shift, so he lay down on his floor pallet while the sun was setting. Though he tried to remember Charlotte's alluring "mistress" performance, he still couldn't forget the blank expression she'd worn earlier when he'd been kissing her.

A couple of hours later he awoke to her incoherent mumbling. He raised himself up and watched her toss restlessly upon her pillow, with expressions of anger and fright chasing across her face.

"Charlotte," he called, giving her shoulder a shake.

When she finally opened her eyes, she looked frightened and unaware of her surroundings.

A tear slid down into her hair, and she angrily dashed it away. "I'm sorry I disturbed you."

"Don't be sorry," he said, getting up onto his knees and leaning his elbows on the bed. "What was your dream about?"

She opened her mouth, probably to dismiss his question, but then a terrible knowledge and resolution appeared in her gaze. "My husband," she whispered.

"What did he do to you?"

When she remained silent, he almost took her hand, but forced himself to remember their relationship. "You should tell me, Char. It'll be better to have it out."

She said nothing for a very long time. He rested his chin on his hands and kept watching her. Finally she gave a great sigh and closed her eyes, as if pretending he wasn't there.

"The . . . things you and I have . . . done to-gether," she began haltingly, "my husband never—"

When she broke off, every instinct in him wanted to fire questions at her, but he held back, waiting, feeling a knot in his stomach twist tighter.

"He never touched me like that," she finally whispered. "When we married, I thought . . . I thought he loved me—or at least liked me. But never once did he kiss me, or care what I felt."

She caught him by surprise when she turned to stare wildly at him.

"I never knew I could feel like you've made me feel when we touch! My mother told me . . . things beforehand, but she said I should trust my husband to please me, and I believed her."

The last came out so bitterly, he wondered if she felt betrayed by her mother.

"It's almost worse now," she continued softly, "knowing that he deliberately denied me pleasure."

"Did he just . . . take you whenever he wanted?"

She shuddered. "I wish it were only that. That was painful, but I could turn my head and it would be over soon. He wanted an heir desper-ately. It was the only thing he wanted from me, and I couldn't give it."

Her hands were gripping the bedsheets at her side, and he finally reached out and covered one of hers with his own. "You know it's not normally like that between men and women."

"I have . . . begun to realize that," she said dryly, with enough humor that he took heart for her recovery.

He stroked her hand slowly, gently, and gradually her breathing eased. She turned her hand over and clasped his.

She frowned as if struggling for words. "He would . . . make me take my clothes off in front of him, and then tell me what displeased him about my form—beside the fact that he was more and more certain that I was barren."

"I'm sorry," Nick whispered. "I told you to take your clothes off, too."

She shook her head. "I shouldn't have reacted so—like the past was still happening."

"You had every right to react when your kidnapper tells you to strip," he said angrily.

"You couldn't have known." She gripped his hand harder, and the next confession poured out of her. "He would make me do things with my mouth."

"Charlotte, there are things that men and women do together to please each other, that when forced on a person are nothing short of cruelty."

She studied him. "Do you like it when a woman does that to you?"

He couldn't lie. "Yes. But I enjoy returning the favor."

Her watery eyes went wide, but she said nothing, only bit her lip and turned away.

"I can tell there's more, Charlotte. Go ahead and say it. You need to tell someone."

"He sometimes . . . tied me up in bed."

He winced at his own treatment of her. "Charlotte, can you forgive me?"

She nodded tremulously, then started crying, great, heaving sobs that she must have kept inside her for years.

He put a hand on her arm. "I don't know what to say, what to do—"

But she kept on crying. He found himself climbing into bed and wrapping his arms around her from behind. She rocked against him, sobbing, until she finally cried herself to sleep. He stayed where he was, gently moving her hair, wet with tears, back from her face. He could tell there was more she hadn't told him, but tonight was a start. He had only two hours remaining, and then he'd have to relieve Cox. He would hate to leave her.

Charlotte barely felt Nick leave the bed at midnight. She heard a whisper promising that one of the men would be in the room with her, but after that she faded back into an exhausted sleep.

It was almost midmorning when she awoke. She lay still, listening to the low murmur of guests far away and the sounds of horses and rumbling carriages from outside her window. Though she still felt tired, she also felt strangely . . . content. She had told Nick the truth about her husband, and she had not died of mortification. Nick had been sad for her, but not repulsed.

She hadn't quite told him everything, though, but there were some things she couldn't bear to share.

Nick came striding in after she'd dressed, looking angrier than she had ever seen him. If she didn't know him well, she'd be very frightened. Sam followed behind, watching Nick with a worried expression.

Nick began to throw his few belongings into his portmanteau. "We're leaving."

"Where are we going?" she asked, quickly opening up her own bag.

When he didn't answer immediately, she turned to Sam, who cleared his throat and said, "Will and Jane left Langley Manor just after dawn this morning, leaving us no explanation."

She paused in the middle of folding a dress. "And why is this bad?"

Sam opened his mouth, but Nick growled, "You don't leave your host's home before most of the guests are even awake. Not unless something has happened."

"And Julia left not long afterward," Sam added.

Charlotte found herself watching Nick. Did he somehow blame himself? Did he think Campbell had done something on the estate that he could have prevented?

"So what are we doing?" she asked.

Nick spared her a glance. "We're following Julia, while Sam follows Will to find out what happened. Keep packing."

She nodded and stopped asking questions, although they continued to bubble up in her mind.

During their silent carriage ride that day, Charlotte had to firmly keep a damper on her fears. It had been a shock to see Campbell so close again, barely ten feet away from her. She had not thought his threat would still affect her so, not with three competent men guarding her, but all the same her stomach ached with nerves. Jane was unaware of any of this, and had only one man with her. How could Charlotte *not* be worried?

Nick was so quiet. He sat opposite her instead of at her side. There was a deep, insecure part of her that wondered if her confession about her marriage had made him think differently of her, but his reaction the previous night had been so sympathetic.

She sighed and turned her head to watch the landscape moving past.

In the afternoon the carriage stopped in the middle of the road. When she would have looked out the window, Nick held her back and did it for her, then sat back. Before she could question him, Sam opened the door and stepped inside.

He sat down beside Charlotte and gave her a friendly smile.

Nick frowned at him. "You were supposed to be following Will."

"I am. We all happen to be on the same road."

Nick's frown intensified, and he leaned forward. "Is Julia following Will? Maybe something happened between the three of them. That might explain why he and Jane left so unexpectedly."

"I'm not sure. Julia left an hour after him, again at a leisurely pace. I haven't seen any of her men moving up and down the road. There are three things she could be doing: heading straight for Leeds, where she'll arrive the day after tomorrow at her speed. She could be following Will to York, though this road could take them to either York or Leeds. But there's also a third option. She could be going home."

"Home?" Nick echoed.

"Her brother's estate is just outside Misterton in Nottinghamshire. She'd reach it by tomorrow."

Nick sat back. "Keep following her. See what you think. Let me know if Will veers off this road. And talk to him as soon as you can."

That evening, in a small inn overlooking the River Devon in Newark upon Trent, Nick paced the length of their room while they waited for word from Sam. He felt agitated, uneasy, wondering if something had happened to Will.

He tried not to look at Charlotte. She asked him no questions, didn't even ask to go down to dinner. It was as if she understood how pivotal the next few hours were to his investigation and was trying to make herself as unobtrusive as possible.

But he might as well ask a diamond not to sparkle. How could he help but notice her? Wasn't that what was muddling up his mind? She was not just a beautiful woman—she was vulnerable and brave. But it was that vulnerability that was playing havoc with his vow to remain at a distance. Her husband had not treated her the way she deserved to be treated. But Nick had to keep reminding himself that it wasn't his job to do so, either.

He desired her, yes. But if lovemaking happened between them, he would have to make sure she understood that there could never be anything else. He would not sacrifice his career for a woman. He could not be the man who put her in the center of his world. This was the very thing he was fighting so hard against, because all it ever did was land him in trouble.

But that was what she needed—what she deserved.

He was watching Charlotte doze in a chair beside the hearth when there was a knock at the door. She came awake and alert so quickly, he couldn't help but be impressed.

"Mr. Black, sir?" called a hoarse, gravelly voice from the corridor.

It was Sam. Nick opened the door and let him in. He watched Charlotte gape at Sam's aged-farmer impersonation, with his rough country garb and the large hat hiding his face. He had a pronounced stoop and a way of shuffling that made him look like he was in constant pain. When the door shut, Sam straightened and tossed his hat on the bed.

"Where's Julia?" Sam asked immediately.

"At an inn nearby," Nick said. "Again, she seems in no hurry."

"Maybe that's because she's waiting to hear the results of what she put in motion yesterday."

"What did she do?" Nick asked in a cold voice.

Chapter 14

When a suspect isn't where he's supposed to be, start looking over your shoulder.

The Secret Journals of a Spymaster

With a sigh, Sam sank down on a chair beside Charlotte. "Will lost track of her yesterday morning for an hour or so, so we can't say for certain what Julia did."

Nick felt his muscles clench. "Just about the time we didn't see Campbell enter the estate."

He was grateful that Sam hadn't asked any pointed questions. But he watched Charlotte blush and drop her gaze.

"But we have a pretty good guess," Sam continued. "Last night Will was attacked as he slept."

Charlotte gasped, but Nick said, "By Campbell?"

"The man wore a mask, so Will can't identify him. That's why he and Jane left so quickly this morning."

"Was Jane hurt?" Charlotte interrupted.

Sam shook his head. "At this point she still doesn't know what's going on, although Will thinks she's now so suspicious, he's going to be forced to tell her some of his past. He promised not to reveal the mission."

Nick frowned. "But if Jane didn't know Will was attacked—"

"But she saw the second attack."

Nick clenched his fists to control his anger. He'd allowed a woman to distract him, and Will had almost paid the price with his life.

When Nick didn't say anything, Charlotte spoke up. "What happened?" she asked anxiously.

"After they reached an inn here in town just a couple hours ago, Barlow—that's Will's coachman," he explained to Charlotte, "was attacked and knocked unconscious. Luckily Will was worried after everything that had happened, so he went to check up on Barlow and ended up surprising the attacker. They fought, but the man got away. Jane saw the whole thing."

"So where is Will now?" she asked.

"He drove northeast of here and is going to spend the night outdoors."

"Outdoors?" she repeated, looking aghast. "My sister won't—"

"Charlotte, please," Nick said, knowing he was being short with her, but it was necessary. "So they're safe for now, Sam? He doesn't think they were followed?"

"Will thinks he lost the man."

"Where will he be tomorrow?"

"In Epworth, a village in Lincolnshire, at an inn called the Crown and the Horse. I told him I'd let him know what happens."

Nick sat down on the edge of the bed to keep himself from pacing. "I just don't understand— why did she have Will attacked?"

Sam shrugged. "Will never said that he confronted Julia, or that she confronted him."

In the silence Charlotte spoke hesitantly. "Nick, you said you had an affair with her. Could you have mentioned Will's name in conversation?"

"No."

"But we were all there in Kabul," Sam said quickly. "Her brother was highly ranked in the army—she could have easily discovered anything she wanted about us."

"She knows she's being followed now," Nick said tiredly. "Yet she still stopped in Newark. Why? There are just too many unanswered questions. Did Will have anything else to report?"

"Just that the duke and Julia aren't officially engaged yet. And that Julia claimed she was heading to her brother's, just like I said."

"But we don't know if she's telling the truth."

"No, we don't," Sam said. "And I don't see

any other way to confirm it but to follow her."

After a few minutes' silence, Charlotte said, "Did you meet my sister?"

Sam shook his head. "Will still had to tell her everything. She's suspicious of him now, and what's interesting is that she likes Julia. Apparently they got along quite well."

"That must have been difficult for Will," she said softly. "He must have wanted to protect Jane."

"That might be his instinct," Nick found himself saying, "but sometimes the mission comes first."

Charlotte straightened and frowned at him. "You can't possibly mean that Will should allow my sister to be in danger."

Sam stood up. "I'll get some sleep."

Nick followed him to the door. "You do that. I think we need to keep a closer eye on Julia at all times, now that we're getting so close to Leeds. I'll take the first watch. I'll come down to speak to you and Cox about it in a minute."

After he shut the door Nick turned to face Charlotte. She had risen to her feet and now stood with her hands on her hips and watched him. That pose enhanced the womanly features he enjoyed looking at, so he quickly went to his portmanteau.

"Don't worry about leaving a guard for me," Charlotte said coolly. "I wouldn't want to jeopardize the mission."

He sighed. "Charlotte, I didn't mean my comments about your sister as literally as they sounded."

"I'm not sure how else I should take them. You'd rather leave my sister unprotected?"

"I meant that the mission came first over Will's worries about two women talking together in the middle of a crowded house party."

"But it was easy for Julia to elude all of you, wasn't it? Who knows why she befriended my sister?"

Nick stiffened as Charlotte cut right to the heart of his guilt.

In a softer voice she continued, "And I know it's partially my fault. I'm not blaming anyone."

"Your fault?" he said, turning to look into her worried eyes. "Did you try to seduce me?" When she said nothing, he bitterly said, "I didn't think so. We both know whose fault my negligence is."

"It's my fault I was there to distract you. But I'm not here to assign blame. It's done."

"Yes, it is," he answered, giving her a direct look he hoped she understood.

She paled but said nothing.

"Will and Jane almost paid the price for my carelessness. It won't happen again."

"We've already agreed on that."

He sighed and felt his shoulders slump. "I can't give you what you need, Charlotte."

"I'm not asking for anything."

"But you are, with every look you give me."

"Maybe you're seeing what you want to see," she whispered, rubbing her arms and turning away. "I'm pretending to be your wife, aren't I?"

Were tears filling her eyes? He couldn't tell— not that he'd meant to put them there.

"Don't you see," he began, "I've tried to stay away from relationships, because inevitably a woman causes me problems."

When she was about to speak, he held up a hand. "Not the woman herself, but my reaction to her. You have to understand that my involvement with Julia in Afghanistan blinded me to what she was doing."

"You don't know that," Charlotte said gently. She heard the pain that Nick was trying so hard to hide and wondered if he knew how deep inside him she was beginning to see. Or was that only because she was growing to care too much for a man who thought soft feelings for a woman were a weakness?

"But I'm allowing you to distract me, aren't I?" Nick said angrily. "Just as it has happened since I was young."

"When you were young?"

But he ignored her question. "I don't want to hurt you, Charlotte, but you cannot doubt how attracted I am to you. I've never lived like a monk, so if something physical happens between us, I would not refuse such a gift."

Something physical? She heard the words and tried not to take it personally, but the pain was there all the same. Though he was vastly different from her husband, she could not deny that in one way, they were as alike as all the rest of the male species: sexual relations did not have to be tied to love.

Though she and Nick had shared some intimate moments, she hadn't thought she truly loved him—yet. Did that make her like a man? Or was she just confused about her feelings for Nick, and letting her heart guide her?

Maybe she was jumping into things too quickly, just as she'd done with her first marriage. She had to get it through her own head that her dreams of being loved and cherished by a man could not happen with Nick.

Silently she watched him leave. No matter what he said, she knew that he worried about her, that he watched over her.

But there was more he wasn't saying. He had mentioned a problem with a woman when he was younger. What had this woman done to him?

Even if he never shared that deep part of himself, Charlotte knew she had to somehow make things easier on him. She would stop making calf's eyes at him; she would be calm and logical and be of help whenever she could. It would make things easier on all of them.

All the next day Nick and Sam kept watch on Julia's slow-moving carriage, leaving Charlotte riding in their carriage in the capable hands of Cox.

By midafternoon Nick veered away from Julia's path to head for his meeting place with Campbell at an old bridge outside an ancient deserted village, which was now surrounded by a vast orchard. Nick was going to have to take him into custody and leave him with the local constable. He didn't want another unaccounted-for man waiting around to take him by surprise. Then if Julia suspected her henchman had been caught, at least she might try to reach Leeds quickly to stop her last accomplice from betraying her to the government. Anything to finish this.

But Campbell never showed up, though Nick waited several hours, until dusk began to blanket the trees. As far as Campbell knew, Nick was now going to go to the authorities about Julia. Didn't Campbell care? It made no sense.

Nick found his own carriage behind the Fountain Inn in Tuxford, which was Sam's guess for Julia's next destination. Cox was still taking care of the horses and looked up when Nick strode into the deserted stable.

"Where's Julia?" Nick asked.

"Other side of the village at the Newcastle Arms Hotel."

"Where's Sam?"

"Off to see how Will's doin'."

"I hate leaving Charlotte alone."

"No one's followin' us, Nick," Cox said. "I

made sure she knew not to open the door for anyone."

Nick sighed. "Very well. When Sam gets back, I want the two of you to come find me. Hopefully, one of the local barkeeps will have seen Campbell and his helpers. There aren't too many decrepit taverns that a hunted man might haunt, so it should be relatively easy to find me. We're going to deprive Julia of help, and us of a threat."

"Anxious are ye, Nick?" Cox said with a grin.

"I want this over. Maybe we can force her into a faster pace. I want you to wait outside, in case our quarries try to escape."

"What about Mrs. Sinclair?"

Nick's stomach tightened at just the mention of her name. "When you've found my tavern, send Sam in and you go back to tell her where we are. Explain what we're doing. Stress that if she needs us, she's to send a servant, not come herself."

"Ye don't want to tell 'er yourself?" Cox asked innocently.

"It will be fine coming from you." He turned to leave, then hesitated. "Did everything go all right today?"

"I think so, sir. I found the lady another newspaper. I don't think she was too bored."

"Thank you, Cox. I'll see you soon."

For an hour Nick strolled through taverns, looking for Julia's henchmen. Finally, at a run-down pub crowded with hunch-shouldered men and thick with the smell of smoke and gin, the barkeep looked up from washing a tankard with a dirty rag. Frizzy gray hair stood out around his head like a halo.

After Nick described the men, the barkeep said, "Sounds like I seen 'em. They took the room over me stable."

Nick's exhaustion fled. He brought forth several sovereigns, watched avidly by the barkeep, and slid them across to him. "There's more where this came from, if you let me wait here and don't alert the men to my presence."

The barkeep narrowed his watery eyes. "And ye'll be drinkin' steady, right?"

"Of course."

The coins disappeared beneath the bar and the man grinned, showing gums but little teeth. "Then I got no problem with ye, guv'nor."

Charlotte woke up alone.

The sun had already risen, though it was just past dawn. She lay still, stretching, breathing in the silence, and tried to remember that just a few weeks ago, she had enjoyed the peace that came from being alone.

That feeling had deserted her.

She told herself it was because she was nervous without protection, but that wasn't completely true.

She missed Nick. She missed the tension of desire between them; she missed the amusing things he said. She hoped she could convince him that she understood his decision regarding their relationship—even though she really didn't. But she wanted the chance to feel at ease with him once again.

But where was he?

A prickle of unease shivered across her skin, and she sat up. Mr. Cox had said that the three of them were looking for Julia's henchmen in a nearby tavern. Surely the tavern was closed by now. So where were they?

She rose and dressed quickly, determined not to panic yet. Nick and Sam had traveled the world together, through more dangerous territory than Nottinghamshire.

Sure enough, she saw a scrap of paper that had been slipped beneath the door. With relief she knelt and opened it. In just a few lines, Nick had informed her that they were keeping watch on the room Julia's accomplices were staying in.

She smiled to herself and held the letter close for a moment. She would not remind him that he'd thoughtfully taken time to tell her where he was. He was good at playing the husband.

All right, so she wasn't really a wife, she thought, humming as she opened the dusty old curtains and looked out on the day. The sky was overcast, threatening rain. Below her window was a village park, with surrounding glass-fronted businesses and even a coffeehouse.

Someone had taken the time to plant flowers

about the green, and she leaned out to see if the scent reached her window.

A carriage pulled up to the coffeehouse next door. The coachman jumped down to open the door and lower the step. She would have ducked back inside so as not to be seen, but something unusual caught her attention about the person descending to the pavement. She was an elegantly dressed woman, but it took a moment before Charlotte realized what was so unusual.

The woman was not wearing a hat or bonnet, and she had the palest blond hair.

When the woman began to look up, Charlotte gasped and leaned back inside her room.

Julia Reed.

Chapter 15

When creating a fictional story, use as much truth as possible. You'll have an easier time remembering.

The Secret Journals of a Spymaster

Who else could it be? They were following Julia Reed, after all. Charlotte slowly peered out, then leaned out farther as she saw Julia disappearing into the coffeehouse. She looked as if she was just having a bit of breakfast on her way out of town. Wasn't this far earlier than she'd set off before?

Where was Nick?

Charlotte gripped the window frame tightly as her mind raced. If the men didn't return soon, they would miss Julia. What if she was going a different way? If they lost her, she could reach

Leeds before them. Nick had said that the town was a journey of but one or two days.

What would Papa do? she wondered frantically. She would have to delay Julia's departure. Finally she could make a difference, instead of just being the woman Nick regretted bringing.

She found the pen and inkwell and paper in Nick's portmanteau and wrote a note, telling him that she was at the coffeehouse next door delaying Julia. He'd figure out what to do from there.

Quickly she put her hair in a simple chignon at the base of her neck, her sister Jane's favorite style. She donned the old shawl Sam had brought for her, and thought she must look very different from her normal self. If she happened to run into Mr. Campbell, surely he wouldn't recognize her as a socialite from a London ball—the witness who was supposed to be dead.

As she opened the door, she hesitated. What was she going to say?

Julia, you can't go yet!

Oh, that would go over well.

Don't I know you?

That at least had more promise.

Or else she could be a bit more direct and say that she recognized Julia because of her description. That was the truth, after all, so it was easier to remember. So who supposedly gave her the description?

She'd let Julia suggest someone, because there wasn't any more time to waste on planning.

Charlotte attracted no attention as she sedately walked down through the front hall of the inn and out the door. She walked down the pavement, then peered slowly through the coffeehouse window. Julia was sitting alone. Mr. Campbell was nowhere to be seen. Perfect.

Taking a deep breath, Charlotte opened the door and stepped inside. It was overly warm with the morning sun shining through the windows, and she felt herself begin to perspire. She'd never really lied to anyone, not with a fictional story. What if in the middle, she forgot what she'd already said? Her breathing was coming fast and panicky as the serving maid approached.

"May I help you, miss?" She was an older woman, with an easygoing smile and eyes that studied Charlotte through tiny spectacles.

"I'd like to dine, but I feel rather self-conscious alone." She looked about and then settled on Julia. "Do you mind if I ask if that lady would share her table?"

The serving maid gestured toward Julia. "Be my guest."

Charlotte clutched her shawl tighter and approached the table. Nick was right—Julia was more physically imposing and taller than even Charlotte's sister Jane. And her hair, though styled demurely, seemed to reflect the sun. It must be difficult to remain anonymous with such an unusual hair color.

Julia put down her coffee and looked up with a smile. "Yes?" she said.

Charlotte cleared her throat and had no problem sounding hesitant, "Miss, are you eating alone?"

"Why yes, I am."

"Would you mind terribly if I joined you? It is so lonely when one is by oneself." Charlotte spoke as she normally did, hoping her accent would put Julia at ease.

If Julia was annoyed at being interrupted, it did not show. "Of course. Please sit down. My name is Miss Julia Reed."

Oh God, what was *her* name to be? She thought of the last person she'd seen. "My name is Charlotte . . . Cox," she said, with only the slightest hesitation. She couldn't take the chance that Julia might know her husband's family.

"What a lovely name," Julia said.

Charlotte wanted to stare at her. This woman had betrayed British soldiers? This woman thought nothing of men dying because of her? She seemed so—normal, so polite.

Charlotte smiled. "Thank you."

Julia handed her the menu. "I hope you don't mind, but I've already ordered."

"How could I mind? I've only just intruded."

And she hoped Julia would politely stay while

Charlotte ate. Charlotte lifted up the menu as if to scan it, but she couldn't imagine forcing food down her dry throat. The danger of what she was doing was daunting. And if Mr. Campbell walked in and recognized her . . .

She casually glanced at the window, wishing desperately that Nick had received her note and would come to rescue her.

But the street was empty except for a milkmaid carrying pails of milk hanging from a bar across her shoulders.

She knew Nick would be furious that she'd disobeyed him, and right now she'd willingly take his anger.

But Julia Reed was sitting across from her, smiling politely while Charlotte could barely read the menu. But when the serving maid came, she found herself ordering eggs and toast. She sounded almost . . . normal.

She forced her shoulders to relax a bit. After all, this was a public place—what could Julia do to her?

"So Miss Cox, where are you from?" Julia asked after her own meal was served.

"I live in London, Miss Reed," she said, remembering to stay close to the truth.

"I just came from there. It is a very gracious city."

Charlotte smiled and sipped her coffee. "You don't sound as if you live there."

"Not until recently. Before this past year I spent much of ten years traveling abroad with my brother, who's an officer in the army."

"How fascinating to see the world," Charlotte exclaimed. "Do tell me the places you've visited."

She let Julia talk, and occasionally asked leading questions to keep her going. After Charlotte's breakfast was served, and she managed to get some of it down, she noticed that more and more, Julia glanced at the clock on the mantel above the bare hearth. Obviously their talk wasn't going to hold Julia back once Charlotte was finished eating.

Charlotte glanced quickly out the window, but saw no sign of Nick and his men.

The conversation went silent as they each paid for their meal. Charlotte thought desperately about another way to delay Julia. Perhaps she should try her first idea and say that she'd recognized Julia right away.

Clearing her throat, Charlotte fiddled with her fork and tried to look humble. "Miss Reed—I wasn't going to say anything—it isn't my place, but you're so pleasant and I can't continue lying to you."

Julia's smile faded and she blinked. "I beg your pardon?"

"I know who you are," Charlotte whispered.

Julia's smile reappeared, and it looked as if she was indulging a simpleton. "Well of course. I told you my name."

"No! I mean—I recognized who you were from a description of you."

"And who gave you that description?"

Charlotte's mind went blank. Who had they been talking about? "Your brother," she blurted out.

Julia relaxed, giving an easygoing grin. "I can imagine what *he* said."

"Besides your hair, he said that you were much larger than myself." Charlotte gasped and covered her mouth. "I—I didn't mean—"

"Please, I've taken no offense," Julia said with a smile. "My brother always called me a horse of a woman."

"That is hardly appropriate!" Charlotte said, feeling almost sorry for her.

"Do you have brothers?"

Charlotte shook her head.

"Then you can't understand what they're like," Julia said indulgently. "Is that why you're in Tuxford?"

"Pardon me?"

"We're only a day's journey from my brother's estate. Were you going to visit him?"

Charlotte nodded, having no other choice. Why else would she be here?

"I'm so sorry you've come all this way, but he's not in residence."

Charlotte's spirits sank as Julia closed her reticule and began to put on her gloves. Julia was going to leave; all Nick's efforts might be wasted.

Charlotte burst into tears.

Julia gaped at her for a moment, then fumbled for a handkerchief. "Oh dear, what's wrong, Miss Cox?"

She pushed the small piece of linen into Charlotte's trembling hands. Some distant part of Charlotte was stunned at how easy it was to cry when one was panicked and frightened.

"It's—it's nothing," Charlotte whispered, blowing her nose softly. Several of the other patrons were glancing their way, and she didn't want to draw any more attention to herself than she had to.

"But it's most definitely something," said Julia. "You needed to see my brother this badly?"

Charlotte nodded forlornly.

Julia's face paled, as if she'd thought of a reason. Charlotte wished she'd share it.

"But Miss Cox, my brother is in London. Didn't you just journey from there?"

"But he told me—" She sniffed several times. "He told me he wouldn't be there, that—that I was not to contact him ever again."

She resumed crying softly, scared that she wouldn't be able to come up with a reason. What would Julia do to her if she discovered Charlotte was lying?

Julia leaned closer and put her hand on top of Charlotte's. "Dear, are you"—she lowered her voice to a whisper—"in the family way?"

A sob of astonishment and relief escaped

Charlotte as she nodded and wiped at her eyes. At least something like *this* would delay the other woman.

Julia rubbed her hand across her face. "Oh my."

"I'm so sorry," Charlotte whispered. "I am a sinful woman. I never should have—should have—"

"And the baby is my brother's? You are certain?"

Charlotte gaped at her, but could only nod. What would Julia do? Think she was after her brother's money? Make her disappear so that there would be no stain on the family honor?

"I won't tell anyone, I promise you, Miss Reed," Charlotte murmured. "I am beyond embarrassment."

Julia returned to patting Charlotte's hand. "You must not blame yourself, Miss Cox. My brother is far older than you and should have known better."

"I just didn't know what to do. I saw you come into the coffeehouse, knew who you were . . . and I was just drawn to talk to you."

"That's because I'm a woman, too, and I understand your predicament. Well, this is something we'd best go tell my brother. Or does he already know?"

Charlotte hesitated. She'd obviously never met Julia's brother, and didn't know how he would behave.

Julia gasped. "He already knows, doesn't he!" she whispered furiously. "And he let you go off alone. Or did he—send you away?"

The last was said in such an appalled voice that Charlotte wondered what kind of man this General Reed was for Julia to think this of him. Charlotte just blew her nose and let Julia draw her own conclusions.

"He can be such a fool sometimes," Julia murmured as if to herself. "I will take care of this matter. You'll come with me."

An hour past dawn, Nick gave up. He, Sam, and Cox had spent the previous evening trying not to get drunk while they waited for Julia's men to show up. Well past midnight the barkeep had finally closed the place down, and Nick and his men took up stations outside the stable, above which Campbell had rented a room.

But although they'd waited until the sun rose, Julia's henchmen had never shown up. Did they know they were being followed, or were they taking precautions just in case?

Nick couldn't waste any more time. Julia usually left each town by midmorning, and they needed to be ready to follow her. It wasn't far to Leeds now, probably by the end of the next day. He was exhausted and anxious all at once. He just wanted it over with.

As he climbed the stairs to his room, he wondered why he wished it all over. Surely it was because he was anxious to return to India.

But for the first time the thought of the many-month journey made him weary. Going back to a place he'd spent thirteen years suddenly had no allure. And he'd have to deal with his family before he went, and he certainly didn't look forward to that.

And he'd never see Charlotte again.

Why was he feeling . . . hollow inside?

He told himself he'd become too involved with a woman as always, but he really hadn't done that with Julia. She'd been a fascination, an enigma, a woman who reminded him of home, yet was unusual enough to seem foreign. He'd lusted after her, but had not spent his hours worrying about her, wondering what she was doing, how she felt.

Charlotte inspired that in him just as once, long ago, Edith had made him feel. He'd been a boy when he met Edith, and maybe now he could recognize his feelings for her as infatuation, as loneliness, but then he'd thought himself deeply in love.

Until his family had stepped in.

He shook the sad memories out of his mind and thought once again of Charlotte, waiting for him, maybe lonely and . . . frightened? No, not frightened. She had too much spirit for that.

He opened the door, feeling in control of his

emotions, ready to hide the smile that she inspired in him—but the room was empty.

He remained frozen on the doorstep, his mind blank, his professionalism gone. Then he shrugged back into Nick the Spy and began a methodical search of the room for clues.

He saw the note on the table almost immediately, and let anger surge to replace the strange emotions he'd battled. She'd left the room! After he'd given her strict orders.

He glanced at the note, and his anger drained away, replaced by an icy feeling it took him a moment to recognize: fear.

He threw open the door and almost collided with Sam.

"What are you—" Sam began.

Nick grabbed his arm and pulled him down the stairs. "We need Cox."

When he had them both alone in the yard of the inn, he told them briefly what Charlotte's note said. Cox looked stoic, Sam looked aghast.

Without saying a word, Nick led them through the alley between the buildings. The walk seemed endless as he told himself he had to change his own behavior and see Charlotte as more than a helpless widow in need of a rescuer. She had chosen to help him; she surely understood the risks. But how could she, when the only evil she'd faced had been her husband?

When they stopped on the walkway outside the coffeehouse, Sam said, "Nick—"

Nick raised a hand. "Let me judge the situation first. Wait here."

He very carefully peered around the corner and through the glass. He didn't see her at first, and his chest tightened, but at the last second he saw her against the wall nearest the alley.

She was seated at a table with Julia—and she was crying.

He pulled his head back before Julia could glance up.

He thought he was in control, thought his face displayed nothing, but Sam grabbed his arm.

"Are you all right? What did you see? Is she—"

Nick pulled away. "She's with Julia. We have to get her away. You and I can't go in there. Cox, it will have to be you."

His coachman straightened with determination and tossed his ever-present black scarf over his shoulder. "I'm ready, Nick."

Chapter 16

Intimacy between captor and hostage sometimes feels inevitable.

The Secret Journals of a Spymaster

"**C**ome with you?" Charlotte echoed as Julia briskly got to her feet. Charlotte pulled her back down. "Oh, I can't do that, Miss Reed!"

"Whyever not? We will have a long talk with my brother about responsibility."

Charlotte couldn't help but admire her determination. "But—but I couldn't . . . couldn't act like I've gone behind his back."

"You need to. We can kick his backside while we're at it."

Charlotte concealed her sudden smile with a forced sob. "No, no, this was the worst idea I've ever had, to—to try to force him into something he's not ready for."

"He was ready about two months ago, wasn't he?" Julia asked grimly.

Charlotte didn't have to fake her shock.

Julia waved her hand tiredly. "Forgive me. That was terribly crude of me. I'm just angry with my brother. I'll feel better when we've made everything right. So come along."

Julia stood up and reached as if to take Charlotte's hand. Stricken, Charlotte remained still. What was she to do?

Suddenly the door opened, and in walked Mr. Cox. He wasn't Nick, but Charlotte was just as glad to see him. She didn't know what he planned to do, so she quickly looked away, but too late.

"Who is that man?" Julia asked.

Charlotte had her first moment of inspiration. She looked at Mr. Cox in horror, and was secretly amused when he looked stunned.

"Oh no," she whispered.

"You know him as well?" Julia asked dryly. "You meet a lot of people, Miss Cox. Unless—unless he was the one who brought you here."

Charlotte quickly wiped the last of her tears away, and her face felt dry and chapped. "Please, Miss Reed, he is why I can't go with you. Please don't tell him what I—" She broke off and donned the falsest smile she could muster. "Oh my dear Mr. Cox, here I am."

He'd already seen her of course, and she was relieved when he began to walk over.

"Mr. Cox—" Julia began, then broke off, her mouth pursing in dismay. "Oh Charlotte, what have you done?"

Charlotte put her arm through Mr. Cox's and spoke in the same falsely cheerful voice. "Mr. Cox, this is my new friend Miss Reed. Miss Reed, this is my husband."

Beneath her arm she felt Mr. Cox stiffen, but he only smiled pleasantly, his well-lined face creasing in seemingly new places. "How do ye do," he said formally, nodding his head.

"Very well, sir," Julia said faintly, eyeing Charlotte with a pitying look.

"I hope you don't mind, dear," Charlotte said, turning to look up sweetly at Mr. Cox, "but I had breakfast with this nice lady while I waited for you. But I understand you're in a hurry."

He tipped his tall hat to Julia and said simply, "Good day, Miss Reed."

"Good day," she answered, fumbling with her reticule. She pulled out a card and pressed it into Charlotte's hand. "Do call upon me, Mrs. Cox. I would like to further our acquaintance."

Charlotte put as much emotion into her eyes as she dared. "Thank you so much, Miss Reed. Have a pleasant trip."

And then she walked outside arm-in-arm with Mr. Cox. He turned down the alley between the buildings, and she saw Nick and Sam waiting. She braced herself for Nick's anger, but his face looked strangely unemotional.

She smiled serenely at them, then whispered, "She could be watching. Do move along, gentlemen."

They turned and together they all walked into the yard of the inn, then up to the room.

Nick couldn't look at Charlotte. His relief was too great. He had to remain professional, to keep these strange emotions locked away. But every time he looked at her, they threatened to erupt, and he didn't want to face them right now.

"Sam, you need to follow Julia immediately," Nick said calmly. "The rest of us will catch up with you. She's leaving early, so something might have aroused her suspicions. Charlotte, is there anything he should know first?"

He had to look at her, only to see her watching him with a wariness he understood.

She shook her head. "We did not discuss anything related to the mission or to you gentlemen." She hesitated, and a faint blush swept her face. "She merely thinks I'm married to Mr. Cox, but carrying her brother's child."

Nick felt his mouth drop open in surprise. For someone used to concealing his emotions, he seemed to have lost that skill around Charlotte. Cox just folded his arms over his chest and looked resigned.

Nick expected Sam to have a good laugh over this, but instead Sam just gave Nick an inscrutable look. "I'll leave you all, then. Charlotte, nice work."

After Sam left, Nick glared at Charlotte. "Start at the beginning and leave nothing out."

"You saw my note," she protested. "I didn't want Julia to escape, so I felt like I should delay her."

"Against my orders."

She flung her arms wide. "Well you weren't here to ask!"

Cox cleared his throat. "Sir, I'll just be harnessin' the horses."

Nick didn't even look at him. "Do that. We'll be down soon."

When he was alone with Charlotte, something happened to his control, and emotions he'd always tried to keep buried came roaring to the surface in a confused rush. All he knew was that she had put her life on the line for his mission. She'd braved an enemy she knew wanted her killed. She'd come up with an impossible story and somehow made it plausible.

And she stood there, looking so beautiful and vulnerable and stubborn—and he'd almost lost her, and the qualities that made her unique, so full of passion, so ready to explore things she'd never done before.

When she opened her mouth to speak, he

kissed her. There was nothing else he could do, no way to assuage this pain, except to convince himself with his every sense that she was alive.

Charlotte reeled from the desperate power of Nick's sudden passion. He caught her face between his hands and kissed her quickly, deeply, over and over again, until the wild emotions she'd gone through that day coalesced into a need for him so powerful she didn't want to resist it, didn't want to question it. He wanted her; she wanted him.

With a moan she slid her arms about him, beneath his coat and up his back, letting her palms slide against hot muscle beneath his shirt. She tasted the recesses of his mouth, suckled his tongue, let herself burn with the raw desire that blazed out of her. She was overwhelmed, lost in her feelings, only aware of a surge of joy that she would finally know the truth of a woman's pleasure. Nick would show it to her, and erase every terrible memory that lurked in the shadows of her mind. There would be no promises, for she needed none.

His kisses suddenly gentled, and his fingers traced patterns across her face. His lips followed, pressing against her eyelids, the tip of her nose, the curve of her ear. Gentle kisses created paths down her throat, and she dropped her head back, letting him do as he wanted. When his tongue swept the hollow at the base of her throat, she groaned.

As he began to undo the buttons of her bodice, she looked into his face. He frowned with concentration, as if he could not disrobe her quickly enough. The backs of his hands brushed her nipples, and she gasped at the sensation that shot through her. He glanced up at her and grinned, then spread her gown wide to push off her shoulders. When it pooled at her feet and she stood in her chemise, she expected him to relieve her of that as well. But instead he slid his hands down her shoulders, then over her breasts, pausing to cup them leisurely as he dropped to his knees, before spreading his hands wide as he spanned her rib cage and waist.

Her breathing came faster with anticipation and longing as his palms skimmed her stomach and his fingers curled around her hips. When through the fabric his thumbs brushed the curls between her thighs, she gave a shudder and had to clutch his shoulders to remain upright.

Then he rose to his feet, the hem of her chemise captured with his fingers. It slid up across her skin, a whisper of fabric. She felt the caress of air across her naked thighs, then the brush of his shirt against her breasts. When her chemise slid up and off her arms, he worked his fingers into her hair until her curls spilled free down her body. He stepped back and looked at her nakedness, and she wasn't embarrassed, only felt proud at his look of approval and desire.

Then he picked her up, took two steps and laid

her out on the bed with a gentleness that brought tears to her eyes.

With the back of his hand, he caressed her cheek and whispered, "How lovely you are."

Then he stood up and began to pull off his clothes, leaving them wherever they landed in his haste. She laughed and lay back among the pillows, knowing that they shouldn't be taking this time, but that he was giving it to her. Her amusement died as his last garments fell and he put a knee on the bed and leaned over her. His body was corded with long, sleek muscles, and his erection proudly showed his desire for her. His dark hair fell forward over his cheeks, and between the strands his black eyes burned her wherever they touched.

"Are you frightened?" he whispered.

She shook her head, then gave a soft gasp as he came on his hands and knees above her. He freely dropped kisses wherever he could reach, from her bent knee to her hip to her toes. Pausing above her breasts, he smiled and passed on to nuzzle her shoulder. She groaned her disappointment and he kissed her mouth, softly biting her lower lip as she pouted.

"You're impatient," he murmured.

"Yesss," she answered, arching her back, displaying herself brazenly.

His smile died, and with a growl he began to spread tiny kisses and licks across her breasts, teasing their peaks with the tip of his tongue. She could hear herself moaning and desperately calling his name, but she was awash in the pleasure that scattered along her skin. She reached for him and he came down on top of her, molding her to him, their chests and hips and thighs undulating against one another. His skin was hot against hers, the weight of him pressing her deeper into the mattress. When she spread her thighs, his hips slid away.

"But—" she began.

He put his finger against her mouth. "Shh. Wait." He lay at her side, kissing her mouth lazily, while he moved his hand from her knee up her thigh. "Now you can open," he murmured against her lips.

And she did. His hand slid between her thighs and he cupped her, gently moving the base of his palm against her in a circular motion. With a groan, she turned her head into his shoulder and squeezed her eyes shut at this new sensation. Every bit of her skin was sensitive, quivering with pleasure and tension in a reach for something higher, for the unknown.

"No, look at me, I want to see you."

She looked up into his handsome face, communicating her urgency with her gaze.

"I know, I feel it, too," he said, as his fingers took the place of his palm.

She cried out in wonder as he caressed her, circling, dipping, even moving inside her. Her every muscle tightened and she arched her back. Just when she thought she could take no more, he lowered his head and licked his tongue in a long, flat caress across her nipple, repeating it as if touching a fuse to a low-simmering flame.

She hovered on the edge of a new wonder, a new understanding of what could exist between men and women.

"Let go," he urged, as his caresses deepened and grew harder, faster.

Then she plummeted, letting herself fall into sensation, feeling shudder after shudder of aftershock take control of her body. When she looked up in wonder, he was there, watching her, smiling.

"Oh Nick," she whispered.

He said nothing, just rose above her and parted her thighs to settle between them. Her newly sensitive flesh came alive again at the touch of him. She felt his hardness pressing against her.

She must have betrayed a touch of an old fear, because he paused.

"I'm not going to hurt you, Char. You know that."

She nodded and looked up into his face, loving the way he shortened her name. It was almost an endearment. With a frown of concentration he moved against her, then sheathed himself deep inside.

There was no pain, only the sense of being filled, of feeling complete. She lifted her knees and he settled deeper, breathing heavily.

"Ready?" he said with an unsteady voice.

Then he pulled out and thrust inside. It was as if every nerve he'd just aroused had only slumbered, ready to be awakened once again. He rocked against her and she found his movement, meeting his hips with hers, feeling that new passion coming to life again.

Their mouths met and their tongues danced together, even as his hand moved between them to capture her breast. This time he joined her in a shuddering fulfillment.

For a moment they simply panted, their lips gently touching, their bodies as one. Then he lifted himself up by the arms and looked down at her. She smiled.

"I could look at you forever," he said.

She stilled, and he must have realized what he implied, because he said, "But there's only today and Cox is waiting."

With a groan she wrapped her legs about his hips and held him still. She put her hands on his strong shoulders, then ran her palms down his chest slowly, enjoying his quick intake of breath when she touched his nipples.

As he trembled, she tightened the muscles deep in her abdomen, the ones that held him inside her.

He groaned. "Witch," he said, but made no move to go.

Very slowly she let her heel caress his backside, and her fingertips danced against his nipples. She gently raked her nails across him, and he twitched and gasped. She could feel him grow hard inside her.

She grasped his head and pulled until he came down on his elbows. Against his mouth she whispered, "Again."

He surged up hard, going deep. His motion was fast but she kept up with him, her legs holding him tight.

When he climaxed again, he groaned and rolled onto his back. "I can't move."

She rose up on her elbow and looked down at his glistening body. "But I thought you said we had to go."

He closed his eyes. "We do. Hold on."

He got to his feet as wearily as an old man, and she giggled. But her amusement faded into a soft smile when he brought her a wet cloth and towel.

"Sorry it's cold," he said, using another cloth on himself.

She cocked her head to the side and watched him until he finally noticed and paused.

"Is something wrong?"

She shook her head. "Just enjoying myself."

She could swear that even with his sun-darkened complexion, a touch of red swept his face. Then she quickly washed herself, and they helped dress each other, which probably took twice as long, but was more fun.

Finally she opened the door for him, since he

carried their two portmanteaus. They raced down the stairs and out into the yard of the inn. Mr. Cox was there to open the carriage door for them, and after handing him their bags, they collapsed next to each other on the bench. A few minutes later the carriage started moving.

"All right," Nick said, "now tell me exactly what happened with Julia."

So she did. During her story he looked alternately amused and angry.

"So you see," Charlotte concluded, "I didn't come up with the whole story so much as allow Julia to lead me on."

"But you told her you knew her *brother*!"

"I panicked! You must admit I kept her attention for well over an hour. And she's very easy to talk to. Nick, she was so nice."

"I know what she can be like," he said dryly.

"I had forgotten—you had . . . relations with her!"

He shrugged. "It was temporary, and we both accepted that."

They were silent for a moment, and she reminded herself that what she had with Nick was also temporary. She'd known that going in, but she had not counted on falling in love with him. Yet how could she not? She'd never felt as cherished, as desired as Nick had just made her feel. But he was a man with a dangerous duty who could be no husband to her. He was constantly fighting his gentler emotions, and that's not what she wanted. She wished she understood him, wished she knew what haunted his past.

But she could still matter in his life by helping him, being a part of this mission she was swept up in. She had now proven herself, and surely he understood that, since he even confided his plans in her.

Charlotte finally said, "So what happened with Julia's men?"

"Campbell never showed at our meeting place," Nick said, his expression turning cold and professional.

"So he *wants* you to turn them in?"

"Who knows? They never came back to the tavern or to the rooms they'd rented, either."

"Maybe they were alerted by someone. Julia *was* leaving town much earlier than she normally does."

"Did she seem frantic or preoccupied to you?"

She shook her head. "She was all courtesy and pleasantness, and eventually concern. She concluded that her brother knew about our *baby* and still didn't want to see me."

"Doesn't think much of him, does she?"

"I guess not."

They were quiet for a moment, jostling gently to the motion of the carriage.

"I have news," he said, giving her a dour look. "You'll consider it good, but I have a bad feeling about it. Sam saw Will last night, and he accidentally revealed to Jane that you're traveling with us."

" 'Traveling with'?" she repeated, smiling up at him.

He didn't smile back, and she knew he'd retreated into his spy persona.

"So they don't know how I came to be with you?"

"Oh, they know," he said. "I heard your sister was very angry. She demanded to see you immediately."

Charlotte couldn't resist clapping her hands together. "How wonderful!"

Nick narrowed his eyes at her, realizing that she didn't understand. "Charlotte, it will be dangerous for all of us to be together. We'll be a perfect target for Julia's men to wipe us out all at once."

"Then we aren't going?" she asked with worry.

He clenched his jaw and spoke through his teeth. "We're going. Sam made the arrangements, so we can't back out now. But you'll only get a few minutes to see her."

"I understand," she said softly.

"I don't know if you do, Charlotte. We're near the end of this mission. We're almost to Leeds. From this point on, we'll get ahead of Julia, leaving Sam to follow behind. We have to be at

Hume's house, waiting for Julia, so we can catch her in the act."

"Not the act of killing him," she said, blinking her eyelashes innocently.

He resisted the urge to smile. "We want to catch her just before. It'll be the last and best evidence in our case. Proof that her treachery was worth killing for."

"And how do you know she just won't send Campbell?"

He glanced at her, grudgingly admiring her intelligence. "Because I think she needs to make sure the job is done right. Her men haven't exactly been able to stop us yet, and she'll know this."

She nodded and looked out the window, and Nick found himself staring at her delicate hand where it rested on the bench. Somewhere inside him, the weak man he was trying to conquer urged him to take her hand, to hold it in his own.

But what idea would that give Charlotte? That there could be more to their relationship than sex? She understood the limited things he could offer her, and he didn't want to confuse her by hinting at more.

But less than an hour ago he'd been wrapped in her arms, held close to her heart. She'd granted him a gift that another man had almost ruined—the gift of her trust.

But he wasn't lying to her—he wasn't betraying that trust.

Then why did he feel so distraught? He didn't

know what he wanted anymore, so it was easier to cling to the past, to the things that made him Nick Wright, political agent. Not Nick Wright, the supposed savior of his family, or Nick Wright, lover.

But there was Charlotte, a warm, giving woman, who'd rediscovered the power of her femininity, who'd demanded his body again instead of waiting for it. Even now he was hard with wanting her.

But his dilemma never changed. He had a job to do, and he'd allowed Charlotte to be a distraction. And now she thought she was a success at spying, because she'd been quick-thinking enough to delay Julia.

But she would only put them all in further danger, because they had to worry about her. Yes, she would see her sister this night, but it would be on his terms, and with everyone's safety in mind. Julia's henchmen were on to them, and would be closing in as all parties met in one place. He would keep Charlotte safe, and in doing so, protect his men, too.

"So Nick," she suddenly said in a cheerful voice, "I have a marriage question for you."

Though he wanted to be somber, he glanced at her, and her mischievous expression made him smile. "Draw upon my wealth of knowledge, my dear."

She elbowed him playfully in the side. "So how often should a husband and wife have relations?"

Stunned, he cocked his head. "Are you suggesting something?"

"Heavens no—we're not married." She batted her eyelashes.

"That's right—you're a merry widow now, and you have used innocent me quite shamelessly."

She gaped at him, as if she didn't know what to respond to first. "Used you—*innocent*?"

"Don't worry, my feelings weren't hurt."

He slid closer to her, and with a groan she pushed him away. "Just answer the question."

"I can't remember it, since you raised up my hopes—and an important body part."

"Oh never mind," she said between gritted teeth.

"Wait, I remember now!" he said brightly. "How often should a husband and wife have relations?"

She gave him a pointed stare that suggested she was only humoring him now.

"Well of course," he continued, "that is up to the husband—I mean wife!" he amended when she scowled. He wondered if he'd said the wrong thing, for certainly everything in her life had been on her husband's schedule.

"Perhaps it should be up to them both," she said calmly. "Whenever either one of them feels like it."

"What a revolutionary idea. But speaking as a

man, I believe the husband would feel aroused every morning waking in his wife's arms."

She glanced out the window, wearing a little smile that said she was imagining just that. "What a romantic thing to say."

"A husband has to be romantic. How else will he persuade his wife that the timing of sex is her idea?"

Her laugh was throaty and alluring, given by an experienced woman. He wanted to pounce on her, to show her that private carriages could be *very* accommodating. Sweat broke out on his brow, and he couldn't wipe it away without revealing too much of his desire to her.

She glanced at him. "So do they each ask—or just seduce?"

He was soon going to need to adjust himself. "Personally, a seduction might be difficult if, in the middle of a party, a wife's low-cut gown inspires a husband's thoughts."

"So you don't think it right for him to whisper his desires in his wife's ear?" she asked. "I would have thought a well-pleasured husband would feel confident in that."

"And what would a well-pleasured wife's response be?"

"Why, she would follow him into the garden, of course, or to a secret, deserted chamber only they know about."

Pleasantly astonished, Nick let himself show

his admiration. "Why, Charlotte, you make marriage sound tempting."

Was that the lesson she was trying to teach him? When she said nothing, only gazed deeply into his eyes, tension once again settled between them.

Chapter 17

Though sometimes a spy is forced to take a hostage, those are the situations he might be least in control of. Because the hostage is treated well, eventually the hostage almost forgets he is one—until reminded.

The Secret Journals of a Spymaster

When the sun slid down behind gray clouds, Nick's mood worsened. Will and Jane had only just escaped Julia's henchmen, and now Nick was about to bring them back into the light. He had no choice but to go ahead with the meeting, for Will and Jane couldn't be left waiting, unprotected.

But damn if he wasn't going to make sure Charlotte was safe first.

Julia went home to her brother's estate, and

when the gates closed behind her, Nick had the carriage wait farther away. Charlotte said she could help them—she suggested she could wear his trousers as a disguise—but Nick firmly insisted that she was finished in the spy business. When he and Sam left to scale the manor wall, he had a picture in his mind of Charlotte breaking her neck trying such a stunt.

It was tricky, because the day hung at the edge of twilight, leaving them no darkness to hide in. But they managed to watch the groom unhitch Julia's carriage horses and lead them into the stable. Through the manor windows they watched as she was greeted by servants, saw her bags taken away, and even caught a glimpse of her in an upstairs corner bedroom.

Only an hour later, when they saw her sitting down to dinner, did they finally sneak away. Sam and Cox would come back when they were finished with Will and keep watch for the night. They climbed into the carriage, and Sam immediately went to sleep. Nick knew Charlotte was watching him expectantly, as if she thought he was powerful enough to keep them all safe. And that was only going to happen with plenty of luck.

A deep fog rolled in after dark, and the road to meet up with Will proved treacherous.

When they stopped to change horses, Nick spoke privately to Sam and Cox outside, explaining his plan for Charlotte. Though Sam seemed strangely belligerent—he normally accepted

Nick's lead—both agreed that Charlotte's penchant for "helping" would get her in worse trouble before the night was through if they didn't do something drastic. They just couldn't trust her to stay safe.

For supper they stopped in a small village, where Cox brought them cheese and fruit and a flask of wine. The four of them shared it in the shadowy darkness of the coach, and the mood was somber, strange. A single lantern hung against the wall, rocking gently with the movement of the carriage as the restless horses stomped and waited.

Nick watched Charlotte, saw the way her gaze became puzzled as it moved among them. He himself felt uneasy, disturbed, and he knew it was because Charlotte would feel betrayed before the hour was through. She'd know he still didn't trust her.

But she'd be safe.

When everyone had eaten his fill, Nick corked the wine and said, "Charlotte, you aren't going to like this, but I'm going to have to tie you up."

He saw her stiffen, then she took a deep breath and looked directly at him. "What are you talking about?"

"Tonight could be dangerous. We don't know where Julia's men are. We need to separate until we've safely found Will, and I can't be worried that you've overtaken Cox and tried to rescue us on your own."

"But I promise I—"

"You promise?" he said, drawing the ropes out of his pocket. "And didn't you promise last night to stay in the room?"

"Yes, I know—but I helped! Julia didn't get away!" She looked at Sam and Cox, neither of whom could meet her gaze.

"There will be no further discussion," Nick continued. "Please hold out your wrists."

Her mutinous look wearied him. He wished he could trust her to obey him unquestioningly. God forbid he should have to fight her. But then she straightened, lifted that fragile chin in the air, and held out her arms. She never said another thing, even as he was about to gag her. But that last indignity made her eyes snap with outrage.

"I'm sorry, Char," he murmured, and unable to help himself, lifted his hand to caress her cheek.

But she reared back so suddenly, she smacked her head into the carriage wall, and part of her hairstyle was knocked askew.

"Are you all right?" he asked curtly, hiding his worry.

She only nodded and turned her back.

They rode on another half hour, then the carriage halted. Sam slipped outside and Nick hesitated.

"Charlotte?"

She only glared at him. Though he tried not to,

he remembered her tearful confession that her husband occasionally tied her up for his pleasure. He felt lower than a toad.

But she would be safe.

After retrieving pistols and swords from beneath the opposite bench, he caught Charlotte's angry stare. He could only shrug and douse the lamp, leaving her in darkness. He descended from the carriage to stand at Sam's side. The carriage wheels squeaked as Cox urged the team on. The vehicle lumbered away, out of sight into the fog.

They were standing beside high walls hung with several guttering lanterns. An open gate led into a courtyard behind a four-story inn, each story with a long gallery overlooking the yard.

Nick offered weapons, and although Sam had a pistol already, he accepted one of the old cavalry swords.

"Are we being a little overly cautious?" Sam asked.

Nick looked around again. "I have a bad feeling about this. I don't like all of us meeting in one place." When Sam guiltily opened his mouth, Nick held up a hand. "Don't apologize again. I understand how it happened. Those Whittington women are hard to resist."

Sam's smile faded. "Are they?"

Nick ignored the unspoken rebuke and quietly asked, "Are we meeting inside the inn or out here?"

They listened carefully to voices raised in merriment on the other side of the wall.

"I thought it best to meet out here," Sam said. "I know this area well, as we're still in my parish. This inn is on the outskirts of the village and—"

He broke off suddenly. "Nick, did you see something?" he whispered.

The two of them backed toward the wall, pistols raised, and Nick thought he saw shadows moving near a stand of trees. The fog swirled around the tree trunks, for once aiding them. Two men were moving steadily toward them, dressed totally in black. One was short and broad.

"Campbell," Nick whispered.

They heard the sudden crack of gunshot, then another, and he and Sam threw themselves to the ground. They each had time for one shot before a man jumped on each of them.

Nick felt hands scratching at his throat, trying to crush his windpipe. His gun was knocked away, but he had his sword strapped at his waist. If only he could reach it. As he rolled to dislodge his assailant, he heard the frantic neighing of horses as another carriage pulled up too close to the fighting.

He staggered as he stood up, losing sight of his opponent in the low fog, fumbling for his sword, only to be knocked from his feet again.

When he was finally upright, he pulled the sword from its steel scabbard with a singing scrape. The man reeled back, and a knife almost as long as a sword glittered in his hand. Nick arced his sword up and brought it down, and the clash of metal on metal reverberated up his arm. Out of the corner of his eye Nick saw a man running toward him out of the darkness, from the direction of the newly arrived carriage. For a crazy moment, he thought he heard the high-pitched bark of a little dog.

"Nick!"

It was Will. With relief, Nick tucked his sword to his side and rolled low into the fog, landing near the wall and his extra sword. He rose up and called Will's name, flinging the sword high over his assailant's head. He never saw if Will caught it, for his assailant was on him once again.

Nick caught a glimpse of another man stalking his opponent from the right. The masked man was distracted, looked to his left, and Nick had him. He felt his sword run through, heard the man scream, then he vanished down into the fog. Nick quickly lifted the body, ripped off the mask, and saw that it was Campbell. Dropping him to the ground, he straightened. He kept his bloody sword raised, unable to tell in the flickering darkness exactly who was near him. And that seemed to be the general problem, because he located Sam and Barlow, Will's coachman, but where was the second henchman?

"He's getting away!" Will yelled.

The masked man had already vaulted onto the

back of a horse and was riding through the village, away from the direction Cox had driven Charlotte. Nick forced his lungs to start working again, let the fear go. He put his sword point into the ground and braced himself on the hilt, gasping for air. His three companions all did the same, tiredly grinning at one another in victory.

They didn't have long to stand around, because they could see several patrons leaning through the gates of the inn to see what was going on.

A woman had descended from Will's carriage, and came running up. She was tall and slender, properly attired yet showing a hint of womanly curves.

Will slung an arm about her shoulder and said, "Nick Wright, this is Jane Whittington, my future bride. I believe you know her sister, Charlotte."

Something set Jane off, whether it was the smiling, slightly bloodied men or Sam's laughter. She angrily pushed Will away from her, and Nick stepped forward to greet her.

When she looked up at him, she opened her mouth, but nothing came out. It was the usual reaction from women caught off-guard by the ungentlemanly size of him.

He gave her a polite society bow. "Miss Whittington, how good to meet you."

Even in the darkness, he could tell her face had paled, and he wondered if she was not quite as brave as her sister.

"Where's Charlotte?" she asked in a haughty voice.

Ah, now that was more like a Whittington woman.

Before he could answer, Will hugged her close. She struggled, but he didn't relent.

"I promised you'll see her, Jane. We need to take care of the body first."

Nick's smile faded and he surveyed the small gathering of people beginning to tiptoe closer. "We should probably go our separate ways for tonight. It's too dangerous to stay together any longer, especially since one bastard got away to warn Julia."

Jane struggled harder. "No! You promised!"

Sam elbowed him. "Didn't I tell you the sisters were alike?"

He nodded, rather enjoying watching Jane as she fought to control her emotions.

"We'll be brief," she said with a hint of desperation. "I just need to make sure she's all right."

Barlow, Will's coachman, was allowed to escape back to his horses.

Nick looked at Sam and Will, then sighed. "Very well. Sam, you and Barlow explain to the innkeeper about being attacked by thieves. Bury the corpse as discreetly as you can. I'll take Will and Miss Whittington to Charlotte. We won't be long."

He glanced at Jane to see if she understood what he meant. She nodded with resignation and moved away from Will to stand alone. Nick turned and began to walk away from the inn, knowing she followed, with Will behind her.

An animal barked nearby and just as quickly stopped.

Nick turned around, frowning. He wanted to be away from the crowds and the danger. "And what is that?"

"You remember Killer," Will said, glancing at the ground around him, where the fog moved. "If I can find him. Ah, there he is." He bent down and came up with a dog.

Nick was stunned. "Killer? *The* Killer? He survived the shipwreck?" The animal had five years' worth of history with Will that had brought the dog into just as much danger. Killer had always acquitted himself well—had frankly been a help more often than not. It was amazing how the animal seemed to understand everything Will said.

"Shipwreck?" Jane repeated, clearly not knowing much about Killer's reputation.

"It was nothing," Will said. "We were almost to Cape Town, so we only floated in the wreckage for two days."

"And Killer survived." Nick shook his head. "That dog has the lives of a cat."

What was wrong with Will that he wasn't telling these things to his betrothed? Then he remembered that Will had been keeping his past a secret to protect Jane. Nick almost felt guilty that he had to be the one to force everything out into the open.

Nick looked at Jane. "Killer was once run over by a barrel aboard ship as he was rescuing a little boy. The dog's broken ribs literally pierced the skin. And still he survived."

"I had to chew his food for him for a week," Will said with a nod.

Jane looked shocked. "Chew his food—"

Nick laughed, imagining that Charlotte would have the exact same reaction. "Has Barlow forgiven Killer for saving his life?"

"You must be joking," Will said. "That man can hold a grudge."

"Can we please just go to Charlotte now?" Jane demanded, stomping her foot as if a tantrum might help.

Will left Killer with Barlow, and he and Jane fell into step behind Nick. He led them away from the inn, out into the darkness on the far side of the road, away from the village. Nick looked over his shoulder and watched Jane trip over the weeds hidden by fog, but she didn't ask Will for help. Already Nick admired her.

A quarter hour later he saw the dark outline of his carriage, and he released a deep breath he hadn't realized he'd been holding. Cox nodded to him from high up in the coach box.

Nick reached for the door handle, then looked over his shoulder at his companions. His decision for how best to protect Charlotte was starting to seem unwise. "I just want you to know that for Charlotte's own protection, I had to bind her."

"What!" Jane said sharply, then looked about as if she finally realized how her voice carried.

"Shh!" Will said, leaning toward her. "I'm certain there is a good explanation."

At least Nick had Will on his side. "Much as Charlotte understands what we're doing, I knew she would follow me and make even more trouble in her attempt to help."

Jane's look was reproachful and angry. "Let me see her at once."

Nick opened the door and as he climbed up inside, he winced at the angry sounds Charlotte was making from behind her gag. Jane wouldn't take this well. In darkness Nick sat down on Charlotte's bench, while Will and Jane stumbled into the seat across.

"I'll light the lantern," Nick said.

He struck a match, found the lantern, and watched a dim light fill the carriage. Charlotte was just where he had left her, propped in the corner, although her hair had seemed to suffer in her struggle. She was glaring at him so angrily he didn't think she saw their visitors. He had hoped she would come to understand his motivations where she was concerned.

Nick leaned closer to her and spoke calmly. "I'm going to remove the gag. Let us not have a repeat of past performances."

When he pulled the gag away, she immediately bit his hand hard.

"Ow!" He let go a string of curses. "I told you not to overreact! You know why—"

"How dare you! You will never—ever!—do that to me again."

"Charlotte—"

"Untie me this instant!"

It was all Nick could do not to use all his physical strength to restrain her as he untied her. When her legs were free she kicked him, when her hands were free she pointed a finger into his chest. He didn't even look at Will, thinking his friend would surely be smirking.

"What happened!" Charlotte turned toward the opposite bench. "And who—" Her voice sank to a whisper. "Jane?"

The women threw their arms around each other, and to Nick's surprise Jane was crying. His Charlotte only laughed and found her sister a handkerchief.

As Jane wiped her eyes, Charlotte turned to Will. "Hello, Will," she said politely, while giving him a searching look.

It must be strange for her to see her sister's betrothed again, now that Charlotte knew the truth.

"Oh, Charlotte," Jane said, "I cannot tell you how I've worried. I had no idea you had been kidnapped!"

"They only tell you what they think you should know," Charlotte said grimly.

Nick smiled.

"Are you hurt?" Jane glared at Nick. "Did he—"

"No, nothing like that," Charlotte quickly said. "I was frightened at first, but he never harmed me. I understand that I might have jeopardized everything if he'd allowed me to escape. But now"—she suddenly leaned toward Nick— "now I can help! And he won't let me."

Crossing his arms over his chest, Nick tried to conceal his fears for Charlotte's safety. Surely Will would laugh that an untrained woman thought she could help in a serious investigation. What did it say about Nick that Charlotte felt herself capable of doing so? But Will only continued to smile.

"Char, see here," Nick began, "I've been trained to deal with such things and you have not."

"But I learn quickly!"

When she put her hand on his arm, did she know how her touch could work magic? How susceptible he was? But he was stronger, and would not let her dictate the relationship between them—certainly not in the matter of Julia Reed.

He stroked her hand. "I killed a man tonight, Charlotte. It is not a thing I want you to see."

He could see her resistance melt in the softening of her gaze. "Were you hurt?" she whispered.

Nick wondered uneasily what Will and Jane thought of the intimate tone of her voice.

Chapter 18

The more one depends on another agent, the more vulnerable one is.

The Secret Journals of a Spymaster

For a moment Charlotte couldn't speak as she noticed the blood that stained Nick's sleeve and thigh. She saw the glitter of fresh blood on the back of his hand, and her fingers trembled as she touched him. The wound was not deep, and seemed to be the only one, but still, she prattled on foolishly about his inability to take care of himself, all to cover up the depth of her relief and love. She ripped the edges of her worn petticoats to use as bandages and set to work. Only once did she glance at her silent sister, but the understanding in Jane's expression had Charlotte wondering. Had Jane also fallen in love? Did she now

259

understand the worry of losing someone to this horrible battle for England's safety?

Charlotte still could not believe how different Will seemed, yet after watching Nick's and Sam's easy assumption of new roles, she shouldn't have been surprised. The monocle Will used to wave about was gone, as were his excitable manner and foppish clothing. He had the same air as Nick, of a man who had faced danger and could count on himself to overcome it.

But they didn't like trusting anyone else. She had to make her peace with the fact that even though she had helped in some ways, she was still a nuisance in others. Nick could never completely trust her in this business he'd given his life to. She could not blame him for tying her up, not when he had a duty to finish.

"We should leave," Will said.

Charlotte still had so much she wished to say to Jane. "But—I thought we could talk."

"I need to tell her the truth about our family," Jane said.

Nick moved his hand away, and Charlotte found herself wanting to hold it close, as if it could reassure her of his safety, his survival.

"Make it fast," he said.

Charlotte rolled her eyes.

Then Jane reached for her hand, her expression troubled. "Charlotte, it will be difficult to bear, but you must know that Papa lied to us. He was more than just a soldier in the army."

"He was a spy," she answered immediately, feeling relieved.

"You knew!" Jane turned to Will. "Did everyone know but me?"

"Of course not. Your mother still knows nothing," he said firmly, though he glanced at Nick. "I think."

Charlotte gripped her sister's hands. "I kept it a secret, Jane. I only found out a few days before you left. I was feeling lost and bored, and I decided to explore the attic. I found a box of journals that I'm certain Papa thought he'd lost. So much of his life was there, Jane, and it was fascinating."

"Why didn't you tell me?" Jane asked.

In her voice was a hurt Charlotte hadn't meant to cause. "Because—because you were focused on this betrothal, and I'll admit, I thought to keep something to myself for a while. It was wrong of me, Jane, and I was going to tell you the moment you returned. His life was so exciting! He did so many dangerous, brave things—"

"So Charlotte thought she could become a spy like your father," Nick interrupted, reminding her of everything that had happened between them.

"I did not!"

"Then what do you call hiding in a wardrobe, listening in on conversations that were none of your business, that could have gotten you killed?"

But that was only the start of their adventures, and she wondered if he would laugh when he told Will how she'd delayed Julia.

"I was doing my duty for England," she said angrily.

"You're lucky it was me who discovered you."

His arrogance could still astound her. "Hardly lucky!"

She locked gazes with Nick, and for a moment the spark of their intimate relationship crackled between them. How boring her life would have been if she hadn't met him!

Will finally spoke up. "Would you like Charlotte to travel with us?"

"No!" Charlotte immediately said, and was relieved when Nick said the same thing.

Nick seemed surprised at his own outburst, and obviously found a rationale. "For one thing, Charlotte has it in her head that she needs to help me. She'd only cause you concern by trying to escape."

Charlotte smiled at his naiveté.

He ignored her. "And the other thing is that the two of you are in just as much danger as we are. So don't worry about Charlotte. I have Sam and my driver aiding me. When this is over, I'll bring her to the colonel and try to . . . explain everything."

Now *Jane* was smiling at him, and Charlotte relaxed, knowing that her sister understood.

Nick looked between them suspiciously. "Now back to the matter at hand," he said. "One of the villains escaped, and could be off warning

Julia right now. Her estate is not far away. Charlotte and I need to stay ahead of her, and you two need to go off to your wedding."

Charlotte hugged her sister tightly, hoping Jane found happiness with Will, a man who was actually ready for marriage.

Jane whispered, "Will you be all right? What if he ties you up again?"

Sighing, Charlotte hugged her tighter. "It will be fine. He doesn't know it yet, but I have everything in hand." If only that were so.

"I'm not sure what Julia is doing at her brother's estate," Nick said to Will, "but I'm certain she'll leave in the morning, headed for Leeds. It will be over soon."

"Take care." Will shook Nick's hand. "Send Sam to tell me when it's done."

"If you need me," Nick added, "send a message to the only inn in Misterton. I'm registered as Mr. Black."

Will stepped down out of the carriage, and with relief Charlotte watched the gentle way he helped Jane down. Jane glanced up at Charlotte, who could see the worry in her sister's face. Charlotte gave her a smile full of a confidence she didn't quite feel.

The carriage suddenly creaked and slowly began to rumble across the uneven field. For a moment Charlotte kept her eyes squeezed tightly shut, searching for control of her emotions. She realized sadly that part of her envied Jane, who had a man who wanted nothing more than to be Jane's husband.

But Charlotte wouldn't be that lucky. She could only enjoy what she had with Nick for a brief time, until he moved on out of her life.

"Are you all right?" Nick asked.

His voice sounded guarded, even hesitant.

She smiled with a confidence she was far from feeling. "I'll be fine."

"Did you want to go with her?" His face was a study in impassivity.

"You didn't hear me hesitate, did you?" She sat back, folded her arms across her chest, and frowned at him. "Are you wishing I would have gone?"

He paused, but this time she immediately understood the reason, for he was looking at her with a hot stare that melted her anger and resistance. He caressed her cheek, then slid his hand back into her hair and roughly tipped her head back until their faces were inches apart.

"I need you to stay," he whispered, then kissed her.

Charlotte wrapped her arms around his neck and straddled his lap, impatiently pushing down the mound of her skirts so she could touch as much of him as possible. They kissed fiercely, greedily, their bodies pressing together with an eagerness they couldn't contain much longer.

"How long until we reach this inn?" she said against his mouth.

"Too long," he answered with a groan.

They both reached for the buttons on the other's garments, and then laughed breathlessly as they fought with their hands between them.

The carriage suddenly slowed.

Nick dropped his forehead onto her shoulder. "That will be Sam. You make me forget everything but you."

She knew he meant it lightly, but somehow the way he phrased his statement sounded almost . . . accusatory. Was he saying everything was her fault? But no, she was trying too hard to ascribe a deeper meaning to what he said.

There was nothing deep between them—at least on his part.

Charlotte scrambled off his lap and had righted her clothing by the time Sam opened the door and jumped aboard. The carriage immediately sped up.

Sam looked between them for a moment, and Charlotte tried to control her breathing and just smile. Sam's answering smile seemed rather forced, and he stared at Nick a moment too long.

"Did everything go okay?" Nick asked casually.

Charlotte admired his easy ability to act as if nothing had happened between them.

Yet it felt like this proved there *was* nothing between them.

"We buried the body without too much inter-ference from the locals," Sam said. "It seems they've been having a rash of burglaries lately, and arc glad we've helped solve their problems."

Nick sighed. "They'll figure out sooner or later that we haven't helped a bit. But we've helped ourselves. There's one less man out there under Julia's control. This must be why Campbell never met up with me yesterday. He already had plans to get rid of all of us."

"He was the one we killed?" Charlotte asked.

Nick gave her a strange look. "Yes, *I* did. I never did see the face of the other man. This will make things difficult." He suddenly frowned and looked at Sam.

"And Will helped you?" Charlotte continued.

"He and his coachman Barlow," he said dis-tractedly. "And yes, Jane was perfectly safe in their carriage. She was quite angry with me for putting you in danger. But wait—Sam, I need you to go back to Julia's, to see if the other henchman returns to report to her."

"He'd be foolish to do that," Sam protested. "It's the first place we'd look for him."

"But we can't take the chance that he might convince her to run in the middle of the night. You go keep an eye on her stables, and I'll take your place in a few hours."

"Very well," Sam said, knocking on the ceiling of the carriage to get Cox's attention.

Even Nick seemed to notice Sam's strange mood.

"Is something wrong?" Nick asked.

"Nothing that can't wait until later. You'll be at the Peacock Inn in Misterton?"

Nick nodded.

"Then I'll await your signal at the Reed manor." Sam turned to Charlotte and smiled more genuinely. "Good night."

When Sam had gone, and the carriage had returned to it's repetitive rumbling, Charlotte thought Nick seemed distracted. Yet even as he appeared lost in thought, he put his arm around her shoulder, and she snuggled against him, breathing in his scent, content to wait.

A half hour later, when they reached the tiny country inn as "Mr. and Mrs. Black," they found a steaming hip tub already in their room. The innkeeper claimed it was for Charlotte, compliments of their friend Mr. South.

"That Sam," Charlotte said, dipping her fingers into the bath, and then flicking droplets at Nick. "He's always thinking of me."

"But not of me," Nick said dryly. "I don't think he thought I'd be a part of this bath."

She inhaled swiftly, suddenly unsure. "But you're not leaving, are you?"

"And leave you to wash alone?" He walked around the far side of the tub, as if stalking her. "How unchivalrous that would make me!"

She laughed softly, then her amusement died as he stopped her fingers from unfastening the buttons at her throat.

"Allow me," he whispered.

And thus began one of the most satisfying, tender hours of her life.

Nick allowed her to do nothing for herself. He undressed her, kissing each inch of skin as it was revealed.

When she was in the bath he washed her slowly, rubbing the wet, soapy cloth into her skin in circular, gentle motions. He washed everything for her, no matter how she protested, then lifted her out of the tub and into a soft nest of towels to dry her.

Then he made her close her eyes, and the wonder of waiting for his caress heightened her feelings. His lips rode the rounded tops of her breasts, and then down below, giving the lower curves of her breasts just as much attention.

She floated in a sea of sensation, her skin sensitized to his every touch. She could tell when he dipped his tongue into her navel, or when his lips brushed her inner thigh. She felt his shoulders separate her legs, then the warmth of his breath across her curls. He kissed her intimately and she cried out her delight as his tongue parted the folds of her flesh and delved deeper. She watched his dark head between her thighs. Too soon he stopped, and she stiffened with frustration.

"Wait," he murmured, then lifted her onto

her knees. He moved behind her, kneeling between her knees, his erection pressing into her lower back.

She tried to turn and look at him.

"No, look ahead," he said.

She followed his pointing hand and saw to her surprise that he'd positioned them just in front of the standing mirror. She could see herself, naked in the flickering lamplight, kneeling with her thighs spread, and Nick just behind her, looking over her shoulder. Her dark hair streamed down about her shoulders, partially hiding her, and he pulled it to her back. When she raised her arms up high to caress his hair, his hands came up to cup her breasts. She moaned and squirmed against him, her eyes half closed as she watched his fingers tease her nipples.

Nick had never seen anything as beautiful as the image of Charlotte in the mirror, aroused, glowing, watching herself be pleasured. He could barely keep himself from bending her over and thrusting inside her. But he wanted her to see how they were with each other, to see that the magic they created banished any thought of her sadistic husband.

When she was panting and writhing with unfulfilled desire, he slid his hand slowly down her body, then between her thighs. She groaned and pushed against his hand, arching her body to instinctively seek the power of her passion. She was wet with wanting him, and it was easy to comb his fingers through the hot recesses of her body. Using both hands now, he spread her wide, so she could see how he touched her, see the little nub of flesh that was the center of her desire. He caressed and circled it, plunging his fingers inside her and back out.

With a groan she came apart in his arms, shuddering, collapsing forward. He entered her swiftly from behind, and she braced herself on her trembling arms to watch them in the mirror.

He could not think what his face showed, or control his reactions as he drove into her. He was consumed with her, driven to possess her, desperate for the powerful release he'd never felt with anyone but her. He held it off as long as he could, listening to her wordless cries as she joined him in the steep climb to oblivion. When he felt her body pulse around his erection, he let go with a hoarse groan and shuddered as he gave everything to her.

He buried his face in her warm neck and chuckled as he finally toppled her over onto her side. They lay spooned together, breathing hard, and he let himself enjoy the feel of her moist skin touching him everywhere.

He'd told her tonight that he needed her. Would she assume he meant for more than sex? Why did he know in his gut that his need for her went beyond the physical? He had to prove to himself—and her—that he could not give her the life she wanted.

Chapter 19

Fellow spies can be objective, where you cannot.

The Secret Journals of a Spymaster

As Nick climbed the wall at the Reed estate and dropped over the side, he felt hollow, exhausted. He wanted to feel nothing but confidence that his mission was almost finished, but all he could think about was Charlotte.

Their affair had gone well beyond sex and into a mingling of their souls. She hadn't asked for anything, but in her eyes he saw the softness of a woman falling in love.

He hadn't ever wanted to see that again.

Yet—it did not alarm him as much as it would have with another woman. Because this was Charlotte, brave, beautiful, strong enough to overcome everything that monster of a husband had done to her.

What would Nick do when he had to leave her?

He found Sam behind the ruins of a medieval dovecote, with a perfect view of the stables and the back entrance of the manor.

Nick hunched down beside him, fully expecting Sam to leave. But Sam seemed to study him in the shadowy darkness.

"What?" Nick finally whispered.

"I'm just trying to figure you out," Sam said softly. "You've bedded Charlotte, haven't you?"

Nick hesitated, but he'd known Sam too long and too well. "Yes. And it's none of your concern."

"Isn't it?"

When Sam leaned toward him, Nick was surprised and sat back.

"I helped you take that girl hostage," Sam said angrily.

"She's not a girl."

"Then she's a young woman, naive about men—"

"She was married!"

"And that makes her an expert on men like you?"

Nick tamped down his cold fury. "What the hell does that mean? She knows more about me than any woman ever has. I told her how things would be between us, but she wants to continue."

"As if she had a choice, once you worked your wiles on her."

"You make it sound as if I forced her!" Nick took a deep breath, reminded himself to whisper.

"A seduction of an innocent isn't far from it. You've taken advantage of her. She's spent every moment with you, and obviously she's never met someone of your experience and adventure in staid old London. What else was she supposed to do?"

"Are you trying to say she'd fall into the arms of any man who took her hostage? I hope you don't think she's that stupid."

Nick kept his anger in line and watched Sam study him. He was not going to feel guilty about what he and Charlotte shared, not when it was so freely offered.

Sam finally sighed. "I don't even think you realize what you're doing."

"And what's that supposed to mean!"

"You . . . have an effect on women. There's something about you. I don't know if it's your wounded air—"

"Wounded air!" Nick echoed in quiet outrage.

"Like I said, you don't even know you're doing it. But you've been hurt, Nick, and some women want to make it all better. I don't know if Charlotte's like that. I don't know what she's thinking."

"I do," Nick said firmly. "She had a bad marriage." He stopped himself before saying anything more.

"So you're trying to heal her," Sam said cynically.

"Yes—no! Stop trying to figure out what this is between Charlotte and me. Even I don't know."

"That's what has me worried, Nick. With that attitude you're going to hurt her."

Nick ran his hand tiredly over his face. "I'm trying not to, Sam. I've explained everything to her. I can't stay here and be a husband to her."

"You can't?" Sam asked gently. "Or you won't?"

Nick opened his mouth but nothing came out.

Sam put a hand on his shoulder. "Just think about this and try not to hurt her. I'm going to go over here under those low trees and get some sleep. Wake me when it's time to leave."

Charlotte came awake at dawn, alone in bed, confused about what had awakened her. She heard another quick knock on the door. Wrapping a sheet about herself, she walked to the door and called, "Who is it?"

"The coachman, ma'am," called Mr. Cox. "I've orders to make sure ye're awake. Mr. Black'll be back soon, I expect."

"Thank you. Could you send up some toast and tea?"

She dressed and ate breakfast slowly. She felt lethargic and hollow, and tears threatened to flow.

She couldn't do this anymore. She'd told herself that she'd be happy to let Nick have her on his terms. And partially that had been true. She'd loved how cherished he made her feel, how right everything was when she was in his arms. She'd never had that with her husband, and thought that alone would be worth anything.

But it wasn't.

Nick didn't love her, didn't *want* to love her, and it was the latter that hurt the most. She didn't blame him; he'd made it clear from the beginning that his mission was the most important thing in his life.

How could she not be grateful that there were men like him to protect their country and keep them all safe?

But she selfishly wanted him for herself, and she could delude herself no longer. She had to let him go. Better now than later, when she might love him so much more.

He didn't trust her even now, and he'd proved that by tying her up again. She kept telling herself these things didn't matter, that this secret hurt he bore could remain his own private pain. But he didn't trust her enough to share that either. She sensed it had much to do with the man he'd become, a man who wanted no close personal relationships. He seemed to feel . . . less a man, because he cared about her the way he did.

But he'd said he needed her, and inside she'd rejoiced that maybe she could help him somehow.

But if it was only going to be a sexual relationship, it would be hurting them both. She couldn't bear to make him unhappy, not when he'd already taught her so much about herself.

Minutes later Nick strode in, all purpose and concentration.

"Are you ready?" he asked as he picked up his portmanteau.

She held up her own packed bag and tried to smile. "Today is the day?"

He hesitated and seemed to study her, but she kept up her cheery front. He would be too focused on his mission for her to discuss her decision with him.

"It should be. It's easily a day's ride to Leeds. I've sent Sam to guard the rear, and today we'll lead the way. Sam will let us know if Julia's going somewhere else. But I don't think so. She's down to only one loyal man. She'll need to get to Hume and make sure he can't betray her."

"Would she truly . . . kill him?"

He shrugged as he opened the door and followed her into the hall. "If he's a threat to her. And he's holding the proof of treason, so I think she'll be motivated to stop him."

"You won't let her," Charlotte said as they walked out into the blue-sky day that promised to be beautiful.

"I'll try to stop her," he said with mock seriousness.

They rode for several hours in peaceful

solitude—or so it must have seemed for Nick, who dozed most of the time. They finally stopped for a midday meal, which he told her they'd be eating on the road in order to stay ahead of Julia.

When she alighted from the carriage she looked around at the small buildings built around an acre of village green. There were children chasing chickens near a stream, and plenty of adults milled nearby, seeming to be dressed in their best clothes. Charlotte was intrigued, but Nick took her arm and firmly steered her inside the two-story tavern.

She retired to the room set aside for ladies, and when she emerged a few minutes later, Nick was ordering their meal. She stood at his side near the public dining room and watched a dozen couples parade past them, talking and laughing as they headed up the staircase.

An older man at the end of the line stopped before them. He let go of his wife's arm and said to her, "Go on up, my dear. I'll be but a moment."

Charlotte could tell from Nick's stern face that he didn't want to be disturbed, but she couldn't help smiling at the gentleman in his plain country clothes and cravat tied in an outdated fashion.

"Good day, ma'am," the man said, giving her a short bow. "Good day, sir."

Charlotte curtsied, but Nick only nodded. She watched him glance impatiently at the door leading to the kitchen.

"You are newcomers to our fair village," the man said.

"We're on our way north, sir," said Nick, using his best clerk attitude, "and my wife thought this a fine place for our meal."

"Aye, it is, sir," said the man, rubbing his hands together. "Today we celebrate the harvest with a village meal. All are invited to the assembly room. You are welcome to join us. Just tell them that Mr. Draper invited you."

Nick smiled. "Thank you for the kind invitation, Mr. Draper, but I've already ordered our meal, and we're in a hurry. It wouldn't do to keep my wife's mother waiting on us for supper."

Mr. Draper raised both hands and nodded. "Of course, of course, we must stay in good graces with family. But if you change your mind, please join us." He gestured to the stairs, gave them a last bow, and then ascended to the assembly room.

"That was kind of him," Charlotte said. She saw Nick's expression and quickly added, "But of course my mother would be worried sick if we were late. You remember what happened last time."

He arched an eyebrow at her. Before she could create a memory out of thin air, Mr. Cox stepped through the door, looked about until he spotted them, then rushed forward.

"Mr. Black," he said loudly, tugging on his hat brim, "there's a problem with changin' the horses."

"Perhaps I should speak—"

"No!" the coachman interrupted. He looked about, then leaned closer and lowered his voice. "*She's* here, sir."

Charlotte understood his reference, and she clutched Nick's arm more tightly than necessary. He abruptly turned them about, facing away from the door.

"Is she passing through the village?" Nick asked softly.

"No, sir. This bein' the only tavern, her carriage has stopped here."

"She mustn't see us," Charlotte said, then winced at her obvious statement. "Did she see *you*?"

"No, Mrs. Black. But she's on her way inside."

"If you can avoid being seen," Nick said, "take the carriage around back to the stable yard. Mrs. Black and I will join the villagers in the assembly room upstairs. Keep watch on Julia, and let me know when it's safe to leave."

After Mr. Cox departed, Charlotte found herself escorted up the staircase by Nick, who wore a grim expression. She knew he was anxious to capture Julia, and this was one more delay he didn't need.

When they entered the high-ceilinged assembly room, Mr. Draper and his wife crossed to greet them and began introducing them to other couples and families. Nick remained at her side, holding her arm firmly, his smile as engaging as ever. Though Charlotte noticed his occasional glances at the open doorway, to others he appeared the epitome of the solicitous husband. He fetched her lemonade and held her plate of refreshments. She knew she was the envy of every lady there as Nick watched her with warm eyes and occasionally let his hand linger on her waist. This saddened and distracted her, for she couldn't help remembering her resolve to end things between them.

As they answered questions about their life in London, she was shocked to hear Nick using details he'd taken from their marriage conversations. He created a second house in the country for them, where "Mrs. Black" could retire to escape the hectic social calendar of London.

When he started in about their four children, she couldn't help thinking, *so much for his talk about preventing pregnancies*. Deep inside she felt the pain of wanting children, the desolation of knowing that such a glowing life would never happen with Nick. Conversation grew harder as every false emotion took a piece of her soul.

Then Nick glanced over her head, and though she saw nothing in his pleasant expression, she felt his hand tighten at her waist.

"Mrs. Black," he said, taking her drink from her hand and setting it on a nearby table, "as much as you'd like to stay, I am really quite concerned with the time. We can't keep your mother waiting."

Charlotte wanted to look over her shoulder to see what he'd seen, but she knew better. It must be Mr. Cox, come to tell them that Julia was gone.

The young couple they'd been conversing with understood their haste, and Charlotte followed Nick's lead as he began their good-byes with several villagers along the wall—the wall closest to the door.

"Nick?" she whispered, before they reached the next couple.

"Julia's here," he answered between his teeth. "The sociable Mr. Draper found another guest."

It was truly awful to keep her back to the enemy. She felt as if her skin itched from being stared at. Nick was surely the tallest in the room, and Julia knew him as intimately as Charlotte did. Though every step they took brought them closer, the door still seemed so far away. She felt as if she was perspiring, but when she looked at Nick, his pleasant expression never wavered. His calm settled over her.

She could hear Mr. Draper's voice as he escorted Julia into the crowd behind them. There were only three more people to pass before they reached the door. Charlotte could have sworn she heard Julia laugh as if she was right behind them.

Then Nick gripped her hand, dragged her behind the last two villagers and down the stairs to freedom.

They found Mr. Cox in the entrance hall, and he bowed his head and sighed when he saw them. "This way, Mr. Black," he said, leading them through the tavern and into the dirt yard behind.

Charlotte practically jumped into the carriage, and Nick fell onto the bench at her side. Silently they swayed as Mr. Cox climbed up into the coachman's box, then jerked backward as the horses began to trot.

She covered her face with trembling hands. "That was too close."

"But exciting," Nick said.

At the laughter in his voice, she frowned at him, and with dismay she watched as his gaze traveled down her bodice.

He loomed over her, his thigh riding hers. "All this talk of marriage makes me think of the fun part of having a wife."

"It's all just a game to you," she whispered, holding back her tears of disappointment.

"Sometimes it has to be," he said slowly, sitting back, "or I'd never be able to function."

"This—this thing between us, it's not a game to me." When he would have spoken, she held up a hand, wanting to get everything out in the open. "I know our relationship can be nothing more than it is. I've appreciated your candor. I thought it would be acceptable to me . . . but it's not." She bit her lip and sighed heavily.

"So what are you saying?" he asked slowly, impassively.

"I can't lie with you anymore. It hurts too much, because it makes me think there's a future for us. You don't want that—"

"Charlotte—"

"No, it's all right. But you must understand that the longer we're intimate, the more I'll risk falling in love with you." It was too late; she already had, but she couldn't tell him that. She thought of the children he'd just pretended they had, and she wanted to sob.

He took her hand and she allowed it, trying to pretend that her heart wasn't breaking. She would have to go back to that false society life, knowing that there could have been so much more.

"I never wanted to hurt you," he murmured, drawing her hand up to kiss it.

"I know. But it's happening, so I have to protect myself. I was never able to do so before. You've given me the courage for that."

"You had it inside you all along."

He sat back, and she watched painfully as his expression closed off, distancing himself— protecting himself. He was good at that.

"I can't leave to take you to your father's," he said.

Her gaze flew to his in surprise. "I wouldn't ask that of you! I'm a part of this, and I need to see it through to the end."

He nodded. "But you'll do exactly as I say."

"Of course."

He turned to look out his window, and she turned to look out hers. She didn't see the countryside; she was blinking furiously, trying to rid herself of tears. It was over.

Had there been a hidden, optimistic part of her that thought he'd protest? It only proved she was even more a fool.

They reached Leeds by the dinner hour, staying ahead of Julia and Sam. Charlotte watched Nick, who must surely feel some satisfaction that Julia was where he wanted her. Nick continued looking out the window, betraying neither worry nor triumph. She wondered if the fact that she'd ended their intimate relationship even bothered him at all.

Because keeping up a normal front was agony for her. She was already grieving for him. She had had no idea how strong her love for him was, how difficult it was going to be to leave him. Her departure was close now, and she almost thought it would be better not to see him anymore.

Because now she found herself staring at him when he wouldn't notice, memorizing the lines of his face, the cocky way he smiled. She watched his hands, so large, so gentle. She would never know their touch again. She so desperately wanted to cry, but now was not the time. Instead she fought the stinging of her eyes and tried to seem interested in Leeds.

The town was bustling with carriages and wagons, surely the largest town they'd visited since they left London. Factory chimneys belched smoke over medieval churches and poor children begged for pennies, the sad part of civilization. She sat back on the bench with a sigh. The reality of life in a town was terrible for many people.

The carriage rolled through street after street, twisting and turning. A man could easily get lost here.

Julia's man Edwin Hume had once tried, but now he was counting on the government—Nick—to protect him from the result of his crimes. And Nick would do it, too, for the chance to put Julia in jail.

"Does Mr. Cox know where he's going?" Charlotte asked, when it seemed as if she'd seen the same church twice.

Nick glanced at her, one side of his mouth turned up in a smile.

"Go ahead, roll your eyes," she said huffily, crossing her arms over her chest. "I'm sorry I spoke."

"Don't be sorry. I just need to think."

"To concentrate?"

He nodded. "That, too. Now Char—Charlotte, you know you aren't coming with us."

"What are you going to do—tie me up on this city street?" Oops, a little too close to the insecurities. She'd been thrown when he'd used his intimate name for her.

"Tempting—but no. Sam knows this town well, and he tells me that there is a genteel tavern frequented by the well-to-do across the street from Hume's. For a servant, Hume has good taste in property."

"Good taste in . . . ah, you mean he makes more money than he should."

"Very good. You will wait in this tavern. You may sit in the front window and watch the house and all that transpires, but you may not leave the establishment until one of us comes for you. Is that understood?"

"I can't wait at Hume's house? Perhaps in a bedroom?"

Nick was looking out the window, already forgetting about her. "No. Bullets travel through wood quite easily."

"You don't want me to die?" she asked.

Startled, he looked down at her. "Hasn't that been what this whole journey has been about?"

Charlotte nodded and bit her lip, turning to look out the window. It was good to be reminded that he had not brought her willingly, had wanted only to save her life and preserve the secrecy of his mission.

But it still hurt so much.

The carriage turned down a quiet, tree-lined street, traveling slowly. She sensed Mr. Cox was looking for the right house. When she saw an elegant eating establishment on her side, she immediately leaned across Nick and looked out.

"Yes, that's it," he said, nodding toward a small house built of limestone with a gravel path leading up between landscaped gardens.

He pushed her away from the window and pointed across her body toward the tavern. "And you'll wait there. Do I have your word?"

She nodded reluctantly.

"Good. We'll get you settled, and then I'll go introduce myself to Hume. He owes me some correspondence."

When the carriage pulled over near the pavement, Charlotte put a hand on Nick's chest to stop him from rising. "I don't need to be settled, like a child waiting for Mama. I'll have dinner. I'll be fine."

Time seemed to stop as he searched her eyes. She tried not to show her heartache, her yearning.

Then he looked away. "Here's a book in case you're bored," he said stiffly, reaching into the bag at his feet.

"I've read it already. And I don't plan to be bored. Surely Julia will arrive any time."

He frowned thoughtfully at Hume's house.

She sighed and stepped out of the carriage. She didn't think he even noticed her leaving. But that was as it should be. He would never forgive himself—or her—if this mission came to naught because of his preoccupation with her. She hoped ending their intimacy now had not been a poorly timed decision on her part.

Without looking back she went inside the tiny

tavern, inhaling the aroma of fresh bread and hot coffee. There was a small table directly in front of the window, and she asked to be seated there, to "feel the last of the sun on my face."

That wouldn't be long, but it was a good enough excuse for the serving maid, who allowed her to pick out her own table. Charlotte slowly perused the menu, all the while keeping an eye on Mr. Hume's home. It was a rather grand place to be hiding out in, she thought skeptically.

She never saw Nick enter the house, of course. The carriage had continued on after she'd gotten out, and turned down a side street she couldn't see.

Nick sat alone in the carriage and tried to tell himself that he was relieved about Charlotte's decision not to sleep with him again. He hadn't wanted to hurt her, and in his selfish need to ease himself with her willing body, he might have just kept going, not knowing what their relationship was costing her.

But that would have been a lie, because he damn well knew what a gentle, caring woman like her expected from a man: marriage, a settled life, children—trust.

His heart twisted with regret.

He had to stop thinking about it—thinking about her. Julia would be here any time. The mission was almost finished.

He told himself he'd fill his empty life with the

next assignment. Why didn't that make him feel better?

Nick entered the back of Hume's home through a narrow cellar window overlooking the alley, making sure his pistol was still in his waist. He kept as quiet as possible, not wanting to frighten Hume into thinking Julia had come for him. Surely the man must have been holed up in here for weeks, dreading every sound on the front steps. Hume was counting on Nick to protect him, but Hume had to know that Julia might be intelligent enough to elude her pursuers.

He made his way up to the ground level of the house, step by step, hearing nothing. Not the creak of a floorboard, not the clink of tableware as someone had dinner.

Silently he pushed open a door that led into the kitchens. Here was the first indication that a desperate man lived alone. Every surface was littered with filth, and the smell of rotting food put him in mind of some of the worst hellholes in Afghanistan.

Or was this the home of a man already dead and rotting away himself?

He brought out his pistol, pulled back the hammer, and held it at the ready as he left the kitchen and went through the dining room. Dirty plates were pushed to the center of the table so more could be added. In the front parlor, empty liquor bottles littered the floor, and water rings from glasses spotted the wood tables.

But there was no sign of Edwin Hume.

Nick cautiously made his way upstairs, and although a bed had obviously been slept in, no one was there.

Where the hell was Hume? Wasn't he claiming to be in fear of his life?

And where was the code letter, the last piece of evidence needed to convict Julia?

Nick began a slow and careful search.

Chapter 20

There are certain things you have to be born with—and ingenuity might be one of them.

The Secret Journals of a Spymaster

Charlotte was biting into a succulent peach tart when she raised her eyes and saw that a carriage had pulled up in front of Mr. Hume's house.

She froze, waiting, and then remembered to put down the tart and wipe her mouth. Though she couldn't see the door to the carriage from where she was sitting, soon she saw a woman's brisk figure start up the pathway. The woman carried a small carpetbag. When she tilted her head up to look at the second floor of the house, the last of the sunset touched her pale blond hair.

Julia. She'd arrived at her destination at last.

And part of Charlotte was sad. Had she wanted Nick to be wrong? Surely she didn't want to see him humiliated. But it was difficult to think of Julia as a traitor when the woman seemed so . . . nice.

And what was in that carpetbag? A pistol?

Charlotte leaned forward, watching across the street as Julia reached for the door knocker and let it bang against the door.

Would Nick open the door and grab Julia? Charlotte had never thought to ask what the exact plan was.

Or would Julia go inside and the door would shut, leaving Charlotte to just wait and wonder.

But none of that happened. Julia knocked again, but minutes went by and no one answered.

Where was Hume? And where was Nick?

Julia turned away from the door and looked about, as if she expected to see Mr. Hume working in the garden. She put her hands on her hips, then her gaze settled across the street.

On the tavern where Charlotte was letting her food get cold.

Julia walked back down the path, called up to her coachman, who only nodded and continued to sit there. Weren't they leaving?

Then Julia marched across the street directly toward Charlotte, who sank back in her chair and tried to disappear. But as her frantic gaze raced around the room, she saw only a steady crowd of customers, some eating at tables, others standing shoulder to shoulder waiting for drinks at the bar. Was there an exit through the kitchen?

Before she could even stand up, Julia was walking through the door. Once again, an eating establishment was bringing them together.

Charlotte immediately turned away to look out the window. Though she pretended to look at passersby, she was frantically searching for Nick or Sam or Mr. Cox. But she would have to rescue herself from this one.

"Mrs. Cox?"

Oh heavens, it was Julia.

Charlotte took a deep breath, schooled her features into worry—which wasn't difficult—and looked up.

"Miss Reed," she breathed, letting her expression show amazement.

Though Julia smiled, there was concern in her gaze. "Mrs. Cox, though I was coming here for dinner, surely our meeting can be no coincidence. Have you been following me?"

Charlotte opened her mouth, then pursed her lips together and frantically dug through her reticule for a handkerchief. She dabbed it into the corner of her eyes and finally nodded.

Julia sat down and reached across the table for Charlotte's hand. "And where is your husband?"

"I don't know," she whispered dramatically. "I—I told him the truth, everything and he—he—"

She quietly cried, the handkerchief pressed to her face. She spared a quick glance at Julia's face.

"Did he leave you?" Julia asked.

Thank goodness all Charlotte had to do was wait for Julia to create the story for her. Charlotte nodded again and blew her nose loudly.

"Then you're alone?"

Her voice was full of sympathy, and Charlotte almost squirmed with discomfort at the guilt she still felt for lying.

"Then I'm glad you followed me," Julia said briskly. "You should have come to me sooner."

"I—I couldn't. You were in that fancy house outside Misterton—"

"That is not my home, but my brother's. You would have been welcomed. Tell me you didn't sleep outdoors."

"No, no, I have some money. I just . . . I just don't know what to *do*."

"I told you that you could leave that to me."

Julia looked about, as if looking for the serving maid. But then her gaze alighted on something that made her look sad, then resolved.

"There's someone here I must speak to before we leave," she said.

Oh heavens, were Nick and Sam here, risking themselves and the mission for her? But she stole a cautious glance around the room and saw no one she knew.

"I just knocked on his door," Julia continued, "but he wasn't at home." Her expression grew distasteful. "And by the look of him, he must have needed his drink badly."

Charlotte looked toward the man she indicated. It could only be Hume. And Nick wasn't here to see their meeting, to catch Julia in the act. Would she pretend she needed to speak to Hume in private, then lure him outside to kill him? Then there would be no witness to her crimes, no code letter.

Charlotte got to her feet so quickly, the table loudly skidded several inches. Julia, who had taken only a few steps, looked back, the threatening carpetbag hanging at her side.

"Oh Miss Reed," Charlotte said tearfully. "I've been alone so long. Do allow me to stay with you."

Instead of protesting, Julia nodded calmly. "I understand. You're welcome to come. I promise I won't be long, and then I'll take you home with me."

Charlotte stayed right at Julia's side as she crossed to the bar and the various men gathered there. Some slumped over their drinks, others leaned toward their neighbors laughing loudly. But one man sat alone, looking down at his full glass as if seeing heaven itself. He lifted it reverently to his lips, and Charlotte noticed that his hands trembled, and that he couldn't be more than thirty years of age.

"Mr. Hume?" Julia said.

He dropped the glass, and it shattered against

the edge of the bar. He stood quickly and turned toward them, while flecks of blood welled up on his arm from the broken glass. He had the red-rimmed eyes of an old man.

He stared at them as if he expected Julia to kill him right in front of witnesses.

Julia pulled a handkerchief out of her sleeve and handed it to him. "I'm so sorry we startled you," she said, motioning to his arm when he seemed to take no notice. "You're bleeding, Mr. Hume."

Absently he put her lacy handkerchief across his wound, and spots of blood welled through it. The barkeep shook his head and came around to clean up the glass.

"Do you recognize me, Mr. Hume?" Julia asked with a smile. "We haven't seen each other since I was a girl. I'm Miss Julia Reed."

Charlotte was fascinated. Neither of them could admit they knew each other in front of this crowd. So what new story would Julia come up with?

Mr. Hume tipped his head nervously. "It's good to see you, Miss Reed."

Julia glanced at Charlotte with a smile. "Mr. Hume's mother was my governess until my parents died. Even after I went to India to live with my brother, Mrs. Hume remained with our estate."

Mr. Hume glanced between Julia and Charlotte nervously, then motioned to the barkeep for another pint of beer. "Have you seen my mother since you came back, Miss Reed?"

Was this how they were connected? Charlotte thought. They'd met as children and she'd lured him into her employ?

Julia sighed deeply and lifted up her carpetbag. Charlotte stiffened.

"My dear Edwin—do you mind if I call you that?" Julia asked. "We used to be very informal with one another."

"Of course," Mr. Hume said.

"Well Edwin, your mother is the reason I'm here. I regret to tell you that she died in her sleep two weeks ago."

Mr. Hume's face went chalk white, and Charlotte was amazed that a criminal could still love his mother. Or was he a man forced into crime, and was now doing his best to repent?

When he didn't speak, Julia said gently, "I've brought some personal possessions of hers that I thought you'd like."

As Julia reached into her carpetbag, Charlotte took a step back, yet noticed that Mr. Hume did not. He simply looked nervously around him.

"Take your hand out of the bag, Julia," said a deep voice just behind Charlotte.

Charlotte whirled around and saw Nick standing close. Sam stepped up to the bar at Mr. Hume's back, and Mr. Cox appeared just behind

Julia. Charlotte's relief left her trembling. Nick took her arm and pulled her behind him, but she stayed nearby where she could see what happened.

Julia looked confused for a moment. "Nick?" she finally whispered. "What are you doing here?"

He took the carpetbag out of her hand and gave it to Sam. "We can't talk here. Let's calmly cross the street and discuss things."

Julia looked at the three men now grouped all around her. "Has something happened?" she asked, her voice rising. "Is my brother all right?"

"This has nothing to do with your brother," Nick said. "Please come with us peacefully. I don't want to have to drag you out of here."

Julia's eyes went wide. "But Nick—why are you threatening me?"

He gripped her elbow. "Let's go."

When Mr. Hume hung back, Sam steered him toward the front door. Charlotte fumbled in her reticule for money to pay for dinner, then caught up with the group outside. The sun had now set, but the gloom of twilight allowed her to see the frantic way Julia looked at the men around her. Julia was doing a good acting job, because Charlotte wanted to pity her.

Together they all walked up the path to Mr. Hume's house. As Charlotte came up last, she almost expected Sam, who held the door open, to refuse her entrance. But he gave her half a smile and gestured for her to go inside.

Though he told himself not to, Nick watched Charlotte enter the room, saw her grimace when she took in the condition of the parlor. He could not believe that once again, regardless of how he tried to keep her out of trouble, she'd managed to meet up with Julia. When he'd seen the two women through the tavern window, pain had clenched his stomach, had made him feel short of breath. Now he might need to use Charlotte's testimony, because he'd missed the beginning of Julia's conversation with Hume. He couldn't stand the thought of having Charlotte appear in court, subjecting her to the dangers of retribution from an unknown faction of Julia's. Maybe Julia would just do them all the favor of confessing.

But his prisoner stood alone in the center of the room, her face pale but her expression proud. She didn't speak, just gripped her hands together at her waist and gave him a wounded look.

He was unaffected. "Hume, I'm here and you're safe. Now where is the letter?" When Hume started toward the stairs to the upper floor, Nick added, "Cox, go with him."

Julia finally spoke. "When are you going to tell me what this is about, Nick?"

She glanced at Charlotte but said nothing to her. Julia was no fool; surely she had to realize that Charlotte's story was now suspect.

Nick studied Julia, tried to forget the good memories they'd once shared, and reminded himself that she had aided in the murder of sixteen thousand men, women, and children. The fact that she was a woman would not matter in his prosecution.

He waited until Hume came down with the letter. He noticed how Hume's hands shook, saw his reddened nose and bloodshot eyes. Hume had obviously taken to the bottle as he waited for protection from Julia. He'd have to be sobered up before the trial.

Nick looked at the letter in his hands. It resembled the one in his possession, except it was dated one day later, and covered different stories Julia had wanted to tell her friend in India. Whereas the first letter had many of the handwritten loops filled in, this one had tiny dots scattered through the text. When you compared this with the first letter, the dots would show which filled-in loop helped form the coded alphabet. Though it would take time, he would finally be able to read the message, with the help of the second code letter.

He held up the letter, out of Julia's reach, but enough that she could see it. "Do you recognize this?"

"Of course," she said angrily. "I wrote it. Doesn't every woman you know write letters to her friends?"

"This was written while you were in Afghanistan."

"I can't see the date from here, but I'll take your word on it," she said with sarcasm. "Why has my letter been stolen from the person to whom it was intended? And why is it any of your business?"

She was good, he thought. His first instinct would have been to deny that he'd written the letter, claim it was a forgery. But clear as day she'd said it was hers. How did she think she would get away with this?

Chapter 21

A spy must be prepared for the inevitability that the object of his hunt is just as smart as he is.

The Secret Journals of a Spymaster

Nick watched Julia closely. "Your letters went exactly where you intended."

"That can't be true," she said, "because Edwin—Mr. Hume had this one."

"Of course he did. He was one of the men you employed to carry your letters."

"He wasn't even in Afghanistan," she scoffed.

"You know he was," Nick said, narrowing his eyes as he studied her.

"If he was, I never saw him, I never employed him. And why should all this matter?" she asked with exasperation, turning around to look at

303

every person in the room. "Will someone please tell me what's going on?"

For the first time she seemed to notice Sam, who had quietly remained at the front door. Sam returned her stare impassively, but Nick knew him well, and knew that this was hard for him. Sam couldn't separate the playful girl Julia had been with the traitor she'd become. Nick well understood his feelings.

"Sam?" she whispered.

Nick stepped closer, interrupting her. "With this letter I finally have enough proof that you betrayed your country, Julia. You are formally under arrest and the charge is treason."

Her mouth gaped open, and she looked caught between hysterical laughter and tears. "This is all in fun, isn't it? A terrible joke gone awry?"

Nick shook his head. "We know everything, Julia. There's no use lying."

"I'm not lying! Who told you these things? Someone wants me punished for something I didn't do. Who is it?"

"You have many accusers, Julia, starting with an informant who saw you at the home of a Russian representative in Kabul. You delivered one of your own coded letters. With that hair, you'd think you'd have taken better care to hide yourself."

"That's a lie!" she cried, looking about her wildly.

"I visited the Russian later," Nick said tiredly, rubbing the bridge of his nose. "I saw the necklace I'd given you there on his table."

She put a hand to her throat and whispered, "But I lost it! I never even met this man!"

"But the most damning evidence were these letters. Your man Hume sent me one and promised me the matching letter to decipher the code if I would protect him from you."

"Protect—"

Julia stared at Hume with incomprehension, while he looked longingly at an empty bottle of brandy.

"Why are you doing this to me, Edwin?" she asked plaintively. "We were friends—you gave me my first kiss! I brought you your dead mother's possessions."

"What?" Nick interrupted.

"Look in my bag! You'll see I'm telling the truth."

Sam opened the carpetbag and began pulling out items: a hairbrush and mirror, a brooch, a stack of letters, and more.

After everything was lined up on the table, Julia said with relief, "Now do you see? Why would I come here to kill him when I was on an errand of mercy?"

Nick didn't give a damn what story she'd concocted to cover her journey, but then Charlotte said, "That was what she was discussing with

Mr. Hume at the tavern." When all the men looked at her, she lifted her chin. "I just wanted you to know what I heard."

"Charlotte, I appreciate your candor, but a cover story is *supposed* to be intricate," Nick said. "Julia was in a public place, with witnesses. She's a smart woman and had carefully thought out a story to explain her movements."

Hume suddenly cleared his throat and blurted out, "It was a code."

Nick nodded. Of course.

But Julia was staring at Hume with incomprehension. "What are you saying?" she finally whispered.

Hume looked at the floor and put his shaking hands deep into his pockets. "That was what we were supposed to talk about if someone overheard us."

Julia literally staggered. "But—he's lying. You must talk to my brother. He knows my old governess recently died."

"I hope you didn't kill her, too," Nick said heavily.

She gasped but couldn't seem to find words.

"Do you remember the massacre at the Khyber Pass?" Nick said, advancing on Julia in his anger. "The information you passed to the Russians helped bring about the deaths of those sixteen thousand British troops and their families. How do you live with yourself?"

Tears finally began to stream down her face as she gaped at Nick. He was unmoved. Thank God he'd finally accepted that a woman could be just as guilty of murder as any man. He would have no trouble making sure she received the ultimate punishment—death.

Julia sank down on the couch, staring blankly forward. "You've all been following me for days now, haven't you?" Then her gaze darted to Charlotte. "Even you. You made up that story about my brother."

Charlotte nodded solemnly. "I couldn't let you leave Tuxford. We weren't ready to follow you yet."

Sam finally stepped forward. "That's enough for now, Nick."

Julia's gaze narrowed in on Sam. "Why would I do this? Someone give me a good reason why I would throw my entire life away for the Russian cause?"

"Money," Nick answered. "You have precious little of it."

Her lips parted. "You think I would help . . . *kill* people, all so I could have a dowry?"

"It happens all the time," Nick said coldly.

Her mouth moved, but no sound came out.

Nick turned back to Sam. "Julia will stay with us here for today. I have an errand to run that directly pertains to her." He looked down at Julia. "Though you tried again to have Will killed, it didn't work. But I'll find the woman you hired, and that will be one more witness against you."

Julia shook her head beseechingly at him and then lowered her face into her hands.

Charlotte walked toward him, and he put an arm about her even though she stiffened. He felt her trembling, but knew she was strong enough to hear the news.

"Nick, what do you mean?" she asked anxiously.

"I left a coded message about our destination for Will at the Misterton inn, in case he needed us. Barlow just found me an hour ago." He lowered his voice. "There's no easy way to say this. Jane and Will were poisoned last night."

Charlotte's eyes filled with tears.

"They're alive," he quickly assured her. "The doctor has already been to see them this morning. Will and Barlow are recovering well, but Jane's recovery is proceeding at a much slower pace."

She sagged in his arms for a moment, then her strength resurfaced, and she straightened. "Do they think she'll die?"

"The doctor is optimistic that she'll improve, but only time will tell."

She wiped a hand across her wet cheeks. "I have to go to her."

"I'll do it, Charlotte. I can move faster without you."

"But—but she needs me, Nick!" she whispered.

"Will is taking good care of her. And you can be of use to us here, by helping watch Julia."

"Me?" She choked on a sob. "I've done nothing but get in your way."

"But with you here, Julia won't be able to claim that we abused her. Can you do this for me, Charlotte? I'll be back as quickly as I can."

"You'll go now?"

"It's already full dark. I promise that I'll leave at dawn."

He wanted to hold her close, to ease her pain, but he'd never earned that right. She walked to the window and looked blankly out, hugging herself.

Sam watched them impassively. "Will we be turning Julia over to the police tomorrow?"

"We'll escort her to London ourselves. She has highly placed connections, what with the Duke of Kelthorpe panting over her, and her brother a general. I don't want accusations of mistreatment. Put her in a bedroom upstairs, and I don't want you or Cox leaving her room, no matter what."

When Cox pulled Julia to her feet, she stiffly turned her face to Nick. "I need to speak with my brother."

Nick shrugged. "Maybe. Now search her for weapons before you take her upstairs."

Sam stepped forward, watching Cox begin to run his hands along Julia's back. "Nick, is this really necessary?"

But when Cox found a pistol strapped to her thigh, Sam nodded and turned away.

As Cox led Julia toward the stairs, she called back, "Sam, what did you expect? That I wouldn't need a weapon to protect myself? I'm a woman traveling alone!"

He didn't answer her.

There was silence in the room for a moment. Then Hume mumbled something and walked slowly into the kitchen.

Nick glanced at Sam, whose eyes were shadowed with sadness and confusion. Nick needed to give him something else to think about.

"Sam, could you make sure Hume gets a decent meal in him and is safely bedded down for the night? Try and steer him away from the bottle. We need him believable when he has to testify."

Sam started to turn away.

"I also wanted to remind you about Julia's last henchman," Nick continued. "Since we killed Campbell and have Julia in custody, he'll probably look after himself and run. But we still have to be careful."

Sam kept his back to him. "I've been doing this as long as you, Nick," he said in a low voice. "I haven't forgotten my duty."

"I didn't mean to imply otherwise."

Sam nodded.

"I'll take the next watch on Julia," Nick called.

Sam didn't answer, and Nick stared after him thoughtfully.

Charlotte's gaze went from Sam's back to Nick. "Are you worried that he might believe Julia's story?"

"No. He knows the evidence. He just can't believe that Julia could commit these crimes."

"Can you?" she asked, studying him closely.

He smiled grimly. "Yes, I can. And I'll see that she's punished for it."

Charlotte rubbed her arms, then looked up at Nick with tears glistening in her eyes. "I'm so frightened for Jane."

"Could I hold you?" he asked.

When she hesitated, he enveloped her in his arms and held her close. It felt so natural, so right to be comforting her, and sex had nothing to do with it.

And it was that final thought that disturbed him the most.

As promised, Nick left for Epworth at dawn. He was confident that Sam and Cox could handle Julia, but he felt less confident about Charlotte. She was trying to be brave, promising to help keep everyone fed, but he sensed a deep fatigue in her. He needed to get her to her father's, to restore her sense of normalcy and her place in life. She'd feel more comfortable that way.

But would he?

Nick arrived in Epworth by midafternoon and found the Crown and the Horse. When he stood outside Jane's door and knocked, he took a deep breath and forced himself to smile cheerfully, triumphantly.

Will opened the door, and he looked so unlike himself that Nick was taken aback. His face was lined with worry and had the sunken appearance of a man who hadn't slept well. This engagement of Will's might have been for convenience's sake, but it was obvious he'd fallen in love with Jane and was suffering along with her.

Will stepped back to allow Nick inside. "I take it everything went well."

Nick froze when he saw Jane lying pale and unconscious on the bed. Where was the vibrant woman who'd stood up to him for her sister's sake? Damn, but he was glad he hadn't brought Charlotte. "Is she doing better? Should we step outside to talk?"

"I'd rather stay here," Will said and sat down in a chair beside her bed.

Though Will took Jane's hand in his, Nick saw that his fingers felt for a pulse at her wrist. Had he spent the night like this, dreading her death as every minute ticked by?

"She's no better?" he asked.

Will shrugged tiredly. "She's been unconscious since last night. The doctor said it would help her to sleep."

Though Nick nodded, he found he couldn't just stand there and look at Jane. He started to pace and tried not to imagine Charlotte in that bed, Charlotte sick from something he himself had led her into, just as he had brought Jane into this mess. He felt guilty for what he'd done to their innocence.

"Don't keep me in suspense," Will finally said. "Did you catch the bitch?"

"Unusually harsh for you." But Nick was grateful to be distracted by conversation.

As Will looked down at Jane, his expression hardened. "I'm not feeling particularly charitable today."

"We have Julia in custody," Nick said.

"Did she go to her accomplice, as you thought she would?"

"She did—though she claimed to be there on a family errand. She said that the man's mother, her governess, had died. To support her story—which she'd obviously thought out well—she had his mother's possessions. But she also had a pistol strapped to her thigh."

"Did she turn herself in without a fight?"

"Yes. Claims she's innocent, of course. We showed her the coded letters, and she had nothing more to say, except that she wanted to speak with her brother, General Reed." Nick didn't bother to tell Will just how persuasive Julia had been, how badly Sam was taking her capture.

"Are you going to arrange it?"

"Maybe. If he even wants to speak to her. Hell, I'll have to go tell the Duke of Kelthorpe the truth, as well." And that was something he didn't look forward to.

"Is Sam guarding her?" Will asked.

"With help from Charlotte."

As Will gave him an intent look, Nick wished he hadn't mentioned her.

"Trust her already, do you?"

"She's proven herself," Nick said impassively. "We'll see what happens next."

An uncomfortable silence hovered between them, and he sensed that Will wanted to talk more about Charlotte.

Nick changed the subject. "So what are you going to do about Jane? Surely you'll make clear to her that she cannot speak about anything that transpired with Julia Reed."

"I have her under control."

When Will got to his feet and led Nick to the door, Nick almost smiled. It seemed Will didn't want to talk about his relationship with Jane, either.

Will opened the door. "Let me know what happens with Julia."

"Of course. You're headed for Colonel Whittington's?"

Will nodded. "Can I tell him what's happened?"

Nick's unease went up another notch. "Yes, but be vague about Charlotte. I'd rather he hear that story from her."

Will wore the ghost of a smile. "He has an extensive gun collection, you know."

Nick glanced back at Jane. "And I guess you should be worried about that, too."

"At least I'm actually engaged to his daughter," he pointed out.

"At least I'm not," Nick shot back, trying to play the carefree bachelor just to see Will grin.

Then Will looked back at Jane, and his smile vanished. "I have to go."

"Of course. Send me a message on Jane's condition. Charlotte is extremely worried."

Will nodded, but his thoughts were obviously on Jane, and Nick couldn't be sure Will even heard him. But he shut the door, and Nick was left standing on the gallery awkwardly, thinking about Will.

He obviously loved Jane. How had Will known? Will's decision to leave the army had had nothing to do with Jane, yet Nick had sensed a restlessness in him the last several meetings, as if Will still wasn't sure he'd made the right decision.

But Will was different now. Though he was worried about Jane, there was a sense of peace about him, as if he'd finally found the life he wanted.

Would Nick ever feel that way?

Chapter 22

Just when you are most confident that your goal is met, disaster can strike.

The Secret Journals of a Spymaster

Charlotte had avoided Julia's room during the day. She knew Sam and Mr. Cox took turns guarding her, and they'd taken up the simple meals Charlotte had prepared.

But Charlotte herself stayed downstairs.

Was she a coward?

The evidence against Julia was overwhelming, yet she couldn't forget the look of disbelief and despair Julia had worn when they took her upstairs.

Those two emotions could very well show on the face of a criminal who thought she was too intelligent to be caught. A criminal who would poison an innocent man and woman.

But Charlotte was thankful it was over for Nick's benefit. He would be a great success with the government. He would be showered with praise and offers of even more dangerous missions. It was what he wanted.

She felt confident in her abilities in a way she hadn't in a long time. Aubrey Sinclair had crushed her youthful confidence and belief in herself. Nick Wright had given it back to her.

But that wouldn't help her during the nights to come. She would be alone. And even though she knew she could easily find a husband, she wanted only Nick.

But she wasn't a coward. She would take Julia's supper tray upstairs herself, and look at the woman who'd tried to kill her sister. She knocked on the door, and Sam opened it.

He smiled. "Thanks, Charlotte. I really appreciate your help—I'm sure Nick does, too," he added quickly.

She nodded stiffly. "That's sweet of you to try to convince me, Sam, but unnecessary."

He reached for the tray, and as she let him take it she said coolly, "Would you mind if I came in?"

He looked surprised. "I'm not sure that's a good idea."

"I've had several conversations with Julia," Charlotte explained patiently. "I think I've handled myself well. Unless you think it would upset her too much."

Julia herself stepped into view. "Let her come in, Sam."

Charlotte froze, trying to find a trace of a murderer in Julia's expression. But all she saw was an exhausted, pale woman. It had been pointless of Charlotte to come. What could she do—confront Julia, who'd already claimed her innocence? Julia wasn't about to explain herself just because Charlotte was the next one to ask her.

Sam stepped back and Charlotte entered. She stood there self-consciously as Julia stared at her and Sam shut the door. He set the tray on the bedside table, and Julia sat down on the bed. There was a feeling of tension in the room that seemed to be more than between a guard and captive. Then she remembered that Sam and Julia had known each other all their lives. She wondered which of them felt more betrayed.

Julia stared at the plate of chicken, then glanced up at Charlotte. "Have you been making my meals?"

Charlotte nodded.

"I appreciate it." Julia began to eat.

When Charlotte continued to stand in the center of the room, feeling foolish, Julia motioned to a chair.

"You could sit down if you want. The men aren't very talkative, and you've always seemed easy to talk to."

Charlotte shook her head and remained standing.

"I know now that everything you said was for my benefit," Julia said dryly.

"Which ended up being for Nick and Sam's benefit," Charlotte reminded her.

"Of course."

Behind them Sam cleared his throat, then went to stand looking out the window as the sun set.

Just when Julia seemed frighteningly normal, Charlotte saw how her fork shook as she brought it to her mouth.

"You don't work for the army," Julia said.

"No."

"Then how did you become involved? Surely Nick didn't pick you out at a dinner party."

"Not quite," Charlotte answered, unsure of what she could say. Sam turned around to look at her and shrugged, so she took that as permission. "I accidentally overheard Nick meeting with your—with Mr. Campbell, who decided I had to die because of what I'd heard."

Julia raised her eyebrows. "So Nick gallantly rescued you."

"No, he kidnapped me. I thought he was in on your—in on the treason. Eventually he convinced me otherwise."

"He's good at that," Julia said with a trace of bitterness in her voice.

Charlotte didn't want to hear Julia's memories

of Nick, and she couldn't bring herself to ask about Jane's poisoning. Why had she come?

After an awkward pause, Julia said, "So they convinced you to help them?"

With his back to them, Sam snorted but said nothing.

"The convincing went the other way," Charlotte said, "and Nick never really was convinced. But I was alone when I saw you in Tuxford, and I couldn't just let you leave."

"You wove a very believable story," Julia said softly.

"You helped with your assumptions."

Julia shot her an unreadable glance.

Sam suddenly cocked his head. Both women stared at him as he moved to the door and bent toward it as if listening.

"Is something wrong?" Charlotte asked.

Sam's face was inscrutable, but to her stunned surprise, he pulled a pistol out of his belt and handed it to her. "I thought I heard something. Stay here with her." He glanced at Julia, but spoke to Charlotte. "Use this if you need to."

Charlotte held the pistol at her side and tried to feign confidence. She knew Julia would assume she knew how to fire it, though that was far from the truth. When Sam left, she backed away from Julia until she was against the door. She couldn't hear anything, not even Sam's footsteps down the stairs.

Julia had stopped eating, as if she, too, was waiting. The women looked at each other, then down at the floor, while the silence in the house grew ominous.

"I swear I don't know what's going on," Julia said softly. "I know you don't believe me. When my brother gets here, he'll make them understand that I couldn't do such terrible things."

Her voice trailed off, and in the growing darkness, Charlotte thought she saw the glistening of tears.

They both jumped when they heard a shout from down below. It sounded like furniture was being toppled, and Charlotte held the pistol in both hands now, though still aimed at the floor. What was happening? Were they being attacked?

She remembered Nick's words about one more henchman still on the loose. She wondered if the man was actually more concerned about Julia than saving himself. A man like that would be . . . desperate.

"We're going to move the desk in front of the door," Charlotte said, sending a sharp glance at Julia. "You're going to do most of the work, because I'll have this pistol trained on you."

"I'm not going to attack you!" she cried.

"But I can't take that chance. It seems someone down below doesn't want you to go to trial."

"Oh God," Julia whispered, covering her face with her hands. "This has to be a bad dream."

"It's not a dream! Those men down there could be injured, maybe even *dead* because of you!" As Charlotte shouted the words, it suddenly became real to her. The pistol started to shake in her hands, but she gripped it tighter and reminded herself that Nick was on his way back. He would arrive in time.

Or he'd walk in unawares and—

Her stomach rebelled, and she wanted to throw up. She couldn't let herself think the worst. Julia took a step toward her, and Charlotte coldly leveled the pistol.

The other woman froze. "You wanted my help," she whispered.

Charlotte nodded and pointed with the pistol to the desk next to the door. Julia went to push it, and Charlotte moved to the other side to pull. She couldn't grip the edge with only one hand—and she wasn't putting down the pistol—so she opened the nearest drawer and wedged her hand inside. Between the two of them, the massive desk began to inch across the wood floor.

Something heavy toppled over downstairs, and there was another incomprehensible shout.

"Hurry," Charlotte ordered, when the desk covered half the door.

By the time they got it where they wanted it, someone was pounding up the stairs.

Julia gasped and backed away, while Charlotte trained the pistol on the door. The door opened an inch and slammed into the desk.

"Who is it!" Charlotte cried.

No one answered. She backed against the far wall, barely noticed as Julia took cover beside the bed. The door slammed harder into the desk and Charlotte fumbled with the pistol, trying to pull back the top piece, as she'd seen her father do when shooting targets.

She started to sob as the door banged harder and harder, and the desk slid. She could see Julia cowering on the floor, covering her head with her hands.

When the desk toppled and a masked man jumped across it, Charlotte screamed and fired. But her shot went wide, and suddenly all she saw was the giant muzzle of the stranger's pistol pointed at her. He fired, and feeling a hot flare of pain, she fell back against the wall. Her pistol tumbled uselessly to the floor, and she slid to the ground.

Feeling dazed and distant, she watched numbly as the intruder grabbed Julia by the arm and pulled her to her feet. Julia screamed and he shoved her toward the door.

"Charlotte!" she cried, trying to turn back, but the man wouldn't let her go. "Are you all right?"

Charlotte wet her lips but she couldn't answer. Pain had begun to radiate all throughout her body, engulfing her mind.

"Go!" the man yelled.

When Julia stumbled over the desk, he roughly dragged her out into the hall.

Charlotte heard the bumping sound of Julia being pulled down the stairs and the woman's hysterical crying. Then Charlotte finally let go of consciousness.

Chapter 23

A fault in your plan is sometimes fate's way of
steering you to the truth.

The Secret Journals of a Spymaster

Just before full dark, Nick was rubbing down
his horse in Hume's stable when he heard the
distant sound of a gunshot. A feeling of terror
he'd never felt before gripped him.

Charlotte was in there.

Another gunshot cracked in the silence.

He grabbed his pistol and went running toward the house. He wanted to burst inside and
shout her name, but he would be calm and controlled or he'd get her killed. The kitchen door
was ajar, so he hesitated, but could not hear any
sounds.

Bending low, he went inside, aiming with his

pistol. But all he saw was Cox sprawled on the ground, unmoving, and Hume unconscious in the corner, with the table upended beside him.

After looking through the doorway into the dining room and seeing no one, Nick bent and put his hand on Cox's chest. He was breathing regularly. In the growing gloom, Nick could make out blood matting his hair. Nick hoped he'd only been knocked unconscious.

"I'll be back," he whispered, patting his coachman.

He heard screaming upstairs, and then pounding as a person—or people—came running down the stairs.

Nick crept through the dining room and as he peered into the candlelit parlor, he saw a black-clad man holding a woman's arm. It was Julia, her face wet with tears. She cried out when she saw another body in the parlor.

Sam had partially fallen across the sofa. There was blood on his mouth, and already his eye was swelling shut. He'd had a more physical en-counter with the intruder than Cox had, but there didn't seem to be a large spill of blood.

Where was Charlotte? Nick wondered franti-cally.

The man pushed Julia out the front door and followed her. Nick spared a glance out the window to see that they were running toward the east, but then he took the stairs two at a time.

The first door—to Julia's bedroom—was broken inward, and a desk was out of place and on its side. He saw Charlotte on the far side of the room, slumped to the side on the floor. When he saw a smear of blood on the wall above her, he tasted bile in his throat. Once again he was the cause of a woman suffering—and not just any woman, but Charlotte, whom he thought about constantly, whom he dreamed about. These last weeks, she had brought him to life.

He fell to his knees and looked at the blood that soaked into her garments along her left side. He called desperately, "Charlotte!"

She stirred and her eyelashes fluttered. When she started to straighten up, she winced and reached for her left arm.

"Be careful," he said quickly, helping her sit upright. "You're wounded."

"He shot me," she whispered, stunned.

"Julia's man?"

"Yes." Charlotte looked up into his eyes and gripped his arm with her right hand. "She didn't know he was coming. He forced her out the door."

"She'd like you to believe that," he said impatiently. "I saw her run willingly once she was outside. But enough of that. Where does it hurt?"

"You saw her just now?" she said hopefully. "Then chase her! Something's wrong, Nick!"

"You're wounded!"

Anger and fright warred inside him. He knew she was right, that he had a duty to go after Julia. But Charlotte could be dying and not know it.

"Nick, I insist you go. My arm hurts, but I think that was all that was hit." She moved her left arm and winced. "See? It's not even broken. Now go!"

"But you could bleed to death!"

"And I can stop the bleeding myself."

And then Nick understood. He had been ordering her around, treating her like the helpless widow, when she was capable of living by her own wits, of making her own decisions. He was not her master, or her husband. He didn't need to treat her—or Julia—like a man, but an equal.

Loving Charlotte was not a weakness. It had become the best part of him. She deserved to be cherished, to be treated lovingly. He had been fighting all the wrong battles where she was concerned. Yet how could he abandon what he was?

But she was worried about him, and he owed it to her not to let her think she'd ruined his career.

Though it was one of the hardest things he'd ever done, he said, "All right, I'll go. But I won't be long. Just let me help you to the bed."

"No, my legs work fine," she said, pushing away his hands. "Just go find Julia!"

"See to Cox and Sam," he called over his shoulder as he ran from the room. "They're downstairs, injured."

Charlotte watched Nick leave, and all her courage and bluster faded out of her. It would be so easy to have allowed him to take care of her, something her husband had never done. She'd thought that was what she wanted most in the world—a man who cherished her enough to put her first.

And Nick had wanted to do so, at the expense of his career, his pride, and his honor. But she couldn't let him do it. She would prove that she had the strength to stand alone. Nick was letting her make her own choices, because otherwise he would be no better than her husband was.

Very slowly Charlotte got to her feet and hesitated. But her legs held her; she could breathe in and out with no difficulty. She walked carefully to a mirror and turned up the lamp beside it. She gasped, because now she saw what had caused Nick such alarm. There was a lot of blood soaking her arm, and since it had been against her body, her side was soaked, too.

She found a pair of scissors and cut through the sleeve of her dress until she could see the gouge in her upper arm. Blood still seeped from it, and it made her light-headed and dizzy with pain when she washed it out with soap and water. She wrapped a long strip of linen about her arm and secured it with a knot. Her heart was pounding and the pain was making her nauseated, but then she remembered Sam and Mr. Cox. Were they bleeding even worse than she was?

Hesitantly Charlotte descended to the ground floor and paused to listen. There was no sign of

Nick, no other sound in the house. She found Sam in the parlor, half lying on the sofa, nearly trapped behind a fallen display case, as if he'd tried to use it to protect himself. He was already beginning to stir.

"Sam?" she called, giving his shoulder a gentle shake.

He groaned and lifted his head. She could see a small amount of blood on his face, and his eye was turning colors as it swelled shut. When he put a hand to his head, she brushed his hand aside and felt the bump.

"Are you all right?" she asked.

He nodded and almost fell over as he tried to rise from his knees. She steadied him and helped him sit on the sofa.

"I'll be fine," he said, wincing. "A bloody headache, but nothing else. Where's Julia?"

"She's run away. Nick is chasing her now."

When she tried to touch his face, he pulled away. "Charlotte, what about Cox?"

They found Mr. Cox unconscious on the kitchen floor. Mr. Hume sat huddled in the corner, his eyes vacant, a bottle of brandy at his lips, blood trickling from the back of his head and down into his collar. When they asked if he was all right, he only shrugged, but allowed Charlotte to wrap a bandage about his head. Between Sam and Charlotte, they woke Mr. Cox and saw to the nasty cut on his head. Considering what could have happened, they'd all emerged relatively unscathed.

But had her sister Jane? Charlotte had never had the chance to ask Nick how she was.

He was still out there somewhere, she thought, looking out the window into the darkness. All she could see was her own worried reflection.

It wasn't difficult for Nick to follow Julia and her henchman, which surprised him. Though it was near dark, he could see the light color of her dress as she ran through quiet, deserted streets, hear her heavy breathing. Gaslights intermittently illuminated the fleeing pair. Before them loomed the darkness of a park, perfect for them to elude him.

Nick picked up his pace, his pistol in his hand. It was easy to want her captured. He had only to think of his injured men—of Will and Jane, of Sam and Mr. Cox.

And Charlotte.

He thirsted for revenge, for an end to what had begun years before.

As he got closer, he saw that Julia was being helped by her cohort. He had a hand on her arm, pulling, but she could move only so fast in her heavy gown and petticoats.

They crossed the last street before the park, and as they moved through the gates, Julia's partner took one last look behind him. Nick had been ready and kept himself motionless, out of sight, away from the gaslights. He heard what he thought was a sob, but surely that was wrong.

Running swiftly, silently, he entered the park behind them, hiding near the brick columns of the gate. As he took a deep breath, ready to pursue them, he heard a muffled scream, quickly silenced.

Nick peered around the column, and only ten yards into the trees he saw Julia's henchman with his hands around her neck. She struggled, dangling from his grip like a rag doll.

It was too dark to use his pistol. Nick launched himself at the two and dragged the man down to the ground. Julia collapsed beside them, coughing and sobbing.

Nick fought more with his other senses than with his eyes, dodging blow after blow and inflicting several of his own. In the glimmer of gaslight through the overhanging trees, he saw the glitter of a knife and caught the man's grip in his own. They struggled, the knife between them. Nick concentrated all his energy, his will to stay alive. At the last moment he twisted his opponent's hand, and the knife sank into the man's chest.

As his opponent crumpled, Nick turned and caught Julia's dress in case she tried to flee. But she was crying hoarsely, her shoulders hunched and trembling. Nick pulled her to her feet, and she cried out as her legs gave way.

"I'm so tired," she moaned. "Let this be over with."

"It will," he answered shortly, then bent and tossed her over his shoulder. "I'll make sure of it this time."

Charlotte had stationed herself at the front windows, so she was the first to see Nick carrying Julia up the path. The relief inside her was so great that she could have wept with joy. But she knew that wasn't what he wanted from her. In a time of danger and excitement, they'd come together for a brief moment of passion. But it was over.

Sam flung open the door, and Nick strode inside, dropping Julia onto the nearest chair. She sat still, with her chin almost touching her chest.

"Is she . . ." Charlotte began.

Nick rubbed his neck. "She's rather heavy, is what she is. But enough about her." With just a step he stood before Charlotte, taking her hands and rubbing them. "Shouldn't you be lying down? Did you send for the doctor"—he turned and looked at Sam and at Mr. Cox, who'd come to stand in the kitchen doorway—"for any of you?"

But his gaze returned to her, and she felt the warmth of his concern, and though she told herself not to hope, inside she melted at the way he cared about her.

"I'm fine," she reassured him. "It was merely a shallow scrape along my arm."

"But it could have been worse," Nick said.

He lifted her arm, and his warm fingers found the ragged edge of her sleeve to stroke over the bandages and over her skin. Just that innocent touch moved her.

"My God," he continued, "when I think about him pointing a pistol at you . . ."

Though she shuddered at the memory of her terror, she forced a cheerful smile. She would not allow some of his last memories of her to be full of self-pitying tears. "We are all fine, Nick. What happened with Julia?"

His hands dropped away from her, and his expression became coolly professional. "She's lucky to be alive—if you can call it that. Her henchman didn't rescue her to save her. He wanted her dead."

Charlotte gasped and couldn't help but look at Julia, who listlessly turned her head away. There was something terribly sad and pitiful about the way her shoulders shook with her sobs.

But the woman could have easily cost Nick his life, so Charlotte could not grant her sympathy. Charlotte would never have him, but she had to know that he was alive and well.

Although Sam nodded knowingly at Nick, Charlotte had to ask, "Why would her henchman want to kill her? Didn't he do this to rescue her?"

Nick shook his head. "When I caught up with them, he had his hands around her neck. He wanted her dead."

"So she couldn't testify against him," Sam added.

Nick nodded. "He tried to kill me, so I returned the favor."

Charlotte gaped at him. "Were you hurt?"

"No. But Sam, take Cox and go retrieve the body for me. It's at the entrance to the park a couple blocks east of here. Put it in the barn, and then tomorrow morning we'll take it—and Julia—to the authorities until she can be shipped to London." He looked down at Julia, though she didn't look up. "I've let your femininity and your high-placed connections sway my judgment, but no more. You belong in jail with the rest of the criminals. I'll let the government answer questions from your brother and the Duke of Kelthorpe."

When Sam and Mr. Cox had left the room, Nick said to Julia, "It's back to the bedroom for you. There's no one left to rescue you."

Her bleak expression never changed.

Charlotte could hold back her fears no longer. "Nick, how is my sister?"

She was gratified when he held her hands and looked into her face. But the worry in his eyes told her the truth. "I'm sorry to say that her condition hasn't changed, Charlotte. But she's asleep, which the doctor said is the best thing for her. Will is taking good care of her, and promises to send word the moment anything changes."

Charlotte had felt so certain that Jane would

be better. She blinked at the stinging in her eyes and was gratified when Nick pulled her gently against him.

"I'm so sorry, Char," he murmured into her hair. "Will you be all right?"

She nodded and gently pushed him away, when all she wanted to do was clutch him and sob. She had to deal with her own problems, because Nick would no longer be there. How had she come to depend on him in so short a time?

"I'm fine," she said, wincing as her voice broke. "Please let me know the moment you hear anything."

"Of course," he said softly. "I have to go."

"I know," she whispered bleakly.

That night Charlotte slept alone in a small bedroom in Mr. Hume's house. Sam came up an hour after she retired. A message had come from Will saying that Jane had awakened and would be fine. Charlotte thanked him gratefully, and when she was alone burst into relieved tears. Would she ever stop crying?

In the morning Nick had Sam escort her to a nearby hotel. Nick was keeping his distance from her, and although it had been what she asked for, the pain tore her apart.

Sam made sure Charlotte had money for meals, and brought her books and newspapers before he left. She listened almost impatiently to his instructions to remain at the hotel until she heard from them.

She was shattering slowly from the inside, and each crack was an added wound to her heart. She just wanted to be alone.

When Sam was gone she closed the door, and the dam holding her tears burst. She hugged herself and slid to the floor with her back to the bed. If only she understood what drove Nick, what made him the man he was. It might make their separation understandable.

During the day a doctor came to visit and inspect her wound. A deliveryman from a fashionable modiste arrived with several new dresses and undergarments, even a nightdress for her to sleep in. Nick's thoughtfulness warmed her as well as saddened her.

That night she put on the nightdress and thought of him. The material was so sheer, so fine. Would she ever find a man to care for her as he did? Did she even imagine someone could take his place? Why couldn't she just accept him on his terms?

Because her pride wouldn't let her.

But oh, she wanted to see him one last time. They never even had the chance to say good-bye.

Chapter 24

The last secret uncovered can be the most revealing.

The Secret Journals of a Spymaster

Charlotte waited through the evening, clothed in her elegant nightdress. She paced to keep herself awake, then when her limbs would no longer carry her, she curled up on top of the bedcovers and slept.

She came awake as she was lifted in someone's arms.

"Nick," she breathed, opening her eyes slowly.

His beloved face showed wistfulness and regret. "I've turned down the covers," he said softly. "You'll sleep better there. We can talk tomorrow."

"No!"

"Have I hurt your wound?" he asked, looking at her arm where the bandages made her bulky.

She didn't answer, just wrapped her arms around his neck and pulled his head down for a kiss. She invaded his mouth with her tongue, wanting every taste because she knew it would be her last chance. She was weak where he was concerned.

"Sit down on the bed," she whispered. When he hesitated, she nipped at his lower lip with her teeth. "Please."

With a groan he followed her order. She pushed him back and straddled him, making quick work of removing his coat and shirt. He was already hard beneath her, and she rocked her hips and rubbed herself against him as she caressed the broad muscles of his chest.

"You look beautiful," he said hoarsely. "I knew the nightdress would compliment you."

She sat up and arched her back, reveling in his admiration. When he slid his hands up her ribs to cup her breasts, she moaned. He kneaded her flesh through the sheer material, and the rasp of it across her nipples made her shudder.

She had to have him, had to feel him inside her one last time. She undid his trousers and pulled them down around his thighs. His erection lay heavy against his stomach, so large and hard. She touched it, letting her fingers caress his smooth, hot skin, enjoying the way he tensed beneath her, the way his breath shuddered out of him.

And then she took him in her mouth because she wanted to give him pleasure. He groaned and shuddered as she used her lips and tongue.

"Charlotte!" he gasped as he pulled her up to kiss her.

"But—"

"I can't take any more. Let me—"

When he would have rolled her onto her back, she held her ground, straddling him again. When the nightdress got in her way, she pulled it over her head and was rewarded by the way his eyes flamed with appreciation and passion.

"Charlotte," he groaned as their naked hips came together.

His erection pressed along the length of her, hot and pulsating with need. She could wait no longer to have him inside her, filling her. She lifted herself up and he was there, at the entrance of her womb. He pulled her hips down hard, and they were one.

Seductively she leaned over and licked at his nipple. Beneath her his hips rolled, and he surged up inside her again.

"Wait," she whispered against his moist skin, "I'll tell you when."

She clasped him with her knees, her thighs, and even the muscles inside her. He came up on his elbows and took her breast in his mouth, sucking hard, then licking rapidly with his tongue until it took all her will not to lift her hips and sink down once more.

When his fingers explored between her legs, she whimpered and clasped his head even closer. They trembled against each other, and she enjoyed the heat and moisture and the incredible feel of him inside her.

"Char, let me move," he said against her breast, and then bit her gently.

But she held off as long as she could, until they were both groaning their need.

"Now!" she cried, and rode him until her climax crested and shuddered through her.

Nick thought he would surely die. He continued to thrust into her again and again, watching her above him, the way her breasts trembled, and the way her thighs clutched him. With a shout he joined her in fulfillment, grinding against her until she, too, cried out.

She fell forward on top of him, and he wrapped his arms around her, careful of her wound. Never had a woman taken him to such heights, pleasured him first instead of wanting more for herself.

"Char," he murmured into her ear, kissing wherever he could reach.

They lay entwined for many minutes, until their breathing slowed. He was still hard inside her, but he let her slide to the side and just held her.

Charlotte suddenly let out a soft chuckle.

"What?" he asked. "I can give you something to giggle about." He tweaked her nipple.

"No—no, I was just remembering something my mother told me."

"You're thinking of your mother at a time like this?"

She laughed again. "Well, only that she told me I would have to trust my husband—I mean the man—to give me pleasure. I never understood what she meant before I met you."

"You could give yourself pleasure," he whispered into her ear, then bit her lobe gently.

He could feel her slide her hands up to cover her face.

"There's nothing to be embarrassed about," he assured her.

"Every day has been a revelation with you," she said, looking up from where she rested her head against his shoulder. "So tell me, do mothers or fathers tell their *sons* what to expect on their wedding night?"

"I think most fathers assume their sons don't wait until then. They expect their sons to find an experienced older woman and do all the learning firsthand."

"And what do mothers say about that?"

"My mother never said much of anything."

He shouldn't have expressed his thoughts like that. He felt the way she stilled in his arms. The last thing he wanted was her pity, not on their final night together.

She rolled onto her back and looked up into

his face. He thought she did a good job schooling her features into impassivity.

"Your mother didn't talk to you?" she asked. "I thought you said she died when you were fourteen."

"We had a household of servants. She usually let them deal with me."

"Why?"

He shrugged and wished he could look away, but there was something about the directness of her gaze—her wish that he tell her things he'd never told anyone else—that seemed to make him her prisoner.

"I already told you that my father was a cold man. He was forever disappointed that his older brother was the heir, and he took his petulance out on me and my mother. I think she distanced herself from him—and from me—to numb the pain."

Now he sounded like he was whining. But she raised herself up on her elbow to look at him face-to-face.

"But Nick, she could have found the love of a son, though she didn't have the love of her husband. I would have given anything—"

She broke off, and he saw the tears she tried to blink away.

"My mother was nothing like you, Char. If she could not have her husband, she didn't want any part of family. She protected herself, and for that I can't blame her."

"Well I can," she said forcefully.

He smiled and tucked her hair back behind her ear. "Are you my champion now?"

"I would have been then. What about your stepmother? You said she preferred to champion her own children over you. But that does not necessarily make her a cruel woman."

"She wasn't. But she was very focused on the place she and her children held for my father. She didn't have much time for me."

Charlotte bit her lip, her eyes downcast in thought. "You'd think after all that—including Julia's betrayal—you'd hate women, or at least think us inferior."

He shrugged. "Maybe. If it wasn't for the maid, I don't know what I would have done."

"What maid?"

Nick groaned and rolled onto his back to drop his arm over his face. She prodded him.

"What maid?" she demanded again.

Charlotte sensed that she was uncovering secrets that Nick had never told anyone. She was poised on the edge of understanding everything about him, and she had to fight not to show her eagerness.

"Her name was Edith," he said.

Though he stared at the ceiling, she knew he wasn't seeing it.

"She came to be a housemaid when I was ten. I was very lonely, for I wasn't permitted to play much with the children of the village. She was seventeen and became my confidante."

"You mean like the mother you'd always wanted," Charlotte said encouragingly.

"Not exactly," he said with amusement in his voice.

It took her a moment to figure out his meaning, and then she gasped. "But Nick—you were only ten!"

"It wasn't like that at first," he insisted. "Don't be so impatient and just listen."

She rested her head on his shoulder and watched his profile.

"She saw at once that I was lonely, and became my best friend. When she could finish her duties early—or sometimes escape them altogether—we would play games or fish, or just run through the woods of my father's estate with abandon. When my father remarried and started another family, he had less and less patience for me. Edith became my eyes, alerting me to my father's moods, warning me when I should make myself scarce."

"She sounds like a good friend," she said quietly, even as she worried about where this story would end.

He hesitated. "As I grew older, I wanted her to be more than my friend. But I was still young and impulsive, and didn't understand the danger to her. I wouldn't let her distance herself. She was my first friend; I wanted her to be my first lover."

"How old were you?" she whispered.

"Seventeen. I was very selfish," he added bitterly.

"You loved her. Surely she loved you."

"And my love ruined her." His voice was harsh with self-loathing. "I had one night with her, and then someone on the staff reported her to my father. My father wouldn't have cared if I had only taken her out of lust. But she meant something to me, and that was her downfall. He sent her away."

"Oh Nick," she whispered, putting her arm across his chest to hold him close. He didn't push her away. "What happened?"

"I was tutored at home throughout childhood, and as I already told you, my father finally relented to my stepmother's pressure and sent me to Oxford. Before I left I tried to get news of Edith from her family, but they wouldn't speak to me, for fear of further angering my father. He could make sure none of them ever worked again in the county. But I couldn't forget Edith. During the summer holidays after my first year, I decided to search for her. I had grand plans about bringing her to school with me, so that we could be together. Again, her family wouldn't talk to me, but I pressured them enough—just like the old man, huh?"

"Don't say that," she said sternly. "You were concerned for her—you loved her."

"If I loved her, I would never have succumbed to my father. I wouldn't have given up on her so easily."

"Nick—"

"She died because of me," he said harshly.

For a moment she listened to his erratic breathing, watching the despair that crossed his face before being hidden by cynicism. She waited, holding tight in case he tried to push her away, but he didn't.

When he finally spoke, his voice was low, raw. "Her family relented and told me she'd been carrying my child. Out of fear of my father, she ran away to London, then died in childbirth along with the babe."

She leaned up and pressed her lips to his cheek, but he pushed her away and sat up, turning until his legs hung over the side of the bed.

"It was my fault," he said hoarsely. "I didn't protect her, and she died thinking she was unloved."

"That's not true, Nick. I'm sure she knew you loved her. But your father was obviously a powerful man."

"And I was weak. After that, I wanted nothing to do with a society of noblemen who could treat a woman so. That's why I joined the army of the East India Company. I didn't need my father's money for a commission, just talent and their military college. Even now, the merest thought of being like him sickens me."

She finally understood his gentleness with her. He had never gotten over his love and guilt over Edith.

"I won't be like him," Nick said fiercely. "And they can damn well shove the title up their—"

"Title?" she interrupted, sitting up to be at his side.

He glanced at her, his mouth tilted sardonically. "When my father died, I became the Earl of Folkestone."

"But—but you said he was always disappointed in being the younger brother."

He shrugged. "I found out that just last year my uncle died childless, leaving my father the earl. In his foolish jubilation, he went on a wild spending and gambling spree. He was killed over a debt."

"And now you're the earl," she breathed, stunned.

"I don't want the title, but it—and all its responsibilities—are being forced on me. Now you can see why I didn't give a damn about seeing my stepmother when I returned to the country. Suddenly they all need me because they're drowning in debt. Oh, I don't have near enough money to overcome that, but they need me to somehow . . . lead them out of it."

"And you have to, because they're your family."

"I'll do it for my brother and sisters. None of this is their fault."

"And then you'll get to know them," she said encouragingly. "You might find your real family after all."

"You are forever optimistic," he said shortly, and rose to his feet.

He started to pace, and she could see the anger in every flex of his muscles.

"You wish you hadn't told me," she said. "It doesn't make you less of a man just because you have feelings."

"They're feelings I don't wish to dwell on." He turned to look at her.

She saw the flare of passion rise up in his eyes.

"But I could watch you all night," he said hoarsely, walking toward her.

She knew at once that he was going to use sex to distract them both. But she felt even more intimate with him now, and needed there to be no secrets between them, not on this last night.

"That's what my husband used to say." Though her stomach clenched, she forced herself to remember.

Nick pulled up short and just stared at her.

"He enjoyed . . . watching me. But the final, most horrible thing he did to me, I only found out at the end, just days before he died."

Chapter 25

In a spy's life, regrets are legion, but a pointless waste of time.

The Secret Journals of a Spymaster

Nick sat down at her side and took her hand. That's what she loved about him, his willingness to give her support when she needed it. She sent a silent prayer of thanks to Edith for making him the man he was.

She took a deep breath and spoke in a rush. "He so enjoyed watching me that he invited someone else to watch, too."

It wasn't so bad to finally admit it. The painful lump in her throat eased.

Nick spoke hesitantly. "You had to . . . disrobe for someone?"

She shook her head. "I never knew his friend

was hiding in the room. Aubrey and I had . . . relations, and all the time he knew this man was watching us. I only found out when I was lying naked on the bed, relieved it was over, and he—Aubrey's friend—just . . . walked out from behind the draperies. I—I guess he wanted a closer look," she added bitterly.

He kept hold of her hand, and then wrapped his arm around her bare shoulders. "Charlotte, your husband was sick."

"And to think—I had acted the hostess for this man, greeted him as an acquaintance." Her voice rose higher. "I'll never know how many times he watched us, because Aubrey died before I could work up the courage to ask him."

He squeezed her hand tighter, but she wasn't seeing him anymore, but the evil smile of that man who'd stared at her nudity.

"I screamed when I saw him. I screamed and screamed, until Aubrey covered my mouth and held me down. I found out that he later explained my behavior to the servants by saying I'd seen a mouse." She shuddered and let it go, forcing herself to look at Nick, the man who truly cared about her. "I've told you this because I didn't want you to think you needed to hold back from me. I've held nothing back from you."

"I know," he whispered, then pulled her tightly against his side. "Can I . . . hold you like this?"

"Oh please," she whispered, turning her face into his shoulder and letting out a shuddering breath.

He propped pillows up against the headboard and leaned back against it. Charlotte pressed herself against him, holding him tightly in her arms as if she would never let him go.

And she didn't want to let him go. He was a man who could not treat a woman with anything but respect, even if she was his enemy. His past had made him that man, yet he was trying to get beyond it, to see women as dispassionately as he saw men. He was punishing himself over and over again for Edith's death.

Couldn't he understand that his attempt to see women in a different light was impossible? That these feelings for women made him so beloved in her eyes? But he didn't want love for that reason. He wanted no part of such a soft emotion, because he felt weakened by it. He'd been hurt too many times. He had put Julia in jail today, and tomorrow he would walk out of Charlotte's life.

And she had to let him. He had bared his soul to her tonight, and she would never forget that— or him.

When she was almost asleep, she heard him murmur her name.

"Yes?"

"I can't come back here again."

Did he know how bleak his voice sounded? But she only said, "I know."

"Sam will escort you to your father's."

She nodded and held him tighter. "Nick, have Sam come the day after tomorrow. I want to stay another day, just in case you need Sam—or me," she added softly. "To prepare for the trial, of course."

"Charlotte," he began with resignation.

She lifted herself up against the pillows and looked into his face. "I promise I'm not asking anything of you. But I've been of help where Julia is concerned, haven't I?"

He nodded.

"You might need me again. Give me this last day."

"All right," he said.

She took his dear face in her hands, and out tumbled the words she'd never meant to say. "I love you, Nick," she whispered.

She saw the pain he couldn't conceal.

"No, I don't expect anything else," she hurried to say. "I just needed you to know that you've given me back my life, my confidence. And even if I never see you again, I will look back on what we've shared with contentment."

He kissed her softly, gently. "I've enjoyed every moment with you, Charlotte Sinclair."

A tear trickled down her cheek, but she smiled. "Even when you had to tie me up?"

"Even then." He hesitated. "I wish—"

She quickly covered his mouth. "No regrets, Nick. Let's promise each other that."

He nodded and hugged her close.

"Let's sleep," she whispered into his hair. "And don't wake me when you go. Let this be our good-bye."

When Charlotte awoke in the morning she was alone. She lay on her back, looking at the lacy canopy over her bed without really seeing it. She felt drained, too exhausted to even cry. But she was satisfied with the way she'd handled their parting. She hadn't begged Nick to stay, though she'd wanted to. She'd told him the truth, that she loved him, but hadn't asked him to love her in return.

She could live with that.

But would she live happily?

He didn't come back to her that night. The next morning Sam and Mr. Cox arrived promptly at ten to escort her home. At first they were hesitant with her. They weren't blind—surely they knew what she and Nick had done together.

But their concern warmed her, and she wouldn't let them know how truly lost and alone she felt. She forced herself to be a good traveling companion.

They arrived in the bustling city of York the next day, and Charlotte was relieved to be almost home. That afternoon they reached Ellerton House, the ancient family manor that over the centuries had been added to wing by wing, giving it a rather disjointed look. But her father loved it, and though he spent little time there now, he still considered it more a home than their town house in London.

Her sister Jane had been terribly upset and hurt when their father had chosen to come here first, instead of visiting them in London after two long years away. But Charlotte understood her father now; there was something about the peace of being home that could heal a person. She only hoped it was the same for her.

Although she wanted to run to Papa's arms, she forced herself to walk sedately at Sam's side to the front door and knock. When the butler opened the door, he seemed surprised to see her.

"Good afternoon, Mrs. Sinclair. Your father will be most pleased."

"Is he in the library, Smythe?" she asked, already heading across the foyer to the door.

"Of course, madam. I shall announce you," he added, hurrying to catch up while still managing to keep his dignity.

"Not necessary!"

She flung open the double doors and came to a sudden stop as she found her father standing before the globe next to his desk, leaning on a pair of crutches. His right leg was gone below the knee. He straightened and stared at her in surprise.

"Papa," she whispered, already knowing what this injury must have cost him. She'd read his journals, after all. Had he come north, then, to spare himself everyone's pity?

"Charlotte, my little sparrow," he said, a big smile showing beneath his mustache.

She ran and hugged him tightly. He seemed a little more frail than she remembered, but he was still a giant of a figure to her. "Papa, how good to see you! Why didn't you tell us you were injured?"

He kept an arm around her shoulder as he waved his other hand dismissively. "I needed some time to recover, Charlotte. This place is much quieter." Then he spotted Sam and reached out to shake his hand. "Mr. Sherryngton, how good to see you."

"You, too, Colonel," Sam said.

"I'm disappointed in you, sir," said her father.

Sam actually paled. "Colonel?"

"I expected another of your wonderful disguises. Charlotte, have you seen his abilities? Quite remarkable."

"I agree, Papa." Charlotte couldn't help frowning as she studied her father. "You seem to have known I was coming."

"Not really," he answered. Waving them toward the sofa, he followed at a slower pace, then settled himself in a wingback chair. "But after hearing Jane's story, I knew you were nearby, and thought you might remember to visit your old father."

"Jane!" Charlotte cried, clapping her hands in

delighted relief. "She is here? Then she is doing well?"

"Just fine. But I regret to say that her visit was a brief one." Lord Whittington used his finger to smooth his mustache, and his eyes twinkled. "She and Will were in quite a hurry. They left this morning to get married in Gretna Green."

Though Charlotte was happy for her sister, there was a terrible sadness inside her. Jane would have marital bliss with the man she loved. But oh, Charlotte was selfish to think about her own situation, when her sister was finally happy.

She noticed that her father was studying her. She almost felt as if she hadn't done her schoolwork again.

"Jane told me something of what's been going on with the traitor Julia Reed," Lord Whittington said. "Seems you found yourself in the thick of it. Where *is* Nick?"

Charlotte kept a smile on her face by sheer will. "He is busy with establishing the case against Julia, Papa. Sam was kind enough to escort me home."

"I see," he said thoughtfully.

Was it there on her face—the love inside her that would never be returned? She looked down and blinked quickly to hide her tears.

"Jane tells me that you found my journals," her father continued. "Rather took them to heart, didn't you, dear girl?"

She laughed, and it was something of a relief.

"I couldn't quite believe it was you, Papa. What a secret to keep. So tell me how it felt the first time you saw the mountains of Afghanistan."

It was good to hear him talk, for not only did it distract her, but it reminded her how little she'd really known him. She had so much to make up for. She could see herself spending a lot of time in Yorkshire. Maybe the tranquillity would help her to heal, too.

The three of them spent the hours before dinner talking, then continued right on through the meal. Charlotte excused herself early, claiming exhaustion, and encouraged the two men to continue without her.

She found her room exactly as she remembered it, though a maid had obviously lit candles and turned down the bed. Her clothes had been unpacked, and a steaming bath awaited her. Although there were plenty of nightdresses to choose from, she donned the one Nick had given her, because it still had the ghost of his scent.

She lit the candle on her desk and found paper and pen in the top drawer. She dipped the quill in ink and began a letter to her mother. She should have done this in Leeds, but her thoughts had been too full of Nick. Now she was doing her best to chase all those thoughts away. She told her mother the truth of her adventures, leaving out the very dangerous or the very intimate ones.

But finally the letter had to end, and she was alone with her thoughts again. She knew she'd become stronger, but right now all she wanted to do was cry. She put on a dressing gown and went down to the library to find a book instead.

Her father was still awake, seated in his favorite chair, a blanket across his lap. He looked tired and disheveled, and she wondered if he was still in pain. But when he saw her, he smiled with understanding.

Before she even knew what she was doing, she collapsed on her knees at his side and began to sob. He held her, rocked her, let her cry until her tears dried up and she was empty.

"There now, my little sparrow," he murmured, kissing the top of her head. "You've had a horrible year, and I'm sure this brush with danger didn't help."

"But Papa, in a funny way it did," she said, sitting back on her heels and looking up into his face. She took the handkerchief he offered and blew her nose. "I'm capable of a lot, you know."

He smiled. "I never doubted it."

"Well, I did. Jane was always so smart, so interested in the world around her. But I—"

"You were your mother's daughter. You were very good to her when she needed you the most, especially when things between her and me began to . . . sour."

She wiped her eyes. "I thought I only wanted what she wanted, and I think I married Aubrey more to please her than to please me."

Her father hesitated, and she felt the wealth of

his sorrow. "I should have been here for you, Charlotte."

"You couldn't have known, Papa. And England needed you."

"And did you find yourself needing Nick?"

She stared at him, stunned, and found her tears flowing again. Nodding, she blew her nose. "But only England can need him," she whispered sadly. "And I knew that from the beginning— well, as soon as I realized he was working for the government, and not himself."

"I have always found myself worrying about Nick," her father said. "He does not let many people know who he truly is."

She nodded and sighed.

"He has always been very devoted to his duty, but not so to the people in his life. I'm glad you realized that." He cupped her cheek. "But it is not an easy lesson."

When would her crying ever end? she thought, sniffling into the handkerchief.

"It will take time, Charlotte."

She rose to her feet. "I know. But in the meantime I need to read. Do you have something that is bound to make me fall asleep?" She smiled. "And don't suggest your journals, because look what a mess such excitement landed me in!"

A week later Charlotte was walking in the garden, picking flowers to arrange for that evening's dinner table. She felt better, stronger, if not healed. She hoped that would come in time. She wasn't ready to return to London, because that would mean she would be an eligible widow again, and she couldn't imagine looking for a husband. But that would be what her mother wanted her to do. Charlotte would just remain in the country for a while.

When the basket on her arm was full, she turned and began to walk back slowly toward the house. She lifted her face into the wind, let it blow her hair about. She'd taken to wearing it down, and she told herself it wasn't because Nick liked it that way. It was just . . . convenient out here in the country. Her bonnet hung down her back, allowing the late summer sun to touch her face.

She turned down a gravel path, circling a splashing fountain, and as the manor came into view again, she saw someone in the distance walking toward her.

She froze, knowing there was only one man she knew with shoulders that broad, with a walk that was almost a swagger.

Nick Wright had come to call.

Chapter 26

You'll know it's time to move on when the thrill of the chase is not as important as what you've left behind.

The Secret Journals of a Spymaster

Charlotte was angry with Nick as he came closer and closer. They had said good-bye—why did he feel the need to come back again, to make her relive the pain? She almost wanted to shout at him to leave her alone.

But she said nothing, just clutched the basket in both hands and stared at him as her heart raced.

He stopped a few feet away from her and removed his top hat. "Hello, Charlotte."

Distance; she had to remember what separated them. "Good day, Lord Folkestone."

He winced. "Surely I can have a better greeting than that."

She hesitated and then said softly, "Hello, Nick."

He grinned, and as always, his dark, masculine beauty made her weak inside. Did he actually have the gall to let his gaze linger on her in a less than gentlemanly way?

"I didn't think there was anything more to be said between us," she said coolly, beginning to walk back to the manor. "Unless it was to tell me that you're off on another mission."

He took the basket from her hand and fell into step beside her. "No, but I did just return from London."

"You escorted Julia back?"

"No, she's still in jail in Leeds. But I had to speak with my superiors at headquarters."

"I'm sure they were thrilled at your success."

"At our success."

She lifted one eyebrow as she regarded him. "So you told them about me?"

"Not much. It wasn't their business. But I did explain that it was a group effort."

"How decent of you. I'm sure Sam and Will and Mr. Cox appreciate it."

He was smiling at her, as if he knew a secret she didn't. She didn't like it at all—didn't like him for bringing back the feelings she'd tried so hard to repress. Did he feel so little for her that this didn't even hurt him?

"I spoke to my stepmother as well," he said. "She was in London for the end of the Season."

She glanced at him in surprise, but he wasn't looking at her. "And how is she doing?"

"As well as can be expected. She's quite worried about finances—and worried about her children."

"Did you meet them?"

"No, they were at the family seat in Kent."

Was that regret in his voice? She was glad.

"I hope you will take this opportunity to spend some time with them before you leave the country," she urged. "Having close family is such a blessing."

"But I'm not leaving the country."

She stumbled over a pebble. "I'm glad that the army gave you some free time. You deserve it."

"But that's why I went to London. I resigned my commission."

She came to a halt, and if she had been holding the basket, she would have dropped it. She was too afraid to look at him. "What—what will you be doing?"

"I have too many responsibilities now, with the title and all. You can't believe how much property there is to manage. And frankly I've become a bit too prominent to be a spy anymore. Although the Foreign Office did mention something about consulting on matters in Afghanistan."

Was Nick actually . . . rambling?

"I'm not really sure how to go about it all," he

continued, "the title and everything, but I thought if you'd . . . help me, I might make a go of it."

Help him? Her hands started to shake.

His voice softened. "You see, Char, I'm afraid I'm going to turn into my father."

"Oh Nick," she whispered. "You're nothing like him."

"But I almost was. I fled into the army thinking I could become a better man than he was through service to my country. But I never saw that I almost made myself become as distant as him out of fear."

They stopped walking and faced each other, not touching, but yearning.

"I didn't want to feel pain, so I told myself I didn't need love. But there was always this part of me I thought was weak, this part that wanted to look on a woman and . . . protect her. I hated that part of me, until I met you."

Charlotte could barely breathe for the waiting that burned in her. Was he really saying what she hoped he was?

He reached out and gently touched her cheek. "You deserve nothing less than every tenderness I could show you. But I drove you away. You told me you loved me and I froze. How could I deserve—" He broke off as his voice grew hoarse. "But I couldn't get those words out of my mind. I think . . . if you could still . . . love me, after everything I've done, I could prove to you that I'm worth it."

She put both hands on his and held it to her face, breathing in the scent she'd dreamed about for so many nights. "Oh Nick, I do love you. And even if you . . . still need time—"

"No, no I don't need any more time," he said, sliding his arms about her and pulling her close. "I've had too much time away from you. I thought it would be better, but these past days have been the darkest of my life. I missed your optimism, your courage, the way you refused to let me get the best of you. I love the way your face shines with every emotion you feel. I love you, Char," he whispered.

Her tears overflowed at the sweetness of his voice. "I owe Edith so much."

He looked startled at her mention of his first lover.

"Don't you see?" she continued. "She taught you how to love. And the pain of losing her made you the wonderful, tender man you are."

"Thank you," he said simply, smiling.

She could see in his face that he'd never thought of Edith that way, that he had only associated her with his guilt. Maybe he could now let it go.

When he dropped to his knees she gasped. Her hand trembled as he raised it to his lips.

"Char, would you do me the honor of becoming my wife?"

And in the momentary silence, she saw in his eyes his doubt and his hope—and his love. He had thought himself unworthy of true happiness, yet he offered her the world.

"Oh yes, Nick," she cried, and threw her arms around his neck.

With a shout of triumph, he surged to his feet and swept her off the ground, spinning her until she laughed for joy under the sun.

Epilogue

Loyalty to each other and to country is what binds two spies together. Loyalty breeds trust and friendship, very elemental things in any relationship.

The Secret Journals of a Spymaster

Nick and Charlotte were married in a private ceremony with only family in attendance. Standing next to Will and Sam at the altar, Nick looked with amazement as his lovely bride smiled at him. Beside her, Jane, who was already expecting, looked ready to be sick.

But that didn't bother Nick. He was fully hoping his own wife would soon be expecting. He was surprised how much he looked forward to the thought of watching a baby in her arms, to teaching his child to ride a horse and swim in the pond.

These were all things he'd never done before, and the challenges seemed endless and rewarding.

He knew he could count on the colonel, who'd trusted Nick enough to give him his daughter. As for Lady Whittington, she'd almost fainted the first time she saw Nick, but since then was treating him graciously. He was certain his title helped. The colonel stood beside his wife, and although Charlotte had told him about the deep estrangement between her parents, Nick had seen them talking together. Perhaps they could find their way back to each other.

He glanced back at his own family, seated rigidly in their pews. His stepmother wore black, and in the few minutes he'd spoken with her, he sensed that she had now latched on to him in desperation. He had thought he'd resent that, but strangely, he didn't. He felt sorry for what she'd endured in her marriage. He hoped he could someday make her feel comfortable enough so that she could learn to enjoy life for her children's sake.

In his brother and sisters he could see the loneliness of children who never felt loved, their angry desperation to be noticed—he knew those feelings well. He would make sure they understood that he was nothing like their father—like *his* father. He would be a brother to guide them, as he always wished he had had.

And it was all possible because of Charlotte, who looked up at him with trust and love. He was humbled by her faith in him, and he wanted nothing more than to give her everything in life that she deserved. She'd gone from being a frightened widow to being a woman confident in herself. If he'd had a small part in that, he was grateful.

When the minister pronounced them man and wife, Nick looked down into her face and cupped her cheeks. As he leaned down to kiss her, he said the words he would never tire of.

"I love you, Charlotte."

If you enjoyed The Beauty and the Spy, don't miss Sam and Julia's story coming Spring 2005

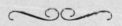

You can never have too much romance, especially when you can choose from these riveting November releases from Avon Books . . .

DUKE OF SIN by Adele Ashworth
An Avon Romantic Treasure

When someone threatens to expose Vivian Rael-Lamont to scandal, she will do anything to preserve her hard-won privacy and peace. But her only hope is an original signed copy of a Shakespearean play owned by the mysterious William Raleigh, Duke of Trent. He is the Duke of Sin, and he is Vivian's only hope . . . and soon, her only temptation.

THE THRILL OF IT ALL by Christie Ridgway
An Avon Contemporary Romance

Try as Felicity Charm might to reinvent her background, the truth will come calling unless she sorts out her nutsoid family—and fast. But first she'll meet Michael Magee, an extreme thrill-seeker who's just as caught up in the antics of the Charm family as Felicity is. He's wrong for her in every single way, but get the two of them together and everything's oh-so right.

CHEROKEE WARRIORS: THE CAPTIVE by Genell Dellin
An Avon Romance

When her headstrong younger brother disappears, Raney is frantic that his life is in danger, so she insists on joining Creed Sixkiller, a man she cannot forget, in a search for the boy. On the trail it becomes all too clear that she still loves him, but Sixkiller is a man who has not yet learned how to forgive. And yet, when he has Raney in his arms, he is willing to try . . .

DARK WARRIOR by Donna Fletcher
An Avon Romance

He calls himself Michael, the Dark One, and he has come to rescue Mary from her abduction by a fearsome warrior. Though they travel through dangerous unknown territory in search of safety, Mary finds she feels safe in Michael's care. But in a moment of vulnerability, can she reach out and know that she—and her future—will be safe in his arms as well?

REL 1004

Avon Romantic Treasures

*Unforgettable, enthralling love stories,
sparkling with passion and adventure
from Romance's bestselling authors*

HOW TO TREAT A LADY   *by Karen Hawkins*
0-06-051405-1/$5.99 US/$7.99 Can

MARRIED TO THE VISCOUNT   *by Sabrina Jeffries*
0-06-009214-9/$5.99 US/$7.99 Can

GUILTY PLEASURES   *by Laura Lee Guhrke*
0-06-054174-1/$5.99 US/$7.99 Can

ENGLAND'S PERFECT HERO   *by Suzanne Enoch*
0-06-05431-2/$5.99 US/$7.99 Can

IT TAKES A HERO   *by Elizabeth Boyle*
0-06-054930-0/$5.99 US/$7.99 Can

A DARK CHAMPION   *by Kinley MacGregor*
0-06-056541-1/$5.99 US/$7.99 Can

AN INVITATION TO SEDUCTION   *by Lorraine Heath*
0-06-052946-6/$5.99 US/$7.99 Can

SO IN LOVE   *by Karen Ranney*
0-380-82108-7/$5.99 US/$7.99 Can

A WANTED MAN   *by Susan Kay Law*
0-06-052519-3/$5.99 US/$7.99 Can

A SCANDAL TO REMEMBER   *by Linda Needham*
0-06-051412-6/$5.99 US/$7.99 Can

Available wherever books are sold
or please call 1-800-331-3761 to order.

RT 0604

AVON TRADE... because every great bag deserves a great book!

ALISA KWITNEY

On the Couch

Paperback $10.95
($16.95 Can.)
ISBN 0-06-053079-0

SONIA SINGH

Goddess for Hire

Paperback $13.95
($21.95 Can.)
ISBN 0-06-059036-X

HELP WANTED, *Desperately*

ARIEL HORN

Paperback $12.95
($17.95 Can.)
ISBN 0-06-058958-2

THE LAST OF THE HONKY-TONK ANGELS

MARSHA MOYER

Paperback $13.95
($21.95 Can.)
ISBN 0-06-008164-3

MICHELLE CUNNAH

Paperback $10.95
($16.95 Can.)
ISBN 0-06-056036-3

MELISSA NATHAN

Persuading Annie

Paperback $12.95
ISBN 0-06-059580-9

Don't miss the next book by your favorite author.
Sign up for AuthorTracker by visiting *www.AuthorTracker.com*.

Available wherever books are sold, or call 1-800-331-3761 to order.

ATP 1004

Avon Romances—
the best in exceptional authors and unforgettable novels!

THREE NIGHTS . . .   by Debra Mullins
0-06-056166-1/ $5.99 US/ $7.99 Can

LEGENDARY WARRIOR   by Donna Fletcher
0-06-053878-3/$5.99 US/ $7.99 Can

THE PRINCESS MASQUERADE   by Lois Greiman
0-06-057145-4/ $5.99 US/ $7.99 Can

IN MY HEART   by Melody Thomas
0-06-056447-4/ $5.99 US/ $7.99 Can

ONCE A GENTLEMAN   by Candice Hern
0-06-056514-4/ $5.99 US/ $7.99 Can

THE PRINCESS AND THE WOLF   by Karen Kay
0-380-82068-4/ $5.99 US/ $7.99 Can

THE SWEETEST SIN   by Mary Reed McCall
0-06-009812-0/ $5.99 US/ $7.99 Can

IN YOUR ARMS AGAIN   by Kathryn Smith
0-06-052742-0/ $5.99 US/ $7.99 Can

KISSING THE BRIDE   by Sara Bennett
0-06-05843-3/ $5.99 US/ $7.99 Can

ONE WICKED NIGHT   by Sari Robins
0-06-057534-4/ $5.99 US/ $7.99 Can

TAMING TESSA   by Brenda Hiatt
0-06-072378-5/ $5.99 US/ $7.99 Can

THE RETURN OF THE EARL   by Edith Layton
0-06-056709-0/ $5.99 US/ $7.99 Can

Available wherever books are sold
or please call 1-800-331-3761 to order.   ROM 0604